Where The

CW00448790

Dougie McHale

Azzie Bazzie
Books

Copyright © Dougie McHale 2023

Edinburgh
2010

He feels it instantly, plummeting through him, a surge of regret, a spasm of unfaithfulness. In the slanting light, her sapphire eyes sparkle, like the gliding seawater of the River Forth that carves the shoreline behind them. It was an immediate reaction; he felt it the moment Zoe looked at him, a definite attraction. Admitting his desire felt a betrayal to his past.

'We were on holiday in St Monans, staying at a caravan park,' Rob tells Zoe, whose gaze is fastened to her shoes as they stroll.

'I was fishing with my dad on the pier and caught a flounder, or a plaice. I'm not sure which. It was a flat fish, anyway. Mum gutted it in the sink, cooked it and we ate it for dinner. Before that, I had my photograph taken with it. It was the late 70s, and I had on these jeans with massive flares, so wide they looked like sails. I couldn't tell you what my shoes looked like. And my haircut, God, it was a typical bowl cut. Horrendous now, but back then, it was your mum that cut your hair and there wasn't a menu of styles on offer.'

Zoe laughs and lifts her head. She glances at Rob. 'I'd love to see that photograph.'

'I'll need to dig it out. It's still at Mums, in the cupboard under the stairs. She's got hundreds of photographs. Not that long ago, she said she was going to throw most of them out. There were too many of them, she said. Luckily, I persuaded her not to. I told her it would be like throwing away your history. They're not just photographs, they're time capsules, captured moments of family and friends, past generations who live forever in images that are precious, that tell the story of where we've come from and who we are. She said she'd never thought about it like that.' Rob smiles. 'A few weeks later, when I visited Mum again, she couldn't wait to show me what she'd done.'

'And what was that?'

'She'd put them in albums, catalogued them, recorded who was in a particular photograph, where it had been taken, and all in chronological order. I couldn't believe it.'

'You must have made a big impression on her. She went from one extreme to the other.'

'She did, but that was her nature.' He smiles at the memory. 'There was never any middle ground with Mum.'

'How is she?' Zoe asks.

Rob thinks for a second. He scratches his head. 'She looks like Mum, but Mum has gone. The person she was no longer exists. She's been erased. I don't know how else to describe it.'

'It's a terrible disease... devastating.'

'I try to visit as often as I can. I know she's in the best place. The staff are amazing. I can't fault them. It doesn't make it any easier, though.'

'You had no choice. She was a danger to herself, wandering outside in the middle of the night.'

'I know. I just thought I'd have more time with her. I didn't expect the dementia to take her from us as quickly as it did. It's not just that. I feel like her whole life has disappeared. The house is going on the market, the furniture is being sold or going to charity shops. I'm sifting through everything just now. It's going to take a while. She never threw anything out. I've found receipts from years ago.'

'What about Sue? Is she helping you?'

'She keeps promising to come up from London, but there's always an excuse, usually work related.'

'She's her mother, too. Has she visited her?'

'Not much. The last time was about two months ago.'

'That's bad. You'd think she'd want to spend time with her.'

'She hardly visited Mum at the best of times. Mum would never hear a bad word against her, always made excuses for her. She'd say, *"A job like that comes with a lot of responsibility."* It was her default for Sue's constant absence. It came with a big salary. It would be nothing for her to jump on a plane and be up here within an hour.'

'I don't understand that. Why wouldn't she want to visit her mum, especially now? And what about her children? It's their gran. When did she last see them?'

'It must be about a year ago.'

'That's dreadful,' Zoe snorts incredulously.

'I know. The thing is, Mum never did get on with Gary, Sue's husband, and the feeling was mutual. Sue was oblivious to it. I'm sure half the time she wasn't even in the room. It was like her head was in a bubble.'

'Maybe that was intentional. Easier to just ignore it.'

'The things Gary used to say to Mum were dreadful at times. He treated mum like she was beneath him. I'm sure that's what he thought, anyway. You could tell he hated having to visit. He made no attempt to hide his disdain. *"The house was too small, the neighbours were too noisy, and why did mum still live in a council estate?"* He seems to forget that's where Sue grew up, too. I'd hate to think about what he used to tell his kids; it would be all lies. It's a shame. They have never really got to know their gran. Gary made sure of that.'

'And it's too late now.'

There is a silence as Zoe's words seep into him.

'They think Mum won't last the month.'

'That's just two weeks.'

A resigned smile crosses his face. They look out over the panoramic cityscape. A slight breeze licks at their clothes; Zoe's hair blows over her face and she flicks the strands from her eyes. The light is fading as a bank of clouds rolls above the River Forth and silver pin prick lights twinkle over the coastline of Fife.

'How did your mum end up living in Elie?'

'My mum's sister, auntie Betty, moved there when she got married to my uncle Max. He was a lawyer and had just become a partner in a practice in St Andrews. Mum loved to visit them in their little mansion, as she called it. It wasn't, it was just a big house, but I suppose it felt like a mansion to Mum back then. Anyway, Betty and Max never had children and when Max died, Mum stayed every weekend. She even went to the church on a Sunday with Betty and, as a result, met a lot of people who became friends. When Betty died, to Mum's disbelief, Betty had gifted the house to her. By then, Dad had passed away, so Mum left her little council house and moved into her little mansion, where she lived for several years blissfully.'

'That's so lovely and I bet it stuck in Gary's throat. I'd have loved to have seen his face.'

'Oh, he never visited Mum. Sue came a few times with the kids, but always had an excuse about why Gary wasn't with her.'

'God, I hate that man and I haven't even met him.'

Rob laughs. 'I wouldn't worry about it; he has that effect on most people.'

They strolled for several minutes until the imposing clock tower of The Balmoral Hotel came into view and the Gothic spires of Scott Monument and St Mary's Cathedral rose above Princes Street towards the early evening sky.

'There's something empowering and calming at the same time when you see Edinburgh on this hill. Don't you think?' Zoe asks.

'She's full of contradictions, but isn't that her charm?'

Zoe's eyes fasten on him. 'Your eyes seem to brighten when you speak about this place. Your face lights up. If Edinburgh were a woman, you'd be madly in love with her.'

'There's only one woman I've ever been madly in love with.'

'Oh Rob. I'm sorry. I still miss Soph every day.' Zoe touches Rob's arm. 'I can't imagine how it must be for you.'

'If I said it gets easier as time passes, I'd be lying. I think I've just got used to living this way, but there isn't a day that goes by that the loss of Soph doesn't stab my heart.'

They walk a little further and then Rob turns to Zoe. 'I'm going to Mum's tomorrow. There're a few documents I need to pick up for the solicitor. Would you like to come?'

'I've nothing planned. I'd like that.'

'I'll show you that photograph if you promise not to laugh.'

She smiles. 'I'll try.'

Rob was married to Sophie for two years when a routine trip to the doctor changed their lives. Sophie had been feeling tired and lost weight and thought she might be iron deficient. Being vegetarian, and ironically, not liking many vegetables, she thought the supplement tablets she took were enough to balance what she otherwise lacked.

The resulting blood test highlighted something more sinister. Sophie was referred to a specialist and after further investigations involving an ultrasound scan and CT scan, they diagnosed her with ovarian cancer. She underwent surgery to remove the cancer, but they discovered the cancer had spread.

Zoe was Sophia's best friend, and they both enjoyed the same social group. They went to the same university, and trained as primary teachers, securing their first job, and starting on the same day in the same primary school. Zoe was the chief bridesmaid at Rob and Sophie's wedding.

Rob had been married for 857 days when his wife was taken from him, and for the next six months, he too felt like he was dead.

Chapter 2

'I've never been to this part of Fife,' Zoe says as she scans the fields that gently descend into a thicket of trees and the wide River Forth and in the distance, she can make out the familiar shape of The Bass Rock.

He turns to look at her, his hands set flat against the steering wheel. 'Really!'

'Yeah. I wasn't expecting it to be...' she pauses, searching for the word.

'So nice.' It is a weak attempt to hide his sarcasm.

'I can't think of the word, but sometimes the simplest expression is best... just beautiful.'

He smiles. 'We're almost there.'

Soon, the flat fields, farm buildings and narrow road are left behind as the wider road and stone and brick houses of Elie engulf Zoe's view. She catches site of a church with a dominant steeple and when they turn into the High Street with its quaint shop fronts; she notices a small deli and café and imagines Rob's mum shopping and meeting friends for lunch. To her surprise, around them, the sky fills with large black birds, gliding, and landing in several small trees that populate the ground amongst picnic tables. She cranes her neck to get a better look.

'They're crows. Look up into the trees. You'll see their nests.'

Zoe sucks in her breath. 'My God! I've never seen so many nests. They're huge and so close to people.'

'I know. I had the same reaction when I first saw them. Here we are, just in here.'

Rob turns right, and the car enters a gate between a garden wall draped with foliage. They stop in front of a red brick house where the bricks around the windows are painted white, as is the prodigious entrance door. They step out of the car and Zoe is delighted to see an apple orchard.

'Mum was famous for her apple pies; she had an endless supply of apples here,' Rob says, smiling at the memory.

'I can't believe you're selling this place.' Zoe takes in the house and garden.

'Sue wants to sell it.'

'And you don't?'

Rob manages a smile. 'What do you think?'

'I think I know who's behind it.'

He puts the key in the lock and opens the door. They step into a black and white tiled mosaic hallway with a dark wooden staircase.

'Wow! This is incredible.'

'It's all original features.'

His expression is hard to read, but she can hear a sadness in his voice.

After a tour of the house, they sit in the kitchen. Rob hands Zoe a coffee and settles into a chair opposite her.

Zoe cradles her cup in both hands and looks around the kitchen. 'There's no way I'd sell this house. It has far too much potential.'

'House prices have gone through the roof, especially for property like this. There's a high demand for this area. There's a lot of city types who'd pay well over the price to have a house in the East Neuk.'

'A holiday home, you mean?'

'It would make an ideal family home.'

'It would.'

'Mum was happy here. She loved it. I'd hate for it to be empty half of the year.'

'It doesn't have to be.'

Rob tilts his head. 'What do you mean?'

'Buy her out.'

'Sue?' His voice rises.

'Yeah.'

'I couldn't afford to. You're talking about four hundred and fifty thousand pounds, maybe half a million.'

He gazes out of the window at the sunshine shafting through the branches of the trees in the orchard.

'I thought you were going to show me that photograph,' she says, attempting to lift his mood.

'They're stored in the cupboard under the stairs. I'll just be a sec.'

He returns with a large box and places it on the kitchen table. The dates 1980 to 1985 written in a felt-tip pen on the lid.

'There're hundreds of photographs in here. Luckily, since Mum catalogued them, it should be easy to find.'

'I love looking at old photos. There's just something special about holding one in your hand. It's handy being able to store them on your phone, but I just feel you're closer to the subject, the person... that sounds weird,' she says dismissively.

'I don't think it does. I'd agree with you.'

Rob opens the box and peers inside. He runs his finger along the spines of the photo albums where specific dates are written. 'This is the one.'

He pulls out a photo album and sits down, grinning to himself. 'Promise you won't laugh.'

'I'll try not to.' Zoe smiles and shuffles to the edge of her chair.

He locates the photo and turns the album so that Zoe can get a better look.

She leans in. 'You look so cute, and your hair is blonde... Wow! Now that's what I call flares and that must be Sue standing next to you.'

'She must be about six.'

'And you. How old were you?'

'I'd be ten.'

Zoe raises her eyebrows. 'The fish isn't the biggest I've seen.'

'No, it's not. It looked big to me at the time. It was probably the first fish I caught.'

'And were there more... fish?'

'I can't remember ever enjoying fishing. It was the only thing Dad and I did together. I was playing football for the school team by then, so the fishing took a back step.'

Zoe flicks through the photographs that sit smugly in their protective sheets. 'Here's one of your mum and dad. He was a handsome man, and your mum looks so young.'

'Let me see.' Rob thinks for a second. 'That was Sue's First Holy Communion. There's a photo of her on the next page looking saintly.'

Zoe moves on to the next page and tilts her head to the side in mild bemusement. Sue is wearing a white top and skirt and a blue sash with a silver pendant pinned to it. Zoe notices Sue's shoes encased in a tidemark of mud, and she grins. 'She looks like she's hating every minute of it.'

'She got grounded for a week. Mum was furious, said she had never been so embarrassed. Before the mass took place, Sue tried to run away right through a field covered in mud. She was caught by a man walking his dog and seeing how Sue was dressed, he brought her right back to the church. That's the last photograph taken of my dad before the accident.'

'It must have been hard for your mum, two young kids to look after on her own and she was so young herself.'

'I don't know how she would have coped if it weren't for Gran and Grandad. Mum had to work, so Sue and I spent a lot of time at their house. My Grandad was like a father to me. He filled a massive hole. He was always there for me. He brought me up like I was a son to him, and when he died, it was like I'd lost my dad. I miss him. In a way, it brings it all back. Grandad, Soph and... well, Mum hasn't got long.'

Zoe looks in the box and tries to sound upbeat. 'There must be hundreds of photographs in here.'

'There's another three boxes under the stairs.'

Zoe hands Rob the photo album, and just as he is about to re-place it in the box, a small envelope drops onto the table. He picks it up and turns it on his fingers, studying its yellow edges. 'I've never seen this before.'

'It must have been tucked in between the pages.'

'How intriguing.'

'It's an old envelope.'

'Well, aren't you going to see what's inside it?' Her voice is louder than she expects.

A small frown creases the side of his mouth and Zoe wonders what he is thinking. Rob runs his finger along the length of the enve-lope before opening it. He sits back in his chair and pulls out a pho-tograph.

Zoe waits for him to speak. His silence seems an eternity. He gazes at Zoe. 'It's an old photograph of a family I don't recognise.' He says, mystified.

'Can I see it?' Zoe stretches out her hand.

Rob hands the black-and-white photograph to her. It is old and not what she is expecting. A couple, in their late twenties, are sitting together on two separate chairs, their postures stiff and formal. The woman is wearing a hat and a nondescript, long dress that almost covers her boots. She is in her twenties, her hair is long, her stare unswerving, her cheekbones prominent. She sets her mouth firm. The man's dark suit, waistcoat and white shirt seem worn and aged. And, at his side, a young girl of about three years of age stands, her hand resting on the adult's shoulder. It is the portrait of a family an-ticipating the flash of the camera.

There is something odd about the composition, and then it dawns on her. None of them are smiling. It was maybe the thing in those days; she thinks.

'Do you know who they are?'

Rob shifts in his chair. 'No. I've not got a clue. It was taken a long time ago.'

'The photograph must mean something to your mum, otherwise why would she have kept it?'

Rob thinks about this. 'I wish I knew.'

Chapter 3

It feels like a bright light has flooded his mind. It is uplifting, important. It feels worthwhile. To do nothing is not an option, this much he knows.

Rob has studied the photograph countless times that his eyes could have, by now, bord a hole in it. He peers into the eyes of the young man and wonders about the man that stares back at him through the grainy image. And his thoughts are always framed with a question - Who are you?

Set in an expanse of farmland and forest, the Georgian country house that was now Leyway Care Home came into view. Rob's stomach always drops when he turns off the country road and swings onto the long driveway that curves through manicured lawns, tall hedges, and mature trees. He feels he has given up on his mum. He has handed her over to strangers, the caring professional. He knows his guilt is a normal reaction, and that she is now in a place with people that can care for his mum in a way that he, or others, could not. But whenever this building comes into view, he cannot help thinking he has abandoned her, and the dreadful feeling in the pit of his stomach is a constant reminder of this.

Rob parks his car. There are another six cars in the visitor's section of the car park. He checks his watch. It is almost two o'clock. It's always busy on a Saturday, more so on a Sunday, so he always visits his mum on a Saturday afternoon. Not that she is aware of what day it is, or the month. Most days now, she does not even acknowledge him. He often wonders if she is aware of who he is. On the few days that she is lucid, she will call him by his name and if he is lucky, she will say a few words in context before the darkness falls behind her eyes and she is gone from him again.

There are two nurses at the nurse's station. Both are familiar to him, although their names are not.

'Hello, Mr Webster.' A nurse stands to meet him. She is squarely built, in her thirties, he supposes, and he notices the skin at the edges of her lips crease as she smiles. 'How are you today?'

'I'm fine, thanks. And you?'

'I'm good.'

The other nurse, a younger woman, is studying a computer screen. 'It looks like Bill is with your mum. If they're not in the day-room, he's probably taken her out into the garden. It's a nice day for it.'

'Thanks. I'll take a look.'

The day room is off a wide corridor with yellow and brown patterned swirls in the carpeting. Rob has always thought it a depressing floor covering that adds nothing to the ambience of the care home.

There are only a few people sitting in the dayroom, two women drinking tea, and a man, his chin resting on his chest, sleeping in front of a television. One woman appears to be listening intently. She nods and smiles, but the other is not talking to her at all, instead she is staring into her lap. A nursing assistant is standing with his back to the room and looking out of the window.

In the garden, Rob can smell freshly cut grass. The sun has broken through the clouds and is already warming the air. He sees his mum sitting on a bench looking over a fishpond. Bill is sitting beside her. She looks shrunken, a tiny version of the woman she has been, and he feels a sudden ache in his throat.

When he reaches them, Bill stands, as if now it is not his place to sit beside Rob's mum.

Bill smiles. 'Jeanie, look who's come to see you.'

Rob bends towards his mum and kisses her forehead.

'Hello, Mum.'

A flash of recognition brightens her eyes.

Bill turns to walk away. 'I'll leave you to it.'

Rob nods an appreciation and sits beside his mum, taking her hand in his. Jeanie returns her stare to the fishpond, retreating from the world around her.

It is enough just to sit with her, to feel her close to him. The familiarity of it sustains him in the absence of conversation.

The air seems heavy; the silence hanging thickly around them. It still catches his breath.

There were always words. His mum was an enthusiastic communicator. If she was not talking to someone, she was absentmindedly talking to herself. She was a tremendous presence that filled the space between people with her infectious personality.

Her eyes flick open and close again.

'Hello Mum.' Rob tries to sound cheery.

She is not here, but she is. The contradiction, the bitter reality, torments him.

'Mum. I've got something to show you. It's a photograph I found in your house. An old photograph.'

'The fish have all gone.'

Jeanie's words startle him. They are unexpected.

'I liked to watch them swimming in the pond. Did you take the fish?' Jeanie's eyes skim the water.

Rob holds her hand. 'No Mum. I didn't take the fish.'

'Well, someone did. Are you sure it wasn't you?'

'Maybe whoever took the fish will put them back again.'

'Yes, I would like that. Did you take the fish?'

Rob squeezes his mum's hand. 'No mum, I didn't take the fish.'

'Oh.' Jeanie looks at him. 'My son Rob is visiting today. Maybe he knows who took the fish.'

A heaviness bore into him. It feels like grief, the bereavement of a loved one. Rob takes an envelope from his pocket and takes out the small photograph. He shows it to his mum.

'Look Mum, I've got a photograph.'

Jeanie stares at the pond.

'Do you know who these people are, Mum?'

She looks, but her eyes glaze, and her expression remains set.

'What about the woman? Do you know who she is?'

Jeanie leans in closer.

'I've never seen them before. Do you know who they are, Mum? I found the photograph in your house amongst all the others?' In his desperation, he is asking her too many questions. He knows this. It only confuses her. It is a gamble he thinks is worth taking.

Jeanie screws her face up.

'Try to remember Mum.'

'He wasn't supposed to be there.'

'The man in the photograph?'

Jeanie stares at the pond.

'Where? Where was he not supposed to be?'

Jeanie leans a hand on the bench, and with an effort, she takes her weight until she is standing. She struggles to keep her balance and sways. Rob stands and takes her by the elbow.

'Careful.'

'I want to see the fish. I always look at the fish.'

They walk the short distance to the pond. Jeanie stares into the murky water. After a while, she looks up and turns to Rob with a questioning look in her eyes. 'The fish have disappeared, just like he did.'

Rob forces a smile. 'Where did he go?'

Jeanie runs her fingers along her forehead. 'An island.'

Rob seizes on the opportunity. 'Try to remember, Mum. I know it's difficult, but it's important.'

He can see she is growing tired. A few seconds pass. He must proceed with patience, yet he is unable to refrain from one more attempt. 'What was the island called?'

Jeanie touches his arm. 'I'd like a cup of tea and some biscuits; chocolate biscuits would be nice.'

He is aware his mum is slightly swaying. A slight breeze has lifted, cold against his face. 'Come on, let's get you back to your room.'

She looks at him then and smiles. 'Corfu. That's what it was called.'

Chapter 4

There is a respectable turnout of family and friends. Not a bad send off for being a daughter, wife, mother, grandmother and friend.

When the coffin arrives in the crematorium, Rob places a single rose onto the coffin. Beside him, Sue wipes away her tears with a handkerchief, as her rose falls from her hand. Gary has not travelled with her, nor have her children.

Uncle Bert bends stiffly and places his rose alongside the others. 'She always loved roses. Jeanie would appreciate the gesture. When it's my turn, don't bother with them. I hate roses.' He taps Rob's shoulder and turns to walk away.

After the service, Rob thanks the priest. 'I'll see you at the reception, Father. Nancy has done a good spread, as always.'

'A cup of tea would be grand and I'm partial to an egg mayonnaise sandwich. Nancy always puts wee bits of cucumber in them.'

'There'll be far too much.'

'There usually is. And your mother was fond of her.'

'Nancy said she wouldn't take a penny for her efforts. She wants me to donate what I would have paid her to a dementia charity.'

'They were good friends, Nancy, and your mother. They grew up together and never lived more than two streets from each other until Jeanie moved to Elie.'

'Nancy visited her regularly, even when Mum went into the nursing home.'

'It will be like she has lost a sister.'

'Yes. I suppose it will.'

At the faraway end of the function suite in the local hotel, a queue has assembled around an assortment of white and brown bread sandwiches: cheese, egg mayonnaises, tuna and cold ham, filling several tables along with miniature sausage rolls, several platters of Indian starters and slices of cold pizza.

Since arriving from the crematorium, Rob has met and chatted with almost everyone in the room, mostly close and distant relatives, and family friends. There are others he hasn't recognised, probably neighbours of Mum's from years ago, he thinks.

He recognises Nancy walking towards him. Now not occupied with preparing the buffet, she has discarded her apron and replaced it with a fitted black jacket. Rob pulls out a chair for her and she eases herself into it.

'Ah, that's a relief. I've been on my feet for hours.' She looks at Rob. 'How are you doing, my love?'

'I'm fine, Nancy. I'll just be glad when this is over. There were people at the graveside I hadn't seen in years.'

'Your mum would have been pleased with the turnout. She's probably looking down at us right now and smiling.'

'She would be if she could see all that food you've made. You've done her proud, Nancy.'

Nancy waves her hand dismissively. 'Nothing's too much trouble for Jeanie. She was the salt of the earth. A wonderful woman. I'm proud to have called her a dear friend.'

'She thought the same of you.'

'I can't believe how quick it was. I only visited her on the Tuesday and by the Friday she was gone.'

'It was a blessing. She didn't suffer.'

'We had some good times together over the years. It was the best thing that happened to her moving to the house in Elie. She was happy there. She loved it. The locals just seemed to adopt her as their own.'

'That's probably who the people are that I don't recognise here today. I never thought of that.'

'They will be. In fact, now that you mention it, I recognise some of them. See the older fella at the bar, the one with the tray of drinks. He was one of your mum's neighbours. He popped in on her a few times a week just to make sure she had enough milk and bread, stuff like that.' Nancy gives a rueful smile. 'Jeanie called him her personal shopper.'

'It's good to know there were people looking out for her.'

'You did too.'

'Not as often as I should have.'

'It's not as if you could just pop round as well. At least you made the effort to visit your mum. Not like your sister.'

'I just had to travel from Edinburgh, not London.'

'It broke your mum's heart that she didn't see a lot of her grand-children. She never said so, but I knew her too well.'

'Your right, there's no excuse.'

Nancy's voice is quiet but sincere. 'You made her happy. She was so proud of you, Rob. You made up for your sister's disappointment. Where is she, anyway? I've not seen her.' Nancy lifts her head and looks around the room.

'She had to get her plane back to London. It's at five o'clock.'

Nancy shakes her head. 'I thought she'd at least stay for a few days.'

'I'm past caring. At least she turned up.'

'God! It's her mother's funeral. You'd think she'd stay for the whole day.'

Rob takes a bite of a tuna sandwich. 'Why do you keep doing this? It's not easy work.'

'What else would I do at my age? I've got a few good years left in me yet. I'm sixty-eight not eighty-eight. I need a purpose, something to keep the grey matter ticking over. It's not as if it's every week. Most of them are funerals these days. Which is a good thing. It guaran-tees a never-ending supply of customers.' Nancy laughs. 'And besides, Cara and Louise, my two granddaughters, help me out. They do most of the preparation. I just make sure it's up to my normal standards.'

Rob longs for the day to be over. He has still to collect his mum's
things from the nursing home. The manager has phoned him to say
they have packed his mum's clothes into bags and sorted out her belongings to be collected. Jeanie has always supported charity shops,
visiting her favourites most weekends. Rob thought she would approve of his decision to donate her clothes to them.

'What's going to happen to the house in Elie?'

'Now there's a dilemma.'

'What do you mean?'

'Sue wants to sell it.'

'Oh! And you don't?'

'I'd rather keep it in the family. I think that's what Mum would
really have wanted.'

'And what does her will say? That's what's important, your mum's
wishes.'

'She knew Sue didn't need the money, but she knew my half
from the sale would be life changing for me. I told her I didn't want
the money. The idea of keeping the house in the family because of
what it meant to her was more important to me. It defined Mum's
sense of identity and her place in the world. It was a place she was at
her happiest.'

'It's getting sold, isn't it?'

Rob nods.

'Have you spoken to Sue about this?'

'To be honest, I think Gary's putting pressure on her to move the
sale along.'

'So, there's still a chance you can change her mind?' Nancy
sounds hopeful.

'I doubt it. As they say, money goes to money.'

Rob sits a little straighter. 'When I was clearing some of Mum's
things from the house, I came across a photograph that... well, let's
just say, it was not what I was expecting.'

'Oh! Why was that?'

Rob rubs his chin. 'It was an old photograph of a family. A man and a woman with a child. It's odd, I've no idea who they are. I know all my relatives and I've seen all the old photographs of the family, but not this one.'

'Oh, I see.' Nancy brushes her skirt with her hand. 'Did your mum know you'd seen the photograph?'

'At the nursing home, they often had sessions where they would look at pictures of the past that were relevant to the clients. You know, try to help them remember. I saw them do it with Mum a few times. So, I took the photograph on one of my visits to see if it would jog her memory.'

'Oh, really. And did Jeanie say anything?' Nancy inhales, unaware she is holding her breath.

'Not at first. She was tired and confused, and I was going to leave it at that.'

'That was probably best.'

'But she remembered.'

'She did, did she? What did she say?'

'Out of nowhere she said, Corfu.'

Nancy's eyes widen. 'Corfu. That's Greek, isn't it? I wonder where that came from.'

Rob stares at Nancy; he can tell she is flustered. 'The other thing she said was he shouldn't have gone there. I can only presume she means the man in the photograph.'

Nany draws in a wavering breath. 'Well, isn't that peculiar?'

'Is there something you're not telling me, Nancy?'

She sighs and reaches out, covering his hand with her own. 'I can't tell you. I kept her trust in life and I will keep it now that she is dead.'

'Why can't you tell me?'

'Just leave it. Walk away from it. It's just a photograph.'

Rob casts his eye around the function suite.

'There's no one here who would know,' Nancy says quietly.

'What about Uncle Bert?'

'Not even him.'

'I don't understand this. This isn't just an ordinary photo, is it? Why did Mum have this photograph and who are the people in it?'

'It's not for me to say.'

'You obviously know.'

'We have just said goodbye to the person who should have told you, and for all these years, she didn't. I'm not going to betray her trust today, of all days.'

Rob scratches his head. 'What does that mean?'

Nancy sighs.

'What?'

'I think it's best if you let the past be just that... the past.'

'I can't do that, not now. Mum has been keeping something from me, and from Sue, something that is making you uncomfortable. I don't understand why she would do that. That's not the woman I know.'

Nancy sighs again, this time deeper and longer. 'I understand Rob. I really do, but believe me, nothing good will come out of it.'

'How can you say that?' Rob can see how Nancy's face changes with his question. It is now dark with apprehension. 'What are you not telling me?'

Chapter 5

'Thanks for coming, Zoe.' Rob hands Zoe a mug of coffee and places a saucer with biscuits on the kitchen table. 'How was the drive?'

'It was fine. It's a lovely drive along the coast.' Zoe hovers her hand over the biscuits and then picks a white chocolate and raspberry one. 'Mm. These are nice.'

'I got them at the local shop and then when I got back to the house and put them in the cupboard, there was an unopened packet. Mum must have liked them too.'

'How did the funeral go? I'm sorry I couldn't make it. I'd hoped to get away a day early from the conference, but it was impossible.'

'Don't worry about it. I know you would have been there if you could. It went well.'

'I'm glad.'

'The crem was packed. Mum had arranged the whole funeral with the Coop several years ago, even down to what handles would be on the coffin. She wanted a religious service, but she also wanted a humanist speaker too. So, when we all got back to the wake, Bill did a moving eulogy. Mum had heard Bill at several funerals and said that she wanted him to do hers. Bill's the humanist, by the way. He was good. He got her down to a tee. About a week before the funeral, he sent me a template of questions to answer about Mum, her past, growing up, meeting Dad, all that stuff, right through her life. I had to ask Nancy about when Mum was growing up and their times together.'

'Did Sue help?'

'I asked her if she wanted to come up to Elie and stay at Mum's and we could share our memories and get something on paper, but she couldn't make it.'

Zoe stared at Rob. 'Surprise, surprise.'

'We spoke on the phone. It's done now. Actually, she was quite good at remembering things I'd forgotten.'

Zoe bites into her biscuit, ignoring Rob's praise for his sister. 'These biscuits are really good. I'll have to buy a packet for myself.'

Rob raises his eyebrows.

'I'm sorry. It's really none of my business. As long as she contributed, that's what matters.' Zoe takes one last drink of coffee and places the mug on the table. 'So, how are we going to do this?'

'Like everything in life, mum has it organised. She left instructions in her will for all her clothes to go to charity shops, The British Heart Foundation, CHAS, Cancer Research...'

'That's a lot of charities.'

'You should see the clothes.'

Zoe smiles. 'We better get cracking, then.'

It feels like packing a life away, his mum's life. There are several cupboards full of her clothes: blouses, skirts, dresses, cardigans, tops, shoes, and jackets. He can still smell the distinctive aroma of her perfume on the collar of some of her jackets, forcing a ball of grief from his throat.

By the time they finish, ten black plastic bags bulge around their feet.

'We'll need to get these in the car.' Rob checks his watch. 'Good. We've plenty of time. I'm sure Thursday is a late opening day. After we've finished at the charity shops, would you like something to eat?'

'Where do you have in mind?'

'Where they serve the best fish in Fife?'

'The famous chip shop in Anstruther?' Her eyes shimmer.

Rob laughs. 'No. This one's in Elie. It was Mum's favourite. It's called The Ship Inn. The fish is amazing and if we get a seat outside, the view is just as impressive.'

'Is it far?'

'No. Once we get back from dropping the clothes off, we can walk there in ten minutes.'

'Sounds perfect.'

The Ship Inn sits in a row of old houses, its white exterior and blue framed windows making it the centrepiece of the street. The outside seating area is opposite, across the narrow street. Rob had pre-warned Zoe that the tables were normally busy, so not to be too disappointed if they had to eat inside. To their relief, a couple are just leaving as they arrive. They weave through the tables towards the vacant one. When Rob goes to order their food, Zoe sits at the timber table in stunned silence, taking in the vast expanse of sand that stretches towards a shadowed headland where the sinking sun sprays the sky in a hue of caramel and a blaze of aureate cloud.

When Rob returns, his face lights up in response to Zoe's glowing smile.

'I can see why your mum loved this place so much,' she enthuses, scarcely containing her appreciation.

Rob sits opposite her. He has bought two glasses of red wine and places them on the table.

'It's a Merlot.'

'Lovely. I meant to ask you. How is work?'

'I'm in between jobs. I've left the college.'

Zoe leans forward. 'Oh! What happened?'

'It was no surprise, really. There've been cutbacks for about a year. I'd heard that the lecturers would be the first to go, not the curriculum heads. There was to be a restructuring. Basically, getting people to do the same job but for less money. To tell you the truth, I haven't been happy for some time. So, they offered me a severance package, and it was pretty decent, so I took it.'

'So, you'll be okay money-wise?'

'I only have to think of me these days, and I'm not leading the most lavish lifestyle. Besides, if I can't persuade Sue that it's a good idea to keep Mum's house, then there'll be the money from the sale.'

'Are you looking for a job? What's the lecturing market like these days?'

'To be honest, I'm enjoying the break. I've been busy with the funeral and the business of putting Mum's affairs in order. I didn't realise what was involved. There's so much to do. At least the funeral took care of itself.'

'Your mum made sure of that, as always.'

Rob smiles. 'She did. When her diagnosis was confirmed, she made sure that everything was in place and organised to the letter before she lost the capacity to do so. She didn't want to be a burden, even when she was dead. Seeing how smoothly it all went, I'm so glad she had the foresight to do so.'

Zoe takes a drink. 'Mm, that's nice.'

'I thought you'd like it.'

'How are you, Rob? Really?' Zoe enquires.

'I'm doing okay.'

'Are you sure?'

'If anything, it's been a bit weird.'

Zoe knows this is a reference to Sophie. 'It's only to be expected. You're human after all.'

'On the day of mum's funeral, when the hearse arrived, it brought it all back. I hadn't really thought about it. I was so preoccupied with what was going on. From when mum passed and up until the funeral, I'd been living in a bubble. It was surreal. That morning, I just wanted the day to be over, and then, instead of seeing mum, it was Sophie's hearse and Sophie's coffin I saw.'

'Oh, Rob.' Zoe shakes her head sadly.

Rob runs his fingers through his hair. 'Even after two years, it can still floor me.'

Zoe smiles fondly. 'I still think about Soph. In fact, I don't think there's a day that passes, I don't think about her.'

'Sometimes, after we'd visited mum, we'd come down here. Sophie always ordered the fish and chips. She loved the view too.'

Zoe wipes her eyes with a napkin. 'I can see why.'

Their meal arrives, and they eat in silence.

Rob looks up from his plate. 'You're really quiet.'

'I can't eat and talk at the same time, and this fish is amazing.' She points her fork at the white flesh. 'I want to savour every morsel.'

Rob smiles. 'I'm glad you like it.'

'I like everything about this place, the food, the view and...' she picks up her almost empty glass, 'The wine.'

'I'll get another. In fact, why don't I get a bottle? It will save me having to go to the bar again.'

A flash of horror crosses Zoe's face. 'I've drunk a whole glass of wine! I can't drive. What was I thinking?'

'It's fine. You can stay the night. Do you have to be back in Edinburgh tonight?'

'Well, no.'

'Then that's it settled. There're four bedrooms to pick from.'

'I'd hate to put you out.' She shakes her head. 'I can't believe I've just done that. I'm always so careful.'

'To tell you the truth, I never gave it a thought. It tells me you're relaxed and I'm glad you're here.'

'You're not just saying that because you're stuck with me?'

Rob smirks. 'Not if it means we can share a bottle of wine.'

For dessert they eat apple pie and cream, and once the server clears their table, another lights scented tea tree candles. It is dark now and yellow lights illuminate the windows of the houses perched above the sea wall that run the length of the beach.

Most people are relaxing, enjoying drinks now that they have finished their meals.

There is a burst of laughter from another table as Rob pours the last of the wine into their glasses and smiles weakly. 'I really want to keep the house. Do you know what I mean? Can you understand that?'

I know exactly what you mean, Zoe thinks. 'I can see why. This place... well, it grows on you.'

'For some, a house is just brick and mortar, but that house meant so much more to mum. It was her life, as Elie was. She was truly happy here. It's funny, you know, but when I'm in that house, it feels like a warm cosy blanket is wrapped around me. There's just something about it.'

Zoe looks at him curiously.

'And I would say that even without all this wine inside me, if you're wondering.'

'I believe you.' Zoe laughs.

'That's why this whole business with the photograph seems surreal. I spoke to Nancy at the funeral.'

'And?'

Rob explains Nancy's reaction. 'She knows, but she's not going to tell me. This whole thing feels unreal. I've just found out my mum was not the woman I thought she was.'

'She's still your mum. That doesn't change. We all have secrets; some are just bigger than others.'

'This is starting to feel quite a big one, otherwise, why wouldn't Nancy tell me, and why is it only Nancy that knows?'

He can see her going over it in her head. 'Because whatever it is that ties your mum to that photograph, the only person your mum felt comfortable sharing it with was her lifelong friend.'

Rob remembers the moment he showed his mum the photograph at the nursing home. 'When Mum said *Corfu,* it was the first time I'd seen her smile in her whole time at that nursing home.'

'The photograph, or to be more precise, the family in it, has some kind of connection to your mum. That's why she had the photograph, but it doesn't explain Nancy's reluctance to tell you what it was. The question is what was that connection? I think that photograph was taken somewhere in Corfu and that could be where the answers lie.'

Rob frowns. 'I can't let this go now. I don't know.'

They finish their drinks, and Rob checks his watch.

'There're a few beers in the fridge if you want to head back?'

Zoe smiles. 'I could do with the walk.'

Rob looks at the sky and points Zoe's attention to a threatening bank of dark cloud. 'I think it's going to rain.'

They make it back to the house just as the first drops of rain fall. As they go through the house, Rob turns on a lamp in the hallway and in the kitchen. Zoe glances outside into the garden where the trees from the orchard loom in the dark, and then fade, as Rob adjusts the dimmer switch.

Rob retrieves two beer bottles from the fridge, plucks a bottle opener from a drawer and as he opens the bottles, suggests they sit on the sofa in the extension his mum had built, which she christened '*the family room*.'

'What's good in your life, Zoe?'

His question is unexpected. She keeps her eye fixed on the bottle of beer in her hand. She examines her fingers and her painted nails. 'I've got a good job, well paid, my own brand new flat, I can afford two holidays a year, my cars decent...'

'What about people, friends... is there anyone special?'

Zoe draws herself up from the sofa and Rob glimpses tiny muscles flicker at the edge of her mouth. 'Not since Greg left, but I'm over it and him.'

Rob thinks she sounds defensive, and he could kick himself for asking her such questions. He has only reminded her of what has gone wrong in her life, of course she would mention Greg. What was he thinking? That was it. He wasn't thinking.

'I'm sorry, Zoe. I shouldn't have asked.'

'It's fine, honestly. It's not as if you don't know all the details. You and Soph were great. You were both my rock. I'd never have got through it without the both of you.'

There is an awkward silence. The tables have turned and unexpectedly, Rob feels the throb of grief.

'Look, if the truth be told, Greg turned out to be one of life's bastards and bullies. It just took me sometime to figure it out. But we were both to blame for what happened,' Zoe continues, to Rob's surprise. 'We created our own little tsunami of destruction. Our rows were like a river of flammable material. It was very effective in destroying anything that was ever good about us. The worst of it was, when he drank too much, he used his fists and I struggled to hide the bruises. I might be small in stature, but I could also give as much as he gave. No one should live like that.'

His eyes haven't left her, and to her shame, she is enjoying the attention.

'Do you still see his family? Do they keep in touch with you?'

'I think there's a saying, when you divorce someone, you divorce their family, too. I never really got on with his sisters. I think they felt Greg was too good for me. They definitely made it plain they felt he was marrying below his station. Apart from Angela, she was the youngest sister. I always got on with her. She wasn't like her sisters. We still meet up now and again. He's bankrupt, by the way.'

'Greg!'

'His business folded. Obviously, his family blames me because of the stress I put him through with the divorce and the financial settlement. Ten grand for every bruise,' she says, bitingly.

A photograph of Sophie, Rob, and his mum catches Zoe's eye, sitting amongst a small gallery of framed photographs on a side unit.

'When was that taken, the one with your mum and Soph?'

Rob turns to look at the photograph. 'Just before she was diagnosed. It was out in the garden. We stayed here for the weekend... it was the last time she was here.'

Zoe touches his arm, and he places his hand over hers. It is a physical urge, an unexpected desire of affection. They stay touching, both stuck in the moment, not knowing what to do next, and then Rob slips his hand from her.

'It's getting late.' Zoe says. She moves to the edge of the sofa and yawns.

Rob wonders if it is exaggerated, a play at the moment that has just passed.

She smiles. 'Too much wine and beer. I'll certainly have no trouble sleeping tonight.'

'You can have the room upstairs. It's the second on the left. There's an en suite in that one. Mum used it as the guest room.'

'Thanks. I'll just go up then.'

'What would you like for breakfast?'

'I don't want to put you to any trouble.'

'Some toast with scrambled egg? I'll even put some cheese in it.'

'Sounds lovely.'

'See you in the morning, then.'

She rises and Rob can see she is hesitant. 'Thank you for a lovely evening. Goodnight, Rob.'

The memories of his day with Zoe swim in his head. He stares at the photograph of Sophie and his mum, and he can't comprehend they are no longer with him: talking, laughing, touching, smiling, eating, sleeping, and breathing. He wants to believe they are somewhere, wherever that somewhere may be. And in his mind, they have found one another; they are together. It is a comforting thought, even just for an instant.

Rob is astonished that he has gone most of the day without mentioning the photograph and Nancy's reaction. Since he discovered it, the image has taken up so much space in his thoughts; it has wormed into his head.

Rob has studied the grainy photograph on countless occasions. He has peered into the eyes of the man and woman and speculated what lies behind the eyes that stare back at him.

The woman has high cheekbones; the skin taught across her cheeks. Her frame is slight and thin, her hair long and dark. There is an elegance in the way she sits, her back straight and her head held high. The man's hand rests tentatively on her shoulder. It is an intimate gesture, shared by two people who are at ease in each other's company and familiar with one another. There is a definite synchronicity. They are a couple. A family.

He has tried to imagine her voice. He has tried to savour every detail and catch glimpses of their story.

His mind floods in a bright light. It is uplifting, important. It feels worthwhile. To do nothing is not an option, this much he knows.

Why has his mum kept her secret from him? It hurts, especially since she can't answer his questions. He feels he suddenly does not know the woman he has known all his life.

At times, he is hesitant, but it is always short-lived and always framed with a question - Who is this family and who is this other woman who was his mum?

Chapter 6

The morning sun washes the kitchen in a delicate light as Rob makes a strong coffee from a Nespresso machine. He remembers giving it to his mum as a Christmas present several years ago. He opens the glass doors that lead into the garden and sinks into one of the wicker chairs that surround a glass table. He feels a slight dampness on the cushion, which reminds him he forgot to take them indoors from last night's rain. Luckily, it had only been a light shower.

Rob takes a sip of coffee, revelling in its strong and bitter taste, as he spots several large snails stuck to the garden wall and he wonders if it has taken them all night to get to where they are.

He glimpses next door's black cat, prowling in the orchard as if it owns the garden. It used to eye him with suspicion, but now goes about its business, ignoring him.

A crow has landed on the wall and wipes its beak on the stone. A sudden noise startles it, and it takes flight in a fluttering of wings.

'I hope you don't mind; I've had a shower, and I made myself a coffee,' she says with an air of apology.

Rob looks up. Zoe is walking towards him, cup in hand.

'Not at all. You don't have to ask either.' He shifts in his chair, an accompanying warmth spreads through his chest at the sight of her.

Her hair is wet, and she has tied it in a bun. She walks barefoot across the stone cladding, smiling a good morning, as she sits next to him. He hasn't noticed before; her toenails are red, and she has a petite tattoo, a rose that sits just above her ankle.

'Did you sleep well?' he asks.

'I did. It's probably the best sleep I've had in weeks.'

Rob smiles. 'You should come more often.' Instantly, he regrets this. It is overfamiliar, and something this situation is not.

She smiles back at him, easing his worry. 'Thanks for the offer.' She leans back in the chair. 'This is a lovely garden. You really have to sit in it to appreciate how beautiful it is.'

'Mum loved it. She spent hours pottering about in it, weeding and planting. She even pointed the wall one year, all on her own. As her health failed, she was forced to get a gardener. I think he came every two weeks, just to keep on top of it. Unfortunately, Mum never handed down the gardening gene to me.'

'It would be a shame for it to not be kept tidy.'

'That reminds me. I need to get in touch with the guy that did the garden. I don't know if he's local, so he might not have heard about Mum. She kept all the important phone numbers in a little book she kept by the phone. His number is probably in there.'

'I remember when you bought that coffee machine for your mum. You were worried that she wouldn't be able to work it.'

'I certainly regretted it to start with.'

'Soph told me you must have shown her a hundred times before she got the hang of it.'

He is mindful of how often they mention Sophie in their conversation, and he wonders if it is deliberate on Zoe's part.

'I've heard nowadays they're putting the ashes of loved ones into lockets and other pieces of jewellery. It's become quite popular.'

Zoe screws up her face. 'I could never do that.'

'I don't think I could either.'

'Have you got you mum's ashes back?'

'They'll be ready to get collected tomorrow.'

'Have you decided what you're going to do with them?'

'Half of her is going beside Dad and the other half is going next to that tree. It was what she wanted, to be in her garden.'

Zoe sat staring at the tree. 'But you're selling the house. Have you told Sue what your mum wanted?'

Rob sighs. 'She thinks I'm making it up to stop the sale of the house,' he says with a trace of exasperation.

'Of course, she would.'

'If I dig the hole deep enough, no one will ever know.'

'Is it legal?'

'I don't know. I've never thought about it. There's only three people that know. Me, you, and Sue. And she's back in London. She's not going to be back up here. What about you, Zoe? Do you approve of it?'

'If that's what your mum wanted, then, of course, as long as it's a big hole, who's going to know?'

'Exactly.' He continues, 'And I promised her I would.'

'Then, the way I see it, you don't have a choice.'

Rob regards his empty cup. 'What about that breakfast I promised you? Are you hungry?'

Zoe raises an eyebrow. 'I thought you'd never ask.'

Zoe picks up her fork and takes a mouthful of the last remaining piece of scrambled egg. 'You really do make a good breakfast.' Zoe says, placing her fork and knife on the plate and dabbing the side of her mouth with a napkin.

'It's a secret family recipe.'

'Really!'

Rob smirks. 'No.'

'You had me there.'

'I do like to cook. I'm not Gordon Ramsay by any stretch of the imagination, but I enjoy it. The only problem is most recipes don't cater just for one. There's always maths involved, trying to work out the right amount of ingredients. Half the time, I end up just guessing and it still turns out okay, well, mostly. What about you? Do you like to cook?'

'Me! No. If I can get away with a microwave meal, I'm happy with that.'

'Now there's a challenge.'

'What?'

'Let me cook you something. Anything you want.'

'Oh, I don't know.'

'What's your favourite meal... well, microwave meal?'

'I'm not very adventurous with food. Let me see.' She stares at the ceiling. 'Shepherd's Pie.'

Rob raises an eyebrow.

'I told you. I like simple food.'

'Shepherd's Pie it is then.'

'You're really going to cook it. I thought you were kidding.'

'What are your plans for today?'

Zoe shrugs. 'I didn't expect to stay here, so I guess I need to get back to Edinburgh. I can't go about all day in these clothes. I need to change. What about you? How long are you staying here?'

'A few more days, at least. There's still a lot to do.' The thought of Zoe leaving deflates him and he wonders if she feels this, too.

For the first time since they have been together, there is an awkward silence between them.

Rob stands and takes the breakfast plates to the sink. He turns on the hot tap and squeezes the washing up liquid into the water. He feels her standing next to him. 'I could always come back.'

'You're thinking of that Shepherd's Pie I promised I'd make?'

'There is that, too. But seriously, if you want, I'd really like to come back.'

He turns to face her. 'I'd like that.'

She takes a deep breath. 'Me too.'

That morning, Zoe returns to Edinburgh. Rob takes a walk along the coastal path, which is in effect a well-trodden track that skirts the coastline. In places, and over time, sand dunes have banked on the edges of the track, formed by the winds that gust from the sea and now bend the long grass. Further along, exposed black rocks shimmer in their coating of seaweed and shelter crystal clear pools where gulls rest and explore.

Rob walks with his head bowed, only lifting it to offer a greeting to fellow walkers that pass. The sun breaks the cloud cover and is pleasant and warm. He looks towards the next village, St. Monans, and decides to turn back towards Elie. He stops to remove his jacket and feels both elated and irritated with himself. He has enjoyed Zoe's company. For the first time since Sophie's death, he has felt comfortable and at ease with himself. He has seemed a different person. He is no longer tense and to his astonishment; he feels like himself, which after such a long absence, is a welcomed encounter.

In the last few days, he has thought of nothing else but the photograph and Zoe. They are both intertwined and connected in his thoughts.

Has he gone too far? He registers a surge of guilt, which would seem to confirm his question. Then, he reconsiders, he has done nothing wrong. And what would *wrong* mean? It has been two years since Sophie died and, in that time, he has not even looked at another woman. Until now, that is. And it is not just any other woman. It is Zoe, Sophie's best friend, and someone Rob has known for as long as he had known Sophie. She is no longer just Sophie's best friend. He sees her differently. It feels like for the first time he has just seen her for who she really is. When he was walking with her on the beach all he wanted to do was slip his hand in hers, he had to resist the temptation to do so.

She has lit a light in his dark place. There is the physical attraction, but there is also a deeper connection. When they are together, it is present. It is tangible in the way they speak; it is a compatibility of ideas, thoughts, and feelings which they share when together. Was it always like this between them? Does it matter? It is the present, the here and now that has manifested this change in him. Then he panics. Is he giving off signs that suggest what he is thinking and what he believes when he is with her?

To tell her what he feels is unthinkable. He hopes there comes a time when it is not.

***

Zoe reverses into the vacant space and places the parking permit on the dashboard. She is glad of the shower she had this morning, but desperate to change her clothes.

In the flat, she habitually places her keys on the sideboard and sweeps up the mail lying on the wooden floor. She walks into the kitchen, checks each letter and groans as she tosses them on the table. They are all bills and junk mail.

Once changed into fresh clothes, she loosens her hair, and it falls in waves around her shoulders. She applies a little makeup in the mirror and considers her reflection. She wonders if Rob pays any attention to the way she looks. Does he read her face with curiosity? Does she fascinate him? Has he deconstructed her face like she has his? His eyes pull her like a magnet, deep with sadness, and at times, alive with light. She finds herself transfixed when he speaks, and when he lowers his head in a moment of thought. She likes the way he crosses his legs. She thought she would die, when that morning, fresh from the shower, she walked out into the garden and Rob was there. Zoe thinks again, as she has since she left Rob this morning, that something is changing. She reconsiders this. Something has changed.

What has come over her? She has succumbed to the most basic of instinct: uncomplicated desire. She has betrayed Soph by her thoughts and feelings. No! She has only ever shown Rob concern and compassion. Her worry for Rob is genuine.

It occurs to Zoe that what has been happening is the making of a connection between Rob and herself. The feeling of being alone, the emptiness she feels, is suffocating. And then that spike again. Is she dishonouring Soph's memory, their forever bond of friendship? A distinct impression takes her then, a hauling from her of hope, of happiness shrinking in the pit of her stomach.

Zoe looks around the room. Her desire to go into town is pulling her towards the door. Right now, she needs to be amongst the hustle of people and escape these thoughts, even if it is just for a momentary reprieve.

Zoe steps out onto Cumberland Street and squints in the dazzling sunlight. She pulls a pair of sunglasses from her bag and slides them over her eyes. She crosses the street and walks steadfastly along the gentle gradient of Howe Street, past shop windows and cafes, and then waits for a break in the traffic before crossing the junction onto Queen Street Gardens West. She turns right onto the long sweep of Queen Street and then left onto North Castle Street, where she smiles at the sight of a seagull standing proudly on the statue of Thomas Chalmers' head. Then, as she reaches Castle Street, she glances at the prehistoric rock where Edinburgh Castle sits atop, unexpectedly; she feels that her life is about to take a pivotal transformation. She wonders if she is about to cry, as she feels a mix of trepidation and happiness shift inside her.

Chapter 7

He came across the name unexpectedly and since then, his heart has raced, and his mind has ruminated over every possibility. He phones Zoe.

'There're a few names in Mum's phonebook I don't recognise. One caught my attention.'

'Why was that?' Zoe asks.

'It was a Greek name.'

'That's very interesting.'

'There was a mobile number next to it. Is it too much of a coincidence? What do you think?'

'There could be valid reasons why your mum knew this person.'

'True. But it's the only foreign name in her book and it's Greek.'

'Are you going to get in touch with them? They can obviously speak English, unless your mum spoke Greek, which I'm assuming she didn't.'

'Now, that would be weird. If she could, she hid it well. No. I'm confident this person must speak English.'

'Is it a British mobile number or does it have an international area code?'

'I didn't think about that. I'll check.' Rob opens the book and flips a few pages. He smiles. 'It's all in alphabetical order. Here we are... you're right, it's a different code.'

'I'll Google the one for Greece.' Her fingers flurry along the small keypad of her mobile phone. 'So, it's zero, zero, then thirty and then a ten-digit mobile number.'

The realisation smacks him in the face. 'It is. It's a Greek number.'

'You didn't tell me their name.'

Rob looks at the page again and places his finger on the name written in his mother's handwriting. 'Damaris. I'm assuming that's a woman. Her name is Damaris Othonos.'

'You need to phone her.'

'I know, but what will I say?'

'Well. I suppose you need to tell her your mum has passed. It's not the best introduction, but it can only get better after that.'

'She might not answer. She doesn't know my number.'

'Did your mum use a mobile?'

'Yes.'

'Then phone her on that, or her landline.'

'I'm not ready. I need to prepare myself, you know, think about what I'm going to say.'

'Of course. You don't have to phone her just now.'

'It has to be right. I need to say the right words. I don't want her hanging up on me.'

'I'm sure she won't.'

Rob nods, taking this in. 'You're probably right. I'll write down some bullet points. That way, it should flow. It's important that it flows, that it's not disjointed. I don't want to confuse her. I don't know how good her English is.'

'Just take your time. There's no rush.'

'I wonder who she is?'

'Damaris Othonos.' Zoe says out loud. 'She has a strong-sounding name. I wonder if the woman reflects it.'

'There's only one way to find out.'

Rob sees vividly the day he showed his mum the photograph. Was this woman, Damaris Othonos, in his mum's thoughts then? He now feels guilty that he may have forced a tremendous weight on her, even through the fog of her fading mind.

Chapter 8

Rob has hardly slept the night before. He is sitting in the garden in one of the wicker chairs and wonders if his mum knew the number off by heart that he is now about to call. How many times has she spoken to Damaris Othonos? He has prepared a list of questions, but in this moment, they feel insignificant, at worst, an inquisition. He breathes deeply. The thought of opening a door that has been hidden and closed to him all his life is both exciting and terrifying. What will lie behind it, and is he prepared for the implications of untangling the threads of... whatever it is that this conversation leads him to?

From the garden, he can see Zoe sitting at the kitchen table, and it is a comfort to him that she continues to visit. His breathing is a flutter in his chest as he taps in the digits on the keypad and turns on the speaker, adjusting the volume. It occurs to him he should have phoned from the landline, the phone his mum would have used. She had a mobile, but never used it much to call people. It was others who called her.

It feels he is waiting an eternity. He is half expecting to hear an answering machine kick in, or at worst, for the phone to ring out. He taps his thigh with his fingers. He glances towards the sky. *She's not going to answer.*

'*Yassoo.*' It is a female voice.

'Oh! Hello. Can you speak English?' It is not the best introduction he has made, but a necessary one given the circumstance.

There is a silence. 'Who is this?' Her voice is heavily accented.

'I'm sorry. I should introduce myself,' *Please don't hang up.* 'My name is Rob Webster. I think you knew my mum, Jeanie Webster.'

Another silence.

'I found your number in her phone book. Are you Damaris Othonos?'

'You said you were her son.'

'Yes. That's right.'

'I am Damaris.'

The sound of her voice saying her name is strangely comforting. 'There's something I need to tell you.'

'I think I already know.'

'You do?'

'Yes. It was agreed between us that she would stop phoning me, as her condition was worsening, and she did not want to embarrass me once her mind began to fail her. I have been expecting your call.'

'You have?'

There is a sharp intake of breath. 'It means Jeanie has died.'

'I'm sorry.'

Her voice begins to break. 'And I too am sorry. She was your mother.'

'Your name and your telephone number were in her little black book. I've been trying to get in touch with people who knew my mum and who may not necessarily know she has passed away.'

It seems to take a moment for Damaris to absorb this, and then Rob can hear her muffled sobs.

She gathers herself. 'It has still come as a shock.'

'It would. I knew that it was only a matter of time, and even though I was prepared for it, when her time came, it was still difficult to take in.'

'Has there been a funeral?'

'Yes. A week ago, now.'

'Oh!'

'Would you have gone if you knew?'

'It would have been difficult. We both knew it was not a possibility.'

'Where do you live? This is a Greek number, and your English is excellent.'

'Kerkyra.'

'I've not heard of it. Is it in Greece?'

'You will know it as Corfu.'

Rob's heart flutters. 'Oh! I see. How long have you known my mum?'

'For a long time.'

A degree of informality has somehow arrived in their exchanges.

'She spoke a lot about you and your sister and, of course, Elie. Over the years, we spoke about our lives, or families and when she moved to the house in Elie, it felt like I lived there, too. I got to know all about the village and her neighbours; your mum had a lovely way of making you feel involved in her life, even though we were thousands of miles apart. And of course, I told her all about my life. Over the years, we grew very close. It has been a long time since I've heard her voice. I miss her very much.'

Rob has not been expecting this. In fact, he has thought little about the relationship the two women might have had. 'This is all very strange.'

'I know, it must be.'

'Since you are friends, you must have met, but you live in Greece.'

'We have met several times. A long time ago, I went to Edinburgh and Jeanie has visited me.'

'She has!' This revelation derails his train of thought. What else does he not know about his mum?

'We shared photographs of our families, sent presents at birthdays and at Christmas.'

Rob almost drops the phone in disbelief. This is a woman Rob does not know. His mum has kept all this from him.

'I've had to clear mum's house and went through all her personal things. I didn't come across any photographs like the ones you've suggested.'

'She may have lost them over time,' Damaris answers quickly.

Rob exhales evenly. 'I'm sorry if I'm asking you too many questions.'

'You are not. I understand. It is hard for me to think that she has gone.'

'I suppose I'm curious how you knew each other? With you in Corfu and mum in Elie.'

That silence again. He knows he is making her feel uncomfortable, and it is not the impression he wants to leave, after all, he has just told her his mum has died and she is upset by this.

'Damaris?'

'Yes.'

'Why don't I phone you another time? In a few days, maybe, just to make sure you're okay.'

'Yes. I would like that, Rob. I need time to... I have lost someone very special to me.'

'It's not a problem. Honestly, I understand.'

'Thank you.'

'I'll phone again on mum's phone. That way, you'll know it's me.'

'Thank you. Goodbye, Rob.' And then she hangs up, and she is gone, a remnant of his mum's other life.

Rob has come into the kitchen from the garden, his mind racing. Beneath all the words they spoke, the bigger question remains unanswered.

'Well. What did she say?' Zoe asks as she hands Rob a cup of coffee.

'She knew my mum and by all accounts they were very good friends.'

'That's something at least, isn't it?'

'It is.' Rob agrees. 'But it raises more questions than answers. I still don't know how they know each other.'

'You didn't ask her?

'It was delicate. She was upset, fragile even. I'd just told her mum had died. I had to be...' He searches for the right word. 'Diplomatic. Sensitive to how she was feeling. I didn't want to upset her any more than she already was.'

'No. That was the best approach given the circumstance.'

Rob sips his coffee. 'She was definitely not telling me everything.'

'She was hiding something from you?'

'It felt that way. No. I'm sure of it. She was hesitant. She said mum had visited her. She went to Corfu to see her.'

'That's interesting.'

'I can't recall mum ever going to Corfu and if she obviously didn't want anyone to know, although I suspect Nancy would have known.'

He clears his throat and compliments Zoe on her hair. She seems taken aback by this sudden interest in her.

'Thank you.'

'There's something different about it.'

She smiles mockingly. 'You mean it wasn't that nice before?'

'No! It's not that.'

'I'm just kidding. I've dyed it.'

'Oh! It does look darker.'

'I dye it every six weeks. You'd see the grey streaks if I didn't. It must be a gene that runs in the family. My mum was totally grey by the time she was in her forties.'

'A lot of women are going natural. It seems the *in thing* at the moment.'

'I'm not ready for that. Maybe in a few years' time.' She looks down at her hands and considers how easy it is to speak to Rob about such things. She could never imagine speaking to another man like this.

'I'm glad you came. I wasn't sure you would.'

'Thanks for asking me and inviting me to stay again. I had a free weekend. I brought a change of clothes this time.' Inside, she squirms. None of what she has just said sounds right.

There is relief in his voice. 'I thought we could go to The Ship Inn again for dinner, or if you fancy, somewhere different, that's fine with me, too.'

'No. The Ship Inn would be nice.' She feels herself relax now, but her guilt will prove a harder task to uproot. At moments like these, it bombards her with deep etched thoughts and memories of Sophie. She wonders if Rob has the same anxieties, then again, that depends on his motivation for asking her to visit again. Maybe, he is just lonely, following a course of his own, where he regards her as someone he can share the mystery of the photograph with. Has she become someone who he knows he can trust and confide in if he discovers things that will upset him, or if Damaris reveals the truth he is seeking? Whatever the ramifications of that truth may be. And what does all this mean in relation to them both? That he trusts her and feels safe in disclosing these things to her? Does he feel a close connection with her?

It could be a combination of all these things, or none, she regretfully admits.

There have been moments when she has been close to telling him of how she feels, but she has found herself holding back, as he may not reciprocate such affections. The thought of embarrassing Rob and possibly ending what has become their frequent time together fills her with dread. Such uncertainties bring an unaccustomed pressure behind her eyes, and she rubs them with a thumb and forefinger.

'Are you feeling alright?' Rob asks, concerned.

'I'm fine.'

'I've got some Paracetamol.'

Zoe shakes her head. 'Honestly, there's no need.'

He holds out his hand.

'I found this yesterday when I was clearing out some more of Mum's personal things.'

Zoe looks at his hand with interest.

'It's a Greek Drachma note. It was the Greek currency before the Euro. I found it in a drawer.'

'It would seem this woman Damaris is telling the truth after all.'

'It seems like she is. In fact, I know she is.'

'How can you be so sure?'

'Because I also found this.'

Rob takes a small blue box from the kitchen table, which Zoe hasn't noticed. It looks like a jewellery box with a golden crest on it.

The hinges are stiff, and Rob must use a certain amount of force to open the lid. He takes out a necklace that unfurls in his hand. Zoe notices a gold heart-shaped locket that Rob carefully opens.

'It's really fragile. I'm scared I'll break it.'

When he opens the locket, Zoe can see a black and white photographic portrait of a young couple. The woman's hair tumbles in waves onto her slender shoulders and even though the image is minute, Zoe can see that she is pretty, and her smile would suggest she is happy. Likewise, the man is also smiling, his hair is greased back from his forehead, and he is wearing a shirt and jacket.

'Can I see it?'

'Sure, but be careful with it.'

'I will.'

Zoe takes the locket from Rob and looks at it for a moment. Suddenly, she puts her hand on Rob's arm. 'It's them. This is real, isn't it? These are not just people in a photograph, they played a part in your mum's life...' Zoe traces her thumb over the image. 'She has a story to tell. I'm sure of it.'

Chapter 9

Sitting opposite the Ship Inn admiring the vast curvature of sand and islands of dark rock that populate the beach, Rob tells Zoe that Elie has a cricket club that instead of playing on grass, play on the very sand they are looking at, making them the only cricket club in Britain to play on a beach. Zoe pushes her sunglasses on top of her thick hair to take in the visual aspect of what Rob has just said. Their meal, fish, and chips with a portion of mushy peas is brought to them on two large oval plates. As they settle down to eat, a silence falls over them, but it is a comfortable one, which both are aware of.

'When are you going to phone Damaris?'

'I thought I'd do it tomorrow. Do you think that's enough time? I don't want to make her upset again.'

'I suppose so. Anyway, she'll be expecting you to call again.'

'I know. It feels like I'm imposing on her grief. She was obviously close to Mum. They must have been good friends. I can't believe I never knew any of this. Nancy knew about Damaris, too. There's no doubt about that. I wonder if she went to Corfu with Mum.'

'Well, if she did, she wasn't going to tell you, was she?'

'Maybe I should tell Nancy I've spoken with Damaris?'

Zoe thinks for a moment. 'I wouldn't.'

'No?'

She shakes her head. 'Wait until you've spoken again to Damaris and see where that lead you.'

Rob rubs his chin. 'The more I think about this, it just raises so many more questions.'

'When you showed me the locket, I noticed that the man and woman were both wearing the same clothes as in the other photograph. Which would mean it was taken at the same time. There could be other photographs. I don't know if they would have just taken one or two, or several at the same sitting.'

'I suppose it would depend on what they could afford.'

'That's probably true. You know, I can't help feeling this woman Damaris is linked to the photograph, too. You must admit, it's more than a coincidence that she's Greek.'

'I know. I've thought about that. Damaris knows, I'm sure of it.' Rob stares out over the sands and sighs heavily.

'I haven't noticed your tattoo before. That little rose above your ankle.'

Rob's voice pulls Zoe from her thoughts, and she stumbles over her words. 'Oh! Haven't you? I've had it for a few years now.'

'What made you get one?'

'I hadn't planned it. When mum died, I felt I wanted to do something that would keep her alive, that would always remind me of her, something that was permanent. So, that's why I got the tattoo.'

'But why a rose?'

'It was mum's favourite flower, a red rose.'

'That makes sense. It's actually quite touching.'

'I would never have got one otherwise. I'm not really into tattoos, but I'm attached to it now.'

'In more ways than one.'

They both laugh.

'And don't even think about it.'

'What!'

'Asking if I should get a tattoo.'

'I hadn't even thought about it.'

Rob sups his pint, and he can feel Zoe's gaze.

'What?'

Zoe twirls the stem of her wineglass. 'Let's just say you were thinking of getting one. What would it be?'

'You mean a tattoo that was significant to the memory of my mum?'

'Yeah. What would you choose?'

He frowns. 'I don't know. It's not something I've ever thought about.'

'Well, think about it now,' Zoe's eyes brighten.

Her enthusiasm encourages Rob to ponder his answer, and Zoe's absorbed smile warms him inside.

Finally, he thinks of something. He clears his throat. 'It would have to be a big fat... question mark.'

'Rob!' Zoe exclaims incredulously.

Rob raises his hands and grins. 'I'm only kidding.'

'I should hope so. That's cruel. So... have you really thought of what it would be?'

'I have.'

'What then?'

'It would have to be a golden sun.'

'Why the sun?'

'Mum always brightened up a room. She had the knack of turning a bad situation into something positive that you could learn from. She always saw the good in people and she would put others first, even if it meant it was detrimental to herself. She was an inspiration. She was my golden sun full of warmth and beauty.'

'That's beautiful, Rob.' Zoe looks hard into his eyes, and for the first time, she feels reluctant to submerge herself in the feelings that stir inside her. They will only complicate what is already an intricate and obscured situation. But can she? Truthfully, it is a question she cannot answer.

'That's what makes this whole thing so hard to accept. I've lost Mum, but who was she? Did I really know the person she was? Why the secrets?'

'She obviously had her reasons.' A strange sense of optimism comes over Zoe. 'You should get it done.'

The lines on his forehead crease. 'A tattoo of the sun?' Zoe seems so enthused and carefree; he finds her infectious and the notion of getting a tattoo is starting to appeal to him. A second ago, it seemed quite outrageous, but now he can even picture what the tattoo will look like. What has come over him?

'Yeah, why not? It can be a small one, like mine.' She grins. 'I'm not saying you should have it engrained on your forehead. It can be discreetly positioned, like mine.'

The appeal of it is sliding into place. 'Maybe on my upper arm.'

'Your deltoid would be a good place.'

'My what?'

She reaches over and touches his arm. 'Just there. What do you think? Discrete enough?'

It is a kind of *tell and dare* game, and he is enjoying colluding in it. It is a game she has initiated. In fact, he can feel the initial distaste for her suggestion that, ordinarily, would seem preposterous, fade from him, as if her fervour has melted it from him.

'It would be discrete,' Rob says, convincing himself.

'It would,' Zoe agrees.

'Do you know a good a tattoo artist?'

'The guy that did mine, Giles, is a good friend. He's got a great reputation; he's won awards, and he is meticulous when it comes to cleanliness. He keeps his studio pristinely sterile. It's spotless.'

'That's always a good benchmark.'

'He's booked up months in advance, but he'd do me a favour if I asked.'

'Okay then.'

'Are you serious?' Zoe tilts her head.

He nods. 'I can't believe it myself, but I think I am. You make the appointment and I'll get it done.'

Rob can't believe the effect Zoe is having on him. He is changing; she is changing him, opening him up to a different way of thinking. In her company, it soothes his fathomless anger at losing Sophie. The burden of his overwhelming loss subsides momentarily. She has enchanted him with her generosity of time and thoughtfulness. She has made him laugh again. He hasn't done that much in a while. He feels happy again. He can now indulge himself in such sentiments that it clothes him in a confidence that has, for so long now, deserted him.

The thought of losing what they have discovered together, or never seeing each other again, would be the worst outcome imaginable. How has it come to this? What stars have aligned that have changed so much? They have entered unfamiliar territory. Something has shifted and neither of them can control it. And for that reason, he is vulnerable to the voice that tells him Zoe was Sophie's best friend and confidant. What would Sophie have made of all of this? Would she rebuff it with deep shock and hurt, or would she give it her blessing?

Zoe reaches for her mobile that is lying on the table. 'I've got Giles' number in my contacts. I'll give him a call and see if we can get you booked in.'

'So soon.'

'You're not backing out?' Zoe's eyes fix on him.

'No. I said I'd do it and I will.'

Zoe smiles. 'Good, because he has just answered. Giles, hello. It's Zoe. I was wondering if you could do me a favour. It's for a friend and he'd like a tattoo done. Just a little one, so it won't take up much of your time.'

Rob listens, and now that it is close to happening a slight pang of regret tugs at him, but he brushes it away. He will do it.

'Saturday at two,' Zoe is saying as she glances at Rob for confirmation.

Rob gives her the thumbs up.

'That's perfect. Oh, his name is Rob Webster.' She listens for a moment. 'Yep. That's not a problem. Perfect. That's brilliant Giles and thank you. See you soon. Bye.'

She turns to Rob and sits back in her seat. 'Well, that's it booked. He had a cancellation. He can do it on Saturday. How lucky was that? No turning back now.'

They smile at each other.

'Now it is going to happen. I'm looking forward to it.'

'Good. All you need to do before the appointment is go onto the website and fill in your medical history and it's good to go.'

'Where is his... tattoo parlour? Is that what you call it? I don't know?'

'It's a tattoo shop, and it's on the Royal Mile.'

'That's good, easy to find then. What's it called?'

'Studio Four. I'll come with you if you want?'

'Would you?'

'Sure. You might need a chaperone after you get the tattoo!' Zoe jokes and they erupt into laughter. Zoe feels it is a significant moment. It suggests there is a blending between them, a bond that is growing with each day they spend together, and she is growing into what they are becoming. Closer.

Chapter 10

'Hello, Damaris.'

'Rob, it's nice to hear from you again.'

'It is? I wasn't sure if you would answer this time, knowing that it was me.'

'Why wouldn't I?'

'I really thought I'd upset you.'

'You didn't upset me. No. It was the news about your mother that did that. I'd been expecting it for a long time. I knew she was too ill to phone me, or even know who I was anymore. I was afraid that I would never know what had happened to her, since Jeanie and I only spoke amongst ourselves. Who would tell me? So, when you did phone, it was a mixture of sadness and of relief that made me cry.'

In some way, hearing Damaris' voice makes Rob feel it is the closest he is ever going to get to his mum again. He squeezes his eyes shut and his eyelashes are wet with tears.

He takes a deep breath. 'There's so many things I don't understand, and I think you are the only person that can answer my questions and help me get to know the part of my mum that was hidden from me all these years.'

'Oh, Rob. That was not what your mother wanted, believe me.'

'But that's how it feels. That's how it was. Neither you nor I can change that.'

'Your mother and I had many difficult conversations over the years. She hated keeping these secrets from you. It troubled her greatly.'

'I don't understand why she kept all this from Sue and me. Sue has no idea about any of this.'

'You haven't spoken to her about me?'

'No. Only Zoe knows.'

'Who is Zoe?'

'She was Soph's best friend. Sophie was my wife she...'

'I know, Rob. I'm sorry. It must have been devastating for you.'

'But of course, you would know. You probably know a lot about me.'

'Jeanie and I spoke a great deal about both our families. You must believe me. Jeanie wanted so much to tell you everything, but it was a difficult choice for her to make. When she found out about her diagnosis, she knew she only had a certain amount of time left. She wanted the moment to be right, and as you know, she deteriorated at a pace that surprised us all. The choice that she struggled with for all these years was eventually and cruelly taken from her. When you contacted me, and we spoke, I knew then the responsibility had fallen to me.'

'So, what do we do now? Do you just tell me, whatever that is?'

'I could, but somehow, that doesn't seem right. I'm sure Jeanie would not have approved. No. There is a better way and one in which I think is best for us all. How would you feel if I invited you to my home? Come to Corfu.'

It startles Rob. He is not expecting this proposition, and for a moment, it leaves him speechless.

'You want me to come to Corfu?

Rob can feel Damaris' smile.

'Yes. After all, this is where I live. It would please me greatly to talk face to face. It is something your mother and I spoke about many times. I know if she was still with us, it would have been something she would have wished for and approved of.'

It takes Rob aback at the pace of how things are developing, and he almost forgets about the photograph. 'I've found a photograph. It's old. Perhaps from the 40s. It's a family photograph, but I've no idea who they are. I showed it to Mum, and she definitely knew who they were, but because of her dementia, she was unable to tell me.'

'Bring the photograph with you. That's if you do decide to visit me.'

'Nothing would make me happier.'

'That makes me happy too.'

Rob can hear the relief in her voice as she must have heard it in his too.

'When will you come?'

'Just as soon as I can get a flight and book a hotel.'

'You can stay with me, I insist.'

'No. I'll book a room... somewhere.'

'It's the middle of the summer. Vacant hotel rooms will be as rare as a shower of rain. I have plenty of room.'

'Are you sure? I wouldn't want to put you out.'

'You wouldn't be.'

'There's just one other thing. I'd like Zoe to come with me. Would that be a problem?'

After the call, Rob tells Zoe about the conversation and Damaris' invitation.

'That's wonderful.' Perhaps it had been inevitable. This was just a necessary step in the process. Zoe hadn't seen it before, but she could see it more clearly now.

Rob is glowing. 'She said that mum had always wanted to tell me, but Damaris didn't elaborate on why she couldn't, not over the phone. That's why she wants me to go over there. She said mum would have wanted this.'

'How do you feel?'

'I'm not sure. I'm a mixture of contradictions. I'm apprehensive, but I'm elated. I'm scared of what she might tell me, but I'm eager to know. It helps that mum wanted to tell me, that sounds more like her.'

'I'm glad. That must be a comfort.'

'It is and a relief.'

Zoe's eyes fall on Rob's tattoo. 'Talking about relief, the tattoo looks amazing. I really like it. Do you?'

'I do. Who would ever have thought? People will think I'm going through an early midlife crisis.'

'Who cares what other people think? You know why you did it and that's all that matters.'

'You know as well, and that matters to me, too.'

Zoe fingers her bracelet and tries to make light of it, even though, at this very moment, she feels like a feather floating in the breeze. 'That's nice of you to say... I can imagine your mum smiling down on you right now.'

Rob grins. 'I'm not too sure about that. She'd use a few choice words that would inform me, in no uncertain terms, what she thought of my tattoo. Believe me, heaven will be turning blue. I can hear her now.'

'Well,' Zoe says, unperturbed. 'I'm going with, I think she would have liked it, given the reason you got it in the first place.'

'He was a nice guy... Giles.' Rob tries to steer the conversation away. 'He told me he was in a few of your classes at high school. I couldn't believe it when he said he has a degree in accountancy but hated every minute of working as an accountant.'

'I know. He'd always been good at art. He'd sketched portraits for family and friends and was encouraged by others' positive comments to give it a go to see if he could make decent money at it. Even at uni, he was always fascinated by tattoos and the art of it, so he thought, why not, and he made the jump, initially working for others, learning the craft until, he was good enough to do it on his own.'

'What an amazing story. You have to respect people like that. No matter the risk, they just go after what their heart tells them.'

'A bit like the pot calling the kettle black.' She bites into a piece of scone that she has quartered, buttered, and jammed. He too takes a piece of scone, his is halved, and he is about to take a mouthful when he sighs and drops the scone on the plate in front of him, covered in crumbs and the occasional sultana.

The air around them has changed, just as the air changes before it is about to rain. You can smell it.

Since the phone call with Damaris, he has been different. She can tell by the way he holds himself, the deep look in his eyes, the set of his mouth. An uneasiness has settled over him as he sinks into the chair and for the first time, Zoe thinks she might be losing him, even before she has gotten to know what she has found.

'What is it, Rob? Tell me.'

He stirs in his chair. 'It's about going to Corfu.'

'What about it? You're still going, aren't you?'

'Yes, but... I don't want to go on my own.'

'What do you mean?'

'I want you to come with me, Zoe.'

'But why?

'You've been with me all through this. You're the only person I can really talk to about it. You understand. You understand me. I know it's a bit sudden, and I'd understand if you can't or don't want to and I know I'm asking you to take time off your work...'

'Rob, stop.'

'I'm sorry, I've put you in an embarrassing position. Of course, you can't come.'

She smiles. 'You haven't and I can.'

Rob fully expected to be disappointed, but Zoe's answer makes his heart pound quicker. 'That's great. In fact, it's more than that, it's fantastic.'

'I'd love to. I've been accumulating leave all year. I haven't been able to use it up with work being so busy, but I've been told I need to use it, or I'll lose it.'

'And don't worry about the money.'

'I wouldn't dream of it. No. I'll pay my own way.'

'But I'm the one asking you to come with me. It wouldn't feel right.'

'If you don't let me pay, then I'm not coming.' Zoe raises her eyebrows.

Rob can tell she means it. 'Then we'll pay for our own flights.'

'And the hotel.' Zoe insists.

'We'll be staying at Damaris.'

Zoe's eyes widen.

'Yeah, she was quite insistent.'

'Oh, I see. And when are you thinking of going?'

'As soon as I can... as soon as we can.'

Chapter 11

She glances out of the taxi window. They are here, in Corfu, and on their way to Damaris' house. They have left the outlying suburbs of the capital and are travelling over the backbone of the island towards the west coast with its lavish display of rolling hills and stunning bays. She has never seen such striking colours, and gasps as each new bend displays a cobalt sea sprinkled with turquoise and crystal clear bays.

Has she been too impulsive? She knew she'd go before Rob had asked the question. Since he told her about Damaris' invitation, she has thought of nothing else. Rob's reason for going to Corfu has an emotional attachment that reaches into the very essence of his family. She, on the other hand, has a different kind of attachment to decipher. An affection exists between them. Is it becoming more than just friendship? Would she like it to be more? She is intrigued by the entire mystery that surrounds Rob's mum and she is flattered that Rob has asked her to accompany him. Obviously, he is pleased he will share whatever it is he is about to discover with her.

Her brows furl. Did Rob ask her because she was Soph's best friend? This troubles her. It is because she is the closest thing to Soph? Apart from Rob, she knew Soph better than anyone.

How the mind plays its tricks.

They are here, and Zoe banishes the thought just as the taxi is slowing to a stop. Something from the corner of her eye distracts her. To her alarm, it is a cat with a dead mouse dangling from its mouth. She squeals and Rob jumps in fright just as he has finished paying the taxi driver.

'That's so gross.'

'That might be, but the house isn't.'

Zoe turns to look at what Rob means. A two storied white-washed house sits at the end of a curved driveway surrounded by immaculately kept grounds. An older woman approaches, with a spring in her step and posture that defy her years. It's Damaris. Her hair is greying but thick bodied and pulled back behind her ears. As she moves, she smiles, a radiant smile that lights up the skin of her face. She wears a light dress that flows with every step and a gold cross that reflects the sun's rays. Something is familiar about her. Maybe her eyes, brown and oval, with a stillness set in them.

With outstretched arms, she envelopes him and pulls him to her. She steps back. 'I can't believe you are here,' she says, her eyes welling.

'That makes two of us.'

'Three of us,' Zoe adds.

'Oh, Damaris, this is Zoe.'

'Welcome, Zoe. Come, both of you, I'll show you to your rooms. Are you hungry?'

Rob detects it is not an enquiry.

'We will eat on the porch.'

'I hope you haven't gone to any trouble,' Rob says.

'It's nothing, just a dish or two.' Her voice catches. 'I can't believe you are standing in front of me. I can see the smile on your mum's face.'

Once unpacked and freshened up, Rob in one room and Zoe in another, they go out onto the porch and stare in amazement at the copious amount of food spread out over the table.

Rob grins. 'I thought you said it was just a dish or two.'

Damaris chuckles. 'It is. Now sit down and eat before it gets cold.'

Between mouthfuls of chicken souvlaki, grilled vegetables, strapatsada and meatballs, Damaris wants to know everything about Rob's life in Edinburgh, the house in Elie and Zoe.

Once they have eaten, she asks Rob about the photograph. She holds it in her hand and her eyes travel the image. 'This was taken just after the war.' She clutches the photograph to her chest and then sets it flat on the table. Her lips curl into a smile. 'I gave this to your mum many years ago now. You have come a long way for answers Rob. I think it is time to tell you the story that lies behind the photograph.'

Chapter 12
Edinburgh
1943

The bar was full of drinkers, groups of young men, some in army uniform, others in suits and ties, and women, dressed in their best skirts and blouses. They had been dancing most of the night in the alcohol-free dance halls and now descended upon the pubs and cafes of The Grass Market.

'Are you sure this is what you want to do?' Archie asked Frank, who sat opposite him in a corner of a pub.

'I've been painting and drawing the effects of the war for months now, the damage of German bombs from Peterhead to the shipyards on the Clyde,' Frank says. 'The War Artists Advisory Group is the government's way of recording the war effort and also the consequences of the war and the sacrifice the country is making.'

Archie had known Frank since they were boys. They played football in the streets of Leith and attended the same primary and high school and then followed separate paths into employment. A reporter for The Scotsman newspaper, Archie was lean, built with a determined chin and pencil thin lips. He stroked his moustache. 'It must feel like an honour to be asked?'

'I prefer to paint than to kill.'

'Still the pacifist, then?'

'My job is to interpret and record in detail what I see. Have you heard of Kenneth Clark, the director of the National Gallery?'

'Friend to the prime minister and the royal family. He's well known in the press.'

'Clark was instrumental in influencing the government's art programmes. It was him, along with the Ministry of Labour, who organised registers of artists who were willing to work as propagandists, publicists, designers, and commercial artists. He also assured the funding and official support. Along with The Ministry of Information, who were also implicit in the plans and the Treasury who are giving it financial support, artists are now able to contribute to the war effort.'

'I hope there're paying you well.'

'A hundred and fifty pounds, plus a daily allowance.'

'That's a fair sum, especially since your accommodation and meals are free.'

'It's not like I'll be staying in a hotel.'

'Do you know where you're going?'

'If I did, I wouldn't be able to tell you. You know that. It's an overseas commission. All I know is it's somewhere in the Mediterranean.'

'That sounds exciting.'

'I'm not really sure how long I'll be away for. I'll be doing important work. It'll be my contribution to the defeat of fascism and at the same time, I'll be producing art.'

'How did you get the commission?'

'I was picked from a list that the War Artists Advisory Committee had drawn up. Their choice of artists was heavily bent towards English artists, I think the term used was *geographic biased*, so the Committee were obliged to solicit suggestions for artists and Hubert Wellington who was the Principal of the Edinburgh College of Art put my name forward, amongst others of course.'

Archie checked his watch and slides his chair backwards on the stone floor. 'It's nearly last orders. I'll get the drinks in.'

Smoke filled the bar. Several drinkers have launched into a singsong. In a corner, two old men studiously studied ebony dominoes in their vein-streaked, tobacco-stained hands while sipping dark half pints. On instinct, Frank reached for the notebook and pencils in his brown satchel bag. But then he straightened his back. The urge to sketch the hunched figures was reined in and tamed, for this time. Instead, he lit a cigarette and drew heavily on the tip, inhaling the smoke, the burn against his throat satisfying one addiction for another.

'Here we go. Get that down you.' Archie slid a pint of beer across the table.

'Cheers.' Frank sipped his beer and licked his lips.

'I forgot to get some ciggies at the bar. Can I have one?'

'Sure.'

Frank offered Archie the cigarette packet on the small round table between them, and Archie took one and lit it.

'When is the train leaving?'

'Seven o'clock tomorrow morning from Waverley station.'

'An early start then.'

Frank scratched his brow. 'The ship leaves Liverpool at five tomorrow afternoon.'

'Not much room for error, then. I hope there's no hold ups with your train.'

'They didn't want me staying overnight in Liverpool. I'm obviously saving them money this way.'

'What does Maggie think of all this? Is she okay about you leaving?'

Frank looked at his shoes.

'Frank, tell me she knows.'

Frank sighed. 'We're having a break. Maggie suggested it. She needed her own space to think about things. It was her idea.'

'To think about what? I thought you were getting engaged.'

'We were. We are. It's just been postponed,' Frank said, flustered.

'You don't sound very sure.'

Frank didn't answer.

'What happened?'

'Honestly, I wish I knew. We had an argument over nothing, really. It was stupid. And then she said she wanted to have time with her friends. I asked her when did I ever stop her from seeing her friends? She said that wasn't the point, and when I asked what her point was, she said something along the lines of she felt suffocated. We were seeing too much of each other and I was sucking the air from her.'

'And were you?'

'I'd been away for a week, painting these villages along the east coast. It was part of a commission. A short-term contract with the ministry of information. It was to be an interpretative record of how the villages looked, preserving their character in case they were bombed by the Germans.'

Frank could tell Archie was thinking. 'Look, I might be way off the mark here, but do you think there might be someone else?'

Frank hesitated over his words. 'Maggie would never do that.'

'I'm not saying she would,' Archie backtracked. 'It's just, well... the way you described what happened, her behaviour's a little odd.'

Frank sighed. He drained the last of the beer in his glass. 'Well, she's getting her break. It's just longer than she anticipated. The War Artists Advisory Committee phoned me yesterday. I was their second placement. The other guy pulled out. He's been rushed to the hospital, apparently. He had a hernia that burst, poor chap. So, it's all been a bit of a rush.'

'Are you going to tell her?' Archie asks.

'Do you think she'll want to know?'

'I'm sure she will. Anyway, you can't just sail off to the other side of the world without seeing her.'

'It's not Australia I'm going to.'

'You know what I mean.'

'She said she didn't want to see me. Maybe this is what we need.'

'But you haven't told her you're heading off to the Mediterranean chasing the German army.'

'I'm there to record what I see and paint it. I'm not going to be shooting Germans.'

'You know what I mean. You should tell her.'

Frank slid his hand through his hair. 'God, I wish I could turn back the clock.'

'Don't we all, believe me?'

'I don't think she'll see me, not after what happened.'

'Write her a letter. You've still got time.'

'I'm half pissed and I'm leaving tomorrow morning. What a mess.'

'Your right, it's a bit of a fuck up.'

Chapter 13

Frank awoke the next morning with a throbbing ache in his head. He washed and shaved and ate a slice of toast accompanied by a cup of tea and a cigarette. With his small suitcase in hand, he walked the short distance to Waverley Train Station. Before boarding his train, he bought a packet of cigarettes and The Scotsman newspaper and checked the accuracy of his watch against the station clock.

To his relief, the carriage was almost empty. While he read his newspaper to pass the time, he came across an article Archie had written about an anti-submarine boom laid across Campbeltown Loch between McCringan's Point and Davaar Island. With a steel net, reaching 90ft deep, about 2,000ft long and weighing nearly 500 tons, Frank thought it an impressive piece of ingenuity and defence.

He sketched a landscape of flushed autumnal colours. At some point, the rhythmical cadence of the carriage made him fall into a deep sleep, only to be wakened when the train pulled into a station. It ignited a sudden flurry of activity. Heavy suitcases dragged and deposited into overhead racks, passengers shuffling in search of seats and a cacophony of voices with the distinct dialect that told him he was now in Northern England. To his relief, no one sat next to him. He was not in the mood for polite conversation. The thought of it tired him.

His thoughts wandered to Maggie. They had been together for nearly two years now. She still lived with her parents in a tenement in Leith, while he rented a flat in Brunswick Street, the spare room doubling up as his studio.

Her father had been gassed in the First World War, leaving him unable to hold down a job for any reasonable length of time until he spent most of his waking days coughing up blood and living as an invalid. Maggie's mother worked at the local bakery while looking after her husband, who resented the life the war had given him. Though academically gifted, Maggie's parents could not afford to give her the education she was capable of excelling in. She attended a small college, then took a job as a secretary working in Jenners Department store.

He can still hear Maggie's voice, her words swimming inside his head. He can still feel that long and soft first kiss sitting on a grass verge in a sunny Princes Street Gardens during Maggie's lunch break.

Was it remorse he was feeling? And was he to blame? He folded the newspaper in front of him, reached for his packet of cigarettes, and lit one. What will become of them? So many questions that would remain unanswered.

All day long, the dockside had seen a flurry of activity. The jibs of cranes carried an endless stream of equipment, vehicles, and ammunition onto the ship. A constant, yet lethargic flow of never-ending young faces, in a sea of soldiers, trundled along several strategically placed brows from shore to ship. To Frank's disappointment, there was no fanfare or dignitaries, no marching bands, and crowds of waving relatives and friends to see them off.

Frank watched in admiration, as the biggest of the dockside cranes, steadily, but surely, lifted a locomotive engine from the dockside and, with only hand signals from a team of riggers, the engine was precisely and delicately manoeuvred onto the ship's port side deck, where it was secured into position and fitted with welding cleats and steel cable.

His cabin was small, but rudimentary functional. At least he had the luxury of a bed, and a wash-hand basin, unlike the soldiers, whose living conditions, Frank imagined, would be considerably worse off than his.

He unpacked his clothes and hung them in a narrow wardrobe. He placed his sketch pads, pencils, crayons, an array of paintbrushes, and tubes of paint on a wooden chair next to his bed.

That evening, as the sun set, Frank watched the coast recede from him, as the ship cut through a heavy swell, joined by a convoy of six merchant navy vessels and two Royal Navy escort destroyers acting as anti-submarine escorts. His heart ached; he'd left Maggie behind.

A summons arrived and Frank met a Captain George Nicholson, a burly officer, with a pencil-thin moustache, who spoke between long drags on his cigarette. He offered Frank a whisky, and Frank noted how spacious the captain's cabin was compared to his own. He even had a writing desk, although small, and a chair. How one's priorities change, he thought.

Once introductions had been formalised, Captain Nicholson informed Frank they were heading for the Egyptian port of Alexandria, an important axis for the transport of troops and ammunition. If the weather was kind to them, they should reach Alexandria within twelve to fourteen days.

'Edinburgh, you say. I had an auntie who lived there. I visited her with my parents when I was about ten. She lived in Stockbridge. Do you know it? It rained for the entire time we were there. Bloody awful weather. That's my only impression of Edinburgh, a decrepit auntie and rain.'

'Sorry to hear it.'

'So, I've been instructed to inform you that as far as you're concerned, you have access to draw and paint the men and the comings and goings on the ship, within reason, of course. There are areas you won't be allowed in, but if you stick to the deck, you'll be fine. We'll be in Alexandria to off load equipment and half of the troops. The rest are heading for the Greek port of Piraeus, where you'll accompany them.'

Frank's eyes widened. 'Greece!'

'You do understand why it was all kept under wraps? Top secret.' Captain Nicholson tapped his nose.

'Of course.'

'Churchill wants to establish a Balkan front with Yugoslavia, Greece, and Turkey. Eden, Dill, and even King George himself have been in negotiations with the Greek government. It's all looking like it could kick off at any minute, I'm afraid. We've intelligence that German troops have been massing in Romania and are now moving into Bulgaria whose army is mobilised and taking up positions along the Greek border. There's a big push on for the transportation of troops and equipment to Greece. It will be your job to record, through your skills as an artist, our boys whipping Hitler's arse.'

'I'd no idea I'd be going to Greece.'

'It doesn't matter where you go. There's no safe place in this war. To the Germans, your brushes and your pencils are just as dangerous as our guns.'

'Good. I want to be useful.'

'Make sure you stay useful. I might be a soldier, but I'm also a man of vision. Unlike some of my fellow officers, I can see the value of having you with us. Your work is of national importance. It's a visual history of the war, recording aspects of war with authenticity that would be, in the main, unseen by others, that is its value and its interest. You have important work to do, as do we all.'

Chapter 14

Two thousand troops lined the ship. Soldiers, airmen wrens, nursing sisters, nuns, and civilians.

When Frank ate his meals in the officer's mess, he noted there were many officers from all the services.

He soon learnt he was fortunate and privileged compared to ordinary soldiers' living conditions. He had the comfort of a cabin, and he ate his meals with the officers. Accommodation for the other ranks was substandard and pitiful in the extreme. Frank often visited the mess-deck several decks deep into the ship, and it was always overcrowded. There, the mechanical drumming and potent smell of the nearby engine room was a constant reminder that if the ship should ever come under attack by a German torpedo, the chances of escape were extremely thin.

The troops ate their meals at dining benches, claustrophobic rows that dominated the floor space. It's also where they slept, overcrowded with two hundred soldiers in canvass hammocks, airless and stiflingly hot with portholes fastened closed. During daylight hours, the soldiers could escape this inclement environment and spend time on the deck. At night, naked lights could be detected by German U-boats and an enforced blackout forbade smoking.

Frank had heard the soldiers' complaints of insufficient and poor quality food. It troubled Frank that only after a week into the voyage, he had heard rumours that some had even begun eating their emergency rations of tinned chocolate and hardtack.

It had been a week now; a constant canvas of sea and sky surrounding him as far as the eye could see. The salty breeze had turned warm. Now they were leaving the Atlantic behind and were making their way towards the Mediterranean Sea.

They moved at a steady six knots, employing a zigzagging formation used by convoys to avoid German submarines and torpedoes and, to Frank's relief, he had not seen a single German aircraft or any submarine activity.

With each passing day, it got hotter, and he had discarded his jacket for the relief of his shirt and rolled-up sleeves. He had become accustomed to the close confines of his cabin, even though, at night, it was uncomfortably hot, and sleep could be fleeting, he reminded himself; he was far better off than most of his travelling companions.

He spent his days getting to know the routine of the ship's crew. He talked with the soldiers, shared the occasional cigarette, and gained their consent to sketch and paint them. Most were obliged, even showed an interest in his work.

Many rumours circulated amongst the troops concerning their destination and how long they would have to suffer the tasking conditions it forced them to endure each day.

The ships-maintained radio silence, and only communicated with each other by exchanging light signals.

Several soldiers knew Morse Code and could read the ships' positions in latitude and longitude. This helped to predict their position, guess at the name of towns they passed when they were close to the shore, and most importantly, their probable destination.

On a warm, clear night, they passed through the Straits of Gibraltar. On one side, Spanish Morocco, on the other, the coast of Spain, flashing lights guided their passage.

They followed the coast of North Africa. On a Sunday morning, they anchored two miles off the coast of Algiers. One of the other ships in the convoy entered the torpedo boom. Frank watched as a small boat blazoned in the red cross approached the ship and several sick soldiers were loaded onboard. Frank scanned the white houses and buildings of Algiers. To once again see patches of green grass and trees brought a special joy, and he thought how wonderful it was to see plumes of smoke rise into the sky as a train snaked its passage along the coast. He drew the scene and hoped it conveyed the emotions he so much wanted to share within its curved and straight lines, its shades and light.

To boost morale, the soldiers constructed a primitive boxing ring on one of the ship's decks. For several hours, the boredom of the voyage receded, with several boxing matches and the inevitable gambling that ensued. It made a change from playing cards and trading cigarettes.

For several days, during his frequent walks around the ship, Frank had noticed a young man, a member of the crew, who intrigued him. Something about him caught Frank's attention. He mulled this over. He was unlike the others. He was younger in looks and stature. And that was it. He was barely a man at all. What was he doing on the ship? So, he made it his business to find out, and what better way than to ask if he could draw him?

One morning, as the young man busied himself checking the chains and slings that fastened the trucks and equipment to the deck, Frank offered him a cigarette. As they smoked, the young man chatted away happily for some time. Frank discovered he was called Angus and once they had finished their cigarettes, he asked Angus if he could draw him while he worked.

Angus' eyebrows furrowed. 'Why would you want to do that?'

'It's my job to draw and paint the soldiers and the people who work on the ship.'

'I see.' No one had ever drawn Angus. 'How did you become an artist?'

'I went to the Edinburgh College of Art and studied there for a few years.'

'Like going to a university.'

'The same, except, instead of studying history or politics, I studied art.'

'So, you just paint all day and draw pictures?'

'There was a bit more to it than that. If you don't want me to draw you, then that's alright. It's not as if there's a shortage of subjects.'

Angus stared at the ground. 'I never said I didn't want you to draw me, you can, as long as I get to see it.'

'I'll show you it the second I'm finished.'

Angus couldn't hide his enthusiasm. 'What do you want me to do?'

'Just carry on doing what you're doing.'

'I thought people posed, you know, sat still when someone was drawing them.'

'Just go about your work as normal.'

Frank pulled his sketch pad and pencil case from his satchel. He watched as Angus checked each chain that secured the trucks and equipment to the deck. Occasionally, Angus self-consciously glanced at Frank, which he returned with a reassuring smile.

As he drew, Frank continually swept his gaze from the boy to the sketchpad in his lap. He worked with quick strokes of the pencil. Several times, he would fish another pencil from the case, a seamless movement that did not interrupt his flow or concentration. Occasionally, he held the end of a pencil between his teeth, contemplating an aspect of his drawing, the angle of a line, the contour of a shade.

Before long, Frank lay the sketch pad in his lap and lit another cigarette. He took a long, satisfying drag and smiled. His effort pleased him, and Frank was curious about Angus' reaction.

Angus gazed at the page with wide eye amazement. He looked at the drawing for some time. He turned his gaze from the drawing to Frank and back again to the drawing, clearly struck by what he had just seen. To Frank's surprise, tears formed in Angus' eyes.

'Whatever is the matter?'

A flush crept across Angus' cheeks, as he looked away, hurriedly wiping his eyes.

'I didn't think it was that bad,' Frank said, trying to make light of the situation.

'It's not,' Angus sniffed. 'It looks like a photograph. It's me on this ship... I miss home, my mum, my dad, even my little brother. I should be with them. I should be at home. I want to go home.'

Frank laid a hand on Angus' shoulder. 'Look around you, Angus. Do you see all these soldiers? Hundreds of faces and every one of them, just like you, would rather be home than be on this rusting ship right now. If I'm honest, I wish I was sleeping in my own comfortable bed tonight instead of that concrete mattress that's masquerading as a bed in my tiny cabin. None of us want to be here, Angus, but we are, and we're amongst friends. Even if we don't know one another, or even speak to each other, we're all in this together.' He squeezed Angus' shoulder and offered a reassuring smile.

Angus regained his composure, and following a moment of silence, he smiled. 'You're right. This is my family now.'

'Would you like to keep the drawing?' Frank asked.

Angus thought for a second. 'I would, but you keep it. You're doing important work too.'

As he watched Angus continue with his work, Frank noticed a new purpose in Angus' demeanour, his posture now straight and determined. Frank smiled to himself and, though he was glad his words had given Angus comfort and a great sense of relief, they left Frank feeling discontent. The irony was, they rang hollow in his head.

That night, Frank lay on top of his bed, smoking a cigarette in his small cabin. Ever since he had sketched Angus, a restless sensation had accosted him. He had tried to put his finger on it and flush out the reason, but to his frustration, it eluded him. He recalled his conversation with Angus earlier that morning.

'Where are you from?' Frank asked.

'Morcombe. What about you?'

'Edinburgh.'

'My names, Angus. What's yours?'

'Frank.'

'Pleased to meet you, Frank.' Angus offered his hand and Frank shook it.

'Like wise. That's a very Scottish sounding name you have for someone from Morcombe.'

Angus smiled. 'My dad's Scottish. He's from Glasgow. He met my mum on holiday and never went back.'

'Very romantic.'

Angus grunted. 'If you say so.'

'I get the feeling you don't get on with your dad.'

'Let's just say, when he has a drink, which is every night, he has a short temper. Free with his hands, if you know what I mean.'

'I see.'

'Mums threatened to leave him a hundred times, but she never does. After it, he always says he's sorry and that he'll never do it again. I begged her, but she wouldn't listen. Till Death Us Do Part, she would always say. And I told her it could come to that. I couldn't stay. Not anymore. I'd had enough.'

'It was a brave thing to do.'

'Do you think so? I've never thought about it like that.' Angus looked at Frank as if he'd noticed him for the first time. 'What are you doing on this ship? You're not a soldier.'

'No, I'm not. I'm an artist.'

'Like that Monet fella. You paint?'

'I do, and I draw and dabble in a little sculpture, but I'm not very good at that.'

'But you must be good at painting?'

'Some people think so.'

'Do you sell your paintings?'

'That's how I make my living.'

'So, what are you doing here?'

'I suppose I work for the government. I've to record in my paintings and sketches the soldiers and people like you. It's part of the war effort.'

'And that's your job?'

'For the moment, it is.'

'It must be great to get paid for something you like doing.'

'I've never thought about it. But now that you've mentioned it, it is.'

Angus shot a glance at the satchel. 'The tools of the trade, I suppose.'

'I take them with me wherever I go.'

'I wish I was good at something.'

'From what you've told me. You're a good son.'

'If I was a good son, I'd have persuaded mum to have left him by now.'

'How old are you?'

'Eighteen.'

'Really?' Frank said sceptically.

Angus shuffled his feet. 'What are you implying?'

'You're very fresh faced.'

'I shave, I'll have you know.'

'I don't doubt it.'

'In fact, I cut myself shaving just this morning. See!' He pulled the skin on his chin to emphasise a slight cut. 'I thought it was never going to stop bleeding.'

'Is this your first job?'

Angus nodded.

'Have you been doing this long?

'This is my first ship.'

'What Merchant Navy School did you train in?'

'Eh... it was.'

'You haven't been, have you?'

Angus furrowed his brow. 'It's that obvious?'

'Not really. I mean, you seem to know what you're doing.'

'Have you been watching me?'

'It's my job, remember? You need to observe people if you are going to draw or paint them.'

'I suppose.'

'How did you end up working on this ship?'

Angus paused and then shrugged. 'I've got my dad to thank for that.'

Frank gave a quizzical *look. 'In what way?'*

'I was working at a fishmonger and on this particular Saturday night my wages were burning a hole in my pocket, so I went out to the dancing at the local Palais, and I met my cousin Bill with his girlfriend. Bill was in the Merchant Navy. He had trained on the Vindatri. His first ship was bombed in port and was unable to sail, so he was now on the S.S.Hopecrown and was on leave as his ship was loading cargo at the Manchester docks.

'By the end of the night, we'd all had a few drinks, so I said my good-byes and went home. When I got home, dad was in one of his moods and he'd been drinking all night. He asked me where I'd been and if I'd I given mum the dig money for the week. When I said I hadn't, he started accusing me of stealing money from him. Mum came down the stairs from bed as she could hear him shouting. When she told dad that I always paid her every week and not to worry, he slapped her across the face. I don't know if it was the drink, or if I'd just had enough. Whatever it was, I just saw red. I pushed him and told him never to hit mum again. He looked at me with a smirk on his face and asked what was I going to do about it? I punched him square on the nose. I heard it crack and there was blood everywhere. He stumbled and fell, hitting his head off the corner of the table. He just lay there, his face covered in blood. Mum was hysterical. She thought I'd killed him. He was still breathing, even though I wish I had. I asked her to pack her bags and come with me. I knew she wouldn't.

'Anyway, Bill, my cousin, just lived a few streets away, so I went to his for the night. He was to be back on board his ship by 7 a.m. on the

Monday and had to leave on Sunday. It was the next morning that me and Bill hatched the plan.

'Bill didn't think I'd have a problem getting a job on a ship if I wasn't too choosey which job I took. He said there were over 20 ships loading on Manchester docks.

'We left on the Sunday for the docks. The only problem Bill could see was getting me past the gateman at the docks, as security was very tight. As luck would have it, on our approach to the dock gate, we met up with the Bosun of the S.S.Hopecrown, along with about 6 other crewmen who were pretty drunk. So, Bill explained the situation to the Bosun. The gateman knew the Bosun well, so he didn't even have to show his pass. The Bosun said we were all his crew and before I knew it, I was at the docks.'

'How did you get on a ship?'

'I spent the night with Bill and in the morning started asking round the ships if they had any jobs. I was given four offers. I couldn't believe it, so I picked this ship. We part loaded in Manchester and then moved on to Birkenhead where we loaded this lot. Did you know, there's two ninety-ton railway engines on the port side? In number three hold there're guns, vehicles, and thousands of tons of ammunition, never mind the hundreds of soldiers on board. If we get hit by a German torpedo, it'll be the best fireworks display ever.'

Frank smiled. 'Thanks for that.'

'By the way, you're right, I'm only sixteen, but I'll be seventeen in September.'

'Does your mum know where you are?'

'I've written to her. Told her not to worry. I regret not telling her. It wasn't right.'

Frank could feel a dullness simmering in his chest. It flamed his guilt. 'I know what you mean.'

Frank should have told Maggie he was leaving. She deserved to know. It wasn't right. It was a selfish thing to have done. It weighed heavily on him. That night, he tossed and turned, and his Catholic guilt, with its retribution and punishment, settled over him like a shawl over his shoulders.

Chapter 15

The convoy passed the town of Bizerte, which was on a section of widened inlet and east-facing coast of the north coast of Tunisia. From this point, rumours spread rapidly amongst the troops that they were heading for Alexandria or even the Suez Canal and beyond. A few days later, excitement and apprehension ran through the ship as a thin line on the horizon, Malta, came into view. Several Corporals went around the decks collecting shillings for a sweep, one of several since they left shore. This one was to guess the time the anchor would drop when the ship had reached its destination. Frank decided on 19.23 hours, the numbers coinciding with the year Maggie was born. He thought it a good omen.

Awakened by a commotion of noise that emitted from the other side of his cabin door, Frank pulled on his clothes. Reaching for the cabin door, he swung it open. Alarm bells shrieked as Frank briskly made his way along the narrow passageway. A man in oil-stained overalls was hurrying towards him.

'What's happening? Is this a drill?' Frank called out to him.

'We've been hit. A great big fucking torpedo has hit the engine rooms on the starboard side. Get yourself onto the deck.'

Frank noticed the dark trail of blood glistening on the man's neck.

Just then, the lights in the corridor flickered and went out. A loudspeaker crackled. 'Watertight doors closed, all crew at action stations, man the lifeboats.'

Frank had counted the lifeboats and knew there were not enough to accommodate for the number of men on the ship.

He ran back to his cabin and slid on his lifejacket. He grabbed as much as he could of his paints, brushes, pencils, crayons, and paper and packed them into his satchel. He snatched up his cigarettes and lighter and hurried out of the cabin and saw the deck jammed with the chaotic mass of hundreds of soldiers, an army who could not see its enemy, an army stranded and paralysed.

Dazed by the frantic commotion that engulfed him, Frank didn't know what to do. Already, men swung lifeboats into the black sea, swaying, and jolting the men crammed inside, waiting to be swallowed by the dark abyss that was the icy waters somewhere below them, a watery roulette wheel that offered salvation or death.

Caught in a river of bodies, the motion dragged him forward in its current. In the crush, he clutched his satchel to his body, and yanked and pushed, breathless and panic-stricken, somehow, he extricated himself and suddenly, in the confusion, he felt hands hauling him into a lifeboat, where he clambered towards the only remaining slither of space.

Frank scanned the faces of those in the lifeboat, searching each one, hoping to see Angus. His heart sank as he clutched his satchel to his chest and willed Angus to have made it safely onto one of the other lifeboats.

He felt the lifeboat sway and then descend towards the foamed waves that lapped against the ship. Above him, the sky curved, alight in a vast display of uninterrupted stars. His eyes found a group of stars known as *The Plough*, as he always did on clear night skies. A burst of exhilaration that chased from him the exhaustion of despair that swamped him. He would not die this night.

As the lifeboat drifted in the swell, Frank saw men jump from the ship into the sea. Were the lifeboats full already? Did fire rage below deck? Was there no other choice but to succumb to the mercy of the sea?

To his horror, another explosion reverberated like an erupting volcano.

Someone shrieked. 'They've hit the ship again. Bastards! It's ripped into number three hold where the ammunition is.'

All were stunned into a breathless silence. A massive plume of smoke rose like a demon and raging fire scorched and engulfed the ship. Those on the lifeboat watched in a paralysed state, their very own image of Armageddon.

Minutes later, the stern and the bow of the ship rose unnaturally in the sky. An unfathomable moment that all watched helplessly as the broken ship seemed to just slip and melt into the sea, taking with it the giant hulk of the locomotive engine, its tenders remaining defiantly solid and firm. Frank knew the images would never leave him.

There were only two more lifeboats in the sea. The few survivors still in the water were hauled into the boats. Frank was horrified as hundreds of bodies littered the sea. Frank drew his knees to his face and wrapped his arms around them. Around him, the injured groaned, while others wept. Some hung over the side and wretched. Frank rubbed his face, as though he could erase the carnage and horror.

Beside him, Frank heard a voice. 'You're the artist, aren't you?'

Frank turned his head. Bleary-eyed with dark dishevelled hair, a young soldier, perhaps only twenty years of age, stared at Frank.

'I am,' Frank replied, almost inaudibly.

'I thought it was you. I've seen you around the ship. You stuck out like a sore thumb.' He shifted and winced in pain.

'Are you alright?' Frank saw the soldier's blood covered hand clutching his stomach. 'You're bleeding.'

The young soldier clenched his teeth. 'It hurts.'

'You need someone to look at it.'

'Well, if you're not a doctor, I don't think that's going to happen any time soon.'

The soldier coughed and Frank noticed a trickle of blood on the soldier's lips. He had never felt so helpless.

Frank knew each lifeboat had a supply of biscuits and fresh water. He feared they would soon run out of both before they sighted land or could be rescued, as since there were no oars or sails to steer the craft, the lifeboat drifted at the mercy of the currents.

During the night, sleep did not come easily. The murmur of voices and the groans of the wounded were the only sounds to penetrate the dark. Frank took out his pencils and drawing pad and sketched the men around him, crammed together. Could he capture their harrowing faces and broken spirits in attempt to make sense of what he witnessed?

When Frank was a child, he often gazed in awe at the night sky, jewelled in a celestial display of wonderment. He imagined he was looking at heaven. Now, all he could do was assign his rage and torment towards it. For now, he had witnessed hell.

That night, the soldier died.

As the sun rose like an orange globe above the horizon, a soldier, in his thirties, said a prayer, and they lowered the body into the sea. Frank feared it would be the first of many. Now it was light. He counted fifteen men in the boat, more than half having suffered life-threatening injuries and trauma.

They discovered a leak where sea water trickled into the boat. The able-bodied men took turns bailing out the water. To the relief of all, a compass was located, and a sail, which was hastily erected. The most senior officer, a sergeant from Gateshead, worked their rations out, which equated to one biscuit and two egg cups of water, per man, each day.

The sun was relentless, the air humid and without a whisper of a breeze. On the fourth day, they slid the fifth man into the depths of the still sea.

Frank thought about Maggie. It allowed a brief escape from this world away from the endless water and continuous horizon. It gave him renewed strength.

It was easy to see her face in his mind, and he hoped this would continue. He drew comfort from it. It fed a sense of hope. It gave him a purpose. He would not die in this boat.

Chapter 16

A golden sun broke the horizon when a voice wakened them. 'Look! A boat.' A soldier stood and pointed towards a darkened shape that steadily moved towards them. Around him, a mixture of anticipation and dread crossed every weary face.

'Is there a flag? Can you see its colours man?' The sergeant's voice cracked, his questions echoing everyone's thoughts.

Minutes passed like hours, as every eye trained nervously on the approaching boat. They could hear the drone of a diesel engine as it drew near.

'It's a *caique*.' The soldier said to no one in particular, relief heavy in his voice.

'And what the fuck is that?' the sergeant barked.

'It's a Greek fishing boat.'

'Fish and chips tonight, boys,' the sergeant grinned.

Frank stood. He scanned the boat as it approached. These were not Greek fishermen.

A rope swirled through the air towards them. Nervous hands caught it, tying the rope, until it was secured to the lifeboat.

'Good morning, gentleman. It looks like you're in need of assistance.' It was an unmistakable Irish accent.

Irish born Captain Finian Doherty was tall and lean with sweeping marmalade coloured hair. He led the elite unit, the Special Boat Squadron unit with the motto 'Stand Boldly On.' They carried out their missions at night under the cover of darkness and spent the daylight hours anchored in remote coves of small uninhabited islands. The small fishing boats were the perfect camouflage for moving in and out of enemy territory.

Concealing their presence was crucial. Each day, just before dawn, they dismantled the mast and draped the hull in camouflage netting, then raised bamboo poles, and swathed more netting over them, forming false contours that simulated rocky outcroppings.

Captain Doherty was a leader of courage, and when needed, cold savagery. His knife was just as effective as his gun. His men called him Fin.

The Sergeant lips curled into a smile. 'Thank Christ.' He scratched his beard. 'A German torpedo hit our ship. There were hundreds of troops on board, most of them dead now. We've been drifting for days. Some of us are injured. We need food and water.'

'I heard about it.' Fin rubbed the stubble on his chin. 'It's not safe to be out here in the daytime. We're not far from our destination. You'll get all the food and water you need.'

'Where are we?'

'You've been floating all the way up the Ionian Sea. You're lucky it was us that saw you first and not the German ships and submarines that infest these waters. Our operations are normally based in and around the South Aegean Islands. We're not normally in this area, so this really is your lucky day.'

The Sergeant wiped his brow. 'There is a God, after all.'

'We'll tow you to Sapientza. It's a small island not far from here. We're staying there until it gets dark. Like I said, it's too dangerous to sail during daylight hours. Then, we'll take you to Pilos, a small town on the coast. It's not far. You'll get all the help you need there.'

'Thank you,' the sergeant said gratefully.

Fin turned to his men. 'Make her scream, Stephanos. Time to move.'

The Levant Schooner Flotilla was formed as a direct consequence of the May 1941 invasion of Crete by German airborne forces. The British had to evacuate thousands of troops from Crete, and in doing so, took over a fleet of caiques, Greek fishing schooners. With Axis forces holding Crete and the other Greek islands, the Royal Navy turned half the fishing fleet over to the Special Operations Executive, who used the fishing boats to maintain contact with British agents working in the eastern Mediterranean and the Adriatic. The other half of the fishing fleet, The Levant Schooner Flotilla were appointed to more hostile operations working together with a special forces brigade of the British Army, the Special Air Service.

A caique averaged 30 feet in length, weighed approximately 20 tons. There was no wheelhouse, no toilet, or protection from the weather. As fishing boats, the holds held thousands of pounds of fish and, although the fish were gone, the smell was still very much present.

Captain Finian Doherty and his men numbered ten in total. Stephanos was the only Greek. It was his boat, and the money he received from the British was far more than he could earn fishing for a living.

They anchored in a small, secluded cove. Fin's men immediately set about camouflaging their boat. Once finished, they smashed several holes into the hull of the lifeboat and, with a hint of sadness, Frank watched it sink into the crystalline water. It had indeed preserved life.

Several hundred yards from the cove and surrounded by trees, they took shelter in an old, abandoned house that Fin's men used when waiting for night to fall.

They kept the shutters closed and lit several candles. Two of Fin's men left the house and within half an hour returned with three rabbits caught in traps set the day before.

Frank ate his first hot meal in over a week, rabbit stew and potatoes, savoured a cigarette from a packet that Fin's men passed around and drank a thimble size of bitter red wine. It felt amazing to be alive.

The sergeant sat next to Frank and burped. 'I think my belly has just wondered what's hit it.' He reached for a cigarette from a packet lying on the table where they ate their meal. 'Do you want one?'

Frank raised his hand. 'I'm fine.'

'Fin has just told me they've made radio contact with the Greek resistance. They'll meet us tonight in Pilos and by tomorrow morning, we'll be on our way to Athens.'

'Wouldn't it be quicker by boat?' Frank asked.

'It would, but beggars can't be choosers.'

Fin sat opposite them and ran his fingers through his yellow corn hair. 'We'll be leaving within the hour. The sea is calm, so it'll be a steady crossing.'

'I've heard the resistance fighters are a formidable lot,' the sergeant asked.

Fin lit a cigarette. 'They're well organised and know the terrain. It's their country and the Italians and Germans were never invited. They're fighting for their heritage, their culture, their religion and most importantly for their families. I wouldn't want them as my enemy. I'm glad they're on our side.'

'You said earlier that you and your men didn't normally operate in this area.' The sergeant puffed on his cigarette.

'That's true. With the Ionian now under German occupation, the resistance fighters need all the help we can give them. The Germans are far more brutal than the Italians ever were. Mussolini made it compulsory that Italian was taught and spoken in schools. They changed the currency to the Lira and exported food to Italy. Overall, life didn't change too much for the Greeks when the Italians were here. With the Germans, there's been many atrocities: villages ransacked, houses burnt and looted, women raped, villagers shot. This is happening all over Greece, not just here. It's about instilling fear and creating a subservient population. The Germans are going to take the lot. Mussolini was just Hitler's puppet.' Fin stubbed out his cigarette. 'It reminds me of what the British did to the Irish. They're all as guilty as each other. German, Italian, British. They're all evil bastards with histories that have covered them in the blood of atrocities and genocide. At the end of the day, its husbands, wives, sons, and daughters that suffer, and that's why we're here, to help the likes of them, not for some bigwig general or politician's ideology or military objective. Fuck them, because they would fuck us in a minute, mind my word.'

The sergeant swallowed the rest of his wine and wiped the back of his hand over his mouth. 'If I could. I'd fight with you.'

'And you'd be welcome.' Fin turned to Frank. 'What about you?'

'I'm not a soldier,' Frank said, a little lamely. 'I'm an artist.'

'As in, you paint.'

'Yes. I'm employed by the government to depict the war through drawings and paintings. I was to record the transportation of the troops into Greece and then their advancement.'

'So, you would be part of the mobilisation, living and travelling with soldiers, engaging with the enemy if need be.'

'I would.'

'Then you're a soldier. Your art is your weapon.'

'I've seen his drawings. He could teach Van Gogh a thing or two.' The sergeant laughed.

'What will you do now?' Fin asked.

'If we can, I'll continue what I started and work alongside the army. It's why I'm here.'

'Up until now, you went down with your ship. Your presumed dead. Drowned. You all are.'

The sergeant laughed. 'We're ghosts.'

Fin smiled. 'Exactly.'

Chapter 17

The crossing was just as Fin said it would be, the boat steady in a calm sea.

With each passing minute, Frank watched as pinprick lights and murky outlines grew more distinct as Pilos unveiled itself from the blackness.

Soon, they would be on their way to Athens. There was there a sinking feeling in his stomach? Ever since his conversation with Fin, he had been troubled. Fin's words unsettled his intentions. Here was an opportunity to experience another side of the war. It was just as dangerous and just as unpredictable, but these men were doing something different. Unlike the battles and the victories and the losses of the army and navy, Fin and his small group of men were the unsung heroes that were never mentioned in the newsreels of the picture houses, or the front pages of the national papers, or the dispatch box in Westminster. Their efforts were no less influential in the direction the war could take. Their stories needed to be told, and Frank felt the prospect of doing so had opened to him.

Everything he achieved had a sizeable chunk of luck attached to it. He knew he didn't want to be a passenger; he wanted to be the driver of his own life. After all, that's what had got him where he was today. He would decide in which direction to turn.

As for Maggie, he told himself; he had lost her; he had to face the reality; she was no longer part of his life, however hard that was to accept. It meant going through the pain, knowing she may no longer love him. It taught him to live his life as if he'd die tomorrow and experience it as if he was going to live forever.

As the others rose to disembark from the boat, Frank remained seated.

The sergeant turned; his eyes screwed. 'Quickly does it, Frank.'

Frank looked up. 'I'm not going to Athens.'

'What are you talking about, Frank? Are you mad?'

Even though he was sitting, Frank was slightly out of breath and his heart raced. 'If he'll have me, I'm staying with Fin.'

The sergeant sensed immediately that Frank meant it. He shook his head. 'Christ, you are mad.'

'I can't allow myself to consider a future and what that might be if I'm not true to myself.'

'And what the fuck is that supposed to mean?'

'For weeks now, we've been living in a constant flux of the unknown. I just want to depict, through my sketches and paintings, what I see, hear, and experience. It's my food and oxygen. They sustain me, and I need to do that here.'

Fin looked at him quizzically. 'Has anyone ever told you, you've a funny way with words? Maybe you should be a writer, as well as an artist. If you come with us, you won't get paid. You will if you stay with this lot as you'll still be fulfilling your contract as a war artist. If you come with us, you are on your own. You do know that don't you? I can't offer you any money, but I can guarantee the unpredictable and constant threat that each new day maybe your last.' A smile flickered across his face. 'Not much of a sell, is it?'

Frank smiled slightly. 'It's about doing the right thing. That's what's important.'

'Sometimes, doing the right thing isn't enough. Life's full of choices, and out here, some of those choices aren't about doing what is right, but what needs to be done, and that can often be brutal. If you come with us, you're going to see a lot of that. Do you understand me? I can't carry baggage, Frank.'

Frank cleared his throat. 'I understand.'

'Good to hear it. I wouldn't mind being immortalised in a painting or two.'

Fin gave them instructions that several resistance fighters would meet them at the end of the street just opposite the harbour and they had put preparations in place to get them safely to Athens.

The sergeant gave Frank a brisk handshake, and with pursed lips he followed the rest of his men off the boat.

As the boat turned towards the open sea, Fin looked at Frank. 'If you're having second thoughts, now would be the time to say.'

'I'm not.'

Suddenly, Frank flinched as the crack of gunfire pierced his ears.

'What the fuck!' Fin's eyes scanned the shore, and his men raised their guns. One of them pointed to the street and in the yellow light from the streetlamps, a truck emerged screeching to a stop. Soldiers dragged lifeless and limp bodies and tossed them unceremoniously onto the back of the truck.

'What's happened?' Frank's voice wavered incomprehensibly, his eyes wide, struggling to take in what he had just seen.

'Stay down,' Fin commanded. 'They've been ambushed. Get us out of here, Stephanos.'

The boat surged, throwing Frank backwards. The sound of the engine alerted the soldiers and a few hurried to the edge of the harbour wall, raising their rifles and firing.

One of Fin's men, who Frank knew as Stu, calmly took aim and fired twice in quick succession, hitting two German soldiers in the head and sending the others scurrying for cover.

Frank stared at Stu and, struggling to understand Stu's calm composure, he was grateful all the same. 'Will they come after us?'

'I doubt it. They'd have to steal one of those fishing boats.'

Everyone was silent for a few minutes as the caique headed out to the open sea. It plunged through the dark waters and a salty spray cooled Frank's face. Fin peered through a small set of binoculars and, when satisfied that they were not being pursued, he turned to Frank, offering him a cigarette. Frank's hands shook as he lit it. He remembered his conversation with the sergeant as they headed towards Pilos. The sergeant had tried to get Frank to change his mind, saying it would be safer going to Athens, safety in numbers, he had said, trying to sound convincing.

Troubled, Frank crouched down. They were all dead. If he had gone with them, he too would be dead. A wave of nausea curdled in his stomach. He turned to look at the receding coastline that now looked serene and soundless. It was difficult to comprehend what they left in their wake. Tears warmed his eyes as he wrestled with the enormity of it. All he wanted now was to be embraced by the darkness they headed towards.

He felt a hand on his shoulder; it was Fin's hardened demeanour softened.

'Are you okay?' Fin asked, concerned.

Frank fumbled with his sleeve.

'There's nothing I can say that's going to change what's just happened.'

'I know.'

'You need to understand. It won't be the last time you see someone dying.'

'These past few days; it seems it's all I've seen.'

'You're still alive and that's all that matters.'

On the boat, Frank awoke with a shudder. He was cold and his back and buttocks ached. He was still on the boat. Most of Fin's men slept, coiled up in blankets. Frank heard muted voices. Stu steered the boat, puffing on his pipe as Fin stood next to him. Frank shifted his weight and stretched his legs. The movement caught Fin's attention.

'There's been a change of plan. We're heading for Paxos.'

Frank's eyes widened. 'Where's that?'

'It's an island South of Corfu.'

Frank's knowledge of the islands in this part of Greece was limited. 'Is it far?'

'We'll be there just before sunrise. There's a smaller island to the south of Paxos. We'll rest up there.'

'Can I ask why we're going there?'

'There's a communications station set up in what used to be the bank in the main town. Our objective is to take it out and retrieve the communications equipment. When I say town, it's more of a village. Then we'll be off to Corfu and deliver it all to the local resistance fighters. Job done.'

'You make it sound easy.'

Fin frowned. 'Nothing's easy in this war. I would have thought what happened tonight would have taught you that.'

Frank dropped his head onto his chest.

Fin lay his hand on Frank's shoulder. 'You'll be staying in the boat. But that's tomorrow. Try to get some sleep.'

Frank did not argue. Today's events showed him how fragile life was and how the brutality of war could be delivered within a few short but devastating seconds.

The light changed as the caique entered the small cove thick with shrubs and trees. The sun appeared on the horizon, softening the sky in buttery clouds and yellow tinged light. In contrast, Frank could sense a buzz of urgency about the men. It was imperative to camouflage the caique in netting so that German planes could not see it from the sky.

The water in the cove was glasslike and through the turquoise and aqua blue, Frank could see the sand and stone of the seabed. He had never seen water so clear. He fought off the impulse to dive into it and cleanse his body of the sweat and grime that coated his skin.

They moved rapidly on foot through the thicket and trees before coming to a clearing and an old, dilapidated farmhouse. Two of Fin's men, rifles drawn, went ahead and cautiously opened the wooden front door. They slid inside and then reappeared, waving the rest to follow. Frank learnt they repeated this with each mission. A suitable building was picked in advance by the local resistance, usually because of its unassuming appearance, and there Fin and his men stayed hidden until darkness fell.

They ate a simple dinner of potatoes and bread that had been wrapped in cloth and left for them, Frank presumed, by those resisting the occupation of their country. It was a simple gesture, but one, he knew, came at a tremendous sacrifice.

After they had eaten, they smoked and waited.

Time passed excruciatingly slowly. The shutters remained closed and the air in the house was uncomfortably hot and suffocating. Games of cards were played. Strong coffee brewed on the ancient stove and Fin asked Frank about his life as an artist.

Frank told Fin about his plans to stage an exhibition after the war in London and Paris. His heart ached as he found himself telling of his regret at leaving Maggie without saying goodbye and making up. He thought now it was too late to think of a reconciliation; they were both living in two different worlds, and he hoped Maggie would find someone who could love her the way he should have done. She deserved to be happy.

'Even at your expense?' Fin tilted his head.

'It would make me happy too.'

'From where I'm standing, you're still trying to convince yourself. Regret eats at you. It crawls into your bones, but you can't undo what has been done.'

'I know.' Frank said, dejected. It was strange hearing this man, who had killed and maimed and lived each day under the threat of losing his own life, talk about the sensitivities of the heart. How strange Frank's life had become.

'The question you have to ask yourself is, would you change it? If you could, would you go back and change what has happened? Be honest with yourself, Frank.'

Frank looked away. 'Sometimes, I feel relieved and then... I feel sorry for her.'

'Feeling sorry is not enough. Do you love her?'

Frank looked away.

'Then, there's your answer.'

Frank slid the back of his hand over his chin. 'What about you, Fin? Is there someone special waiting for you?'

Fin leaned back against the wall and lit a cigarette. 'I've never let myself get close to anyone, but there was one girl I was fond of. We had been seeing each other on and off for several months until I caught her fucking my best mate. She never did that again.'

'That must have hurt. I take it you split up.'

'Well,' Fin grinned. 'Once I cut his cock off, she quickly lost interest in him.'

Frank's mouth fell open. 'Jesus, that was extreme.'

Fin laughed.

Frank shook his head. 'You're pulling my leg.'

'Believe me, the thought had crossed my mind, but I taught him a lesson he wasn't going to forget. By the time I'd finished with him, the only girl that would be interested was the one you had to pay for.'

Frank chortled, and then his face changed. 'How does it feel when you're about to go out on a mission like this?'

'I'd be a liar if I said I wasn't anxious. You never really know how things are going to turn out. There's also the rush of adrenaline. I feed off that. Some do this because they have to, and others because they want to. If a Gerry is going to stick a gun in my face, I'm going to make sure I'm the first to pull the trigger and blow a great big hole in him. Have you ever killed anyone, Frank? There's one thing shooting someone from a distance and another to be that close that you can see the life drain from their eyes. I'd choose the latter every time.

'In war, the normal rules of society disintegrate. You'll have to prepare yourself for things you've never seen before or could ever imáge. It was bad when the Italians were here, but not like this. The Germans have raped Greece. In the cities and countryside, woman and men have been reduced to wearing clothes that hang on them like rags. Their children's stomachs are distended with hunger. They walk bare footed with twig like limbs and deep hollows for eyes. It's not just the Germans people fear. Malnutrition and disease are everywhere. Their livestock have been killed; their crops burnt. Shops are empty. Schools and houses, entire villages have been burnt to the ground, their occupants murdered without discrimination of sex or age. Bodies hang from trees. Even the churches are razed to the ground. It's a world beyond your worst nightmare, yet this is the world you'll be entering. It's a journey into hell.

'Yet, I've never known a people so defiant and independent like the Greeks. Their suffering has become their strength.' Fin rested his hand on Frank's shoulder and, standing, he walked over to the table in the middle of the room where Stu was. Stu puffed on his pipe and stared thoughtfully at a map spread across the tabletop. He scratched his chin and mumbled to himself. He tapped the map with a finger.

'We'll come ashore here.' He glanced at Fin.

Fin nodded in agreement. 'It's a good place to hide the boat.'

Stu returned his attention to the map. 'The town is less than a mile away. There're a few houses not far, a five-minute jog away. It's been arranged. A truck will be waiting for us. We'll go as far as the outskirts of the town, then we'll be on foot again. The bank's in the square. There're never more than ten Jerries guarding the place at night. With luck, most of them will be sleeping. Once we've cleared the place, we've got fifteen minutes to get the communications equipment on the truck and back to the boat. We take as much as we can. There's a small garrison here.' He taps the map with his pipe. 'We need to be well gone before they arrive.'

Chapter 18

Frank watched from the caique as Fin and his men disappeared into the undergrowth, swallowed by the night. With Stephanos' help, they removed the bamboo poles and nets that camouflaged the caique and stored them in the hull.

'Now we wait.' Stephanos said with a slight quiver in his voice.

Frank breathed heavily, beads of sweat glistening on his forehead. His chest heaved; his stomach constricted.

Frank wiped his damp palms on the fabric of his trousers as his shirt stuck to the skin of his back. Around him, the air felt dense with every breath he took.

The cicadas kept a constant pulse, accompanied by the gentle swell of the sea against the caique. Frank raised his head and a solitary cloud, caught in the muted glow of the moon, snagged his eyes. The sounds of the bay and the world around him appeared so tranquil, in stark contrast to the dread and panic that churned inside him.

He gagged and scurrying around Stephanos, he wretched the contents of his stomach into the water below. He hauled himself straight and wiped trails of saliva from his mouth and chin, his eyes moist and red.

'Feel better now?'

Frank struggled to reply, and all he could do was nod.

'Here.' Stephanos handed him a flask of water.

'Drink.'

Frank did as he was told, grateful to wash away the foul taste in his mouth.

'Take this as well.' Stephanos handed Frank a piece of folded paper.

Frank took it from him and unfolded it. It was a list, written in neat handwriting. He glanced at it. Stephanos had written common phrases in English and beside each phrase, he had written the Greek translation. Frank looked up in amazement. 'This is wonderful, Stephanos. Thank you.'

Stephanos pointed to the first line on the sheet of paper. 'Efcharistó. See, it means thank you.'

'Efcharistó.' Frank drawled the word, trying to mimic Stephanos' pronunciation.

'You will need to speak some Greek. In the countryside and villages, few people speak English and not very well. Only the well-educated speak it. If you are to be understood, you will need to learn Greek quickly.'

'You're a fisherman, Stephanos. How did you learn to speak English so well?'

'I was not always a fisherman. When I was younger, in the early 1930s, I lived in Athens. My father was a politician in the government. We lived in a big house in a nice suburb of Athens. I went to the best private schools and got the best education his money could buy. I learnt to speak English and French. But I was dissatisfied. I wanted the education of life, not of books. I wanted to travel. I'd never been out of Athens.' His voice rose. 'I'd never seen my own country. When I told my father about my plans, he was horrified. He had my whole life planned out for me, university, an officer in the military and then, like him, I was to have a career in politics. When I told him that was not going to happen, he cut off my monthly allowance and my inheritance.'

'So, what happened?'

'I followed my heart. I had saved quite a lot of money and that allowed me to travel. I spent months travelling, visiting many towns all over Greece and its many islands, until I came to Zakynthos. I knew then, I had found the place I wanted to live. I had always loved the sea, so the obvious thing for me to do was to buy a caique and I would make a living fishing the waters around Zakynthos. I was happy. I'd never been as happy in my entire life, and then the war came. When all of this is finished, when the war is over, I'll be content just to catch fish again. A simple life. What about you, Frank? What will you do?'

'Paint.' He grinned. 'A simple life.'

They heard it then, the crunch of gears, the slap of pistons and the heavy dull growl of an engine.

'They're back, quickly Frank, get ready to load the radios.'

Frank jumped into the shallow water and waded to the shore. He heard Stephanos crank the caique's engine into life, and then he was standing by his side staring into the night.

The truck appeared from the darkness and in a storm of dust screeched to a stop. A door flew open, and Stu jumped out.

Stu screamed. 'Stephanos, get Fin. He's in the back. Frank, help me load the boat.'

They ran to the rear of the truck. Stu, tense and angry, dropped the tailgate. Frank's eyes shot to Fin and to his horror, Fin was lying crumpled on his back, his chest bloodstained, dark and ominous looking.

'Jesus Christ!' Frank blurted, his heart hammering in his chest.

Stu jumped into the back of the truck and barked, 'Get the fucking radios on the boat. And be careful, they're useless if you smash the valves.'

Desperately, Frank grabbed whatever was at hand: radios, recharging batteries, transmitters, and hand generators and transferred the contents of the truck into the hull of the caique. They ran back and forth, the ground feeling like quicksand beneath their feet. It took them a few minutes to empty the truck, but it felt like an age. Stephanos had lain Fin flat on the deck, who made guttural moans and coughs, and spluttered blood from his mouth.

'Where is everyone?' Stephanos eyes were wide and animal like.

'Either dead or wishing they were dead. Everything went to plan. Until we loaded the truck, a fucking squad of Germans descended upon us. It must have been a night patrol. We need to get the fuck out of here.'

A sound like firecrackers cut through the air. Frank's body involuntarily jerked, and he covered his head with his hands. Another volley of shots split the night air, and Frank glanced at Stu, as the side of Stu's head disintegrated like a melon, and the rest of him hurled into the air and slapped the water below.

The caique surged forwards as its engine howled and Frank lost his footing. He yelped, stumbled, and fell backwards, smacking his head. Around them, the bullets hit the water like miniature torpedoes, flashing overhead and pummelling the caique.

Frank rolled into a foetal position, hugging his legs tightly to his chest. He squeezed his eyes shut, pleading, and bargaining with the God he had never spoken to for years, to save his life. When he opened his eyes, all the while, he kept them fixed on Stephanos. His life now depended on the fisherman.

At dawn, undulating mountains on the Greek mainland appeared to their right. As they neared Corfu, perpendicular white sea cliffs rose from the sea, reminding Frank of the cliffs of Dover. They eased their way up the west coast of the island where Frank glimpsed a pod of dolphins, less than fifty yards from them, cutting through the waves, as if they were escorting and willing Frank to safety.

Frank asked Stephanos about being on the sea during daylight. Weren't they putting themselves in danger from being discovered by a passing German ship? Stephanos gave Frank a reassuring smile. 'Don't worry. We will look like any other fishing boat in the waters of Corfu.'

Throughout the night, Frank periodically checked Fin's chest was still rising and falling. He had managed to stop the stem of blood that had flowed from Fin's wound, but when the first signs of light broke the horizon, he could not stop the flow of life that left Fin's lungs. As he cleaned his hands of blood, he left them dragging in the sea; he had never felt so alone and fearful.

Stephanos remained hunched over the wheel. He told Frank they were heading towards the northwest coast of Corfu and one particular cove where the radios and transmitters were to be hidden in a cave. He again assured Frank. 'Don't worry. We will look like any of the other fishing boat in the area.'

Even as early as it was, the sun pressed its heat against Frank's back. The crystal sea was placid and tamed as the caique made its way at a leisurely pace as not to attract unwanted attention. Frank surveyed a coastline of whitened cliffs towering above a patchwork of turquoise sea. It surprised him how fertile and green the land was, with hills clothed in carpets of luscious pine and cypress trees. He spotted villages, whitewashed walls, and church steeples. The light was different somehow, not like the light back home. It nudged the summit of the hills, hovering like a halo, and melted into the deep blue sky. It was hard to believe the world was strangled by war.

After a while, Stephanos turned to Frank. His face was ashen, and it glistened with sweat. He raised his hand and pointed to a small, secluded cove, the entrance just wide enough for the caique to enter. 'We're here. There's a cave just over there. Everything comes off the boat and into the cave.' Stephanos coughed. He made to move and staggered, the muscles on his face clenched, his knees weakened, and with a deep groan, he doubled over at the waist. His legs gave way, and he slumped forward like a felled tree.

'Stephanos!' Frank approached him, alarmed and hesitant. He knelt beside Stephanos and looked at the vacant and staring eyes. Dread fell upon Frank, so heavy and desperate it took the breath from him. He glared at the gruesome wound, drenched in dark blood. Stephanos had been wounded all this time. Frank held Stephanos' face in his cupped hands in bewilderment. His admiration quickly turned sour with anger. Why had he not noticed Stephanos was wounded? Why did Stephanos keep this from him? His steadfast determination to reach this diminutive, concealed inlet, insignificant in the grand scheme of the occupied territory, was worth more to him than his own life, which he disregarded for the obvious benefit of others. Even in the recesses of his mind, there was no compromise. Frank was both perplexed and amazed. His anger melted, and he smiled in admiration as a lump burned his throat.

He slumped against the side of the caique. His hands shook. Death had been a constant companion. All around him, men had died. He was the only one left. What world had he entered?

In his mind's eye, the streets of Edinburgh consumed him. The familiar sounds he had taken for granted, the distinctive architecture of the buildings, the rattle of the trams on the tracks, the humour of the people. He could smell the distinctive aroma of Maggie's perfume, feel her fingers trail down his cheek, her warm breath upon his skin. He ached to be home. It increased his sense of loss. His heart thumped as he heaved his knees close to his chest. He wanted to close his eyes and shut out this world of death and loss. He ran his hands through his hair and took several deep breaths. Even amongst all the horror of the last few days and the irrevocable situation he found himself in, he owed it to Fin and his men, to Stephanos and, to himself, to finish what had led him to Corfu. Frank felt a surge of urgency and duty. It had been such a short time, yet he had felt a bond develop and mature between himself, Fin, and his men.

Frank pulled himself to his feet. He carefully stepped over Stephanos and jumped down into the hull, heaving every piece of communications equipment onto the deck. Once the hull was empty, Frank transferred it all off the caique and shifted it to the short distance inside the cave. When the last of the radios, batteries and transmitters were piled safely in the cave, Frank slumped to the ground. The sweat on his skin impregnated his hair, his shirt, and trousers. He lay on his back, staring at the rock ceiling of the cave. His fingers trailed through the sand that coated the ground. It was a good hiding place, Frank told himself. Exhilarated and exhausted, there was still one more thing to do.

Back on the caique, Frank took a knife and tore at the sail, cutting it so that there was sufficient length to wrap around two bodies. He held the end of the material close to Fin and rolled him along its length, covering his entire body in several layers. He did the same with Stephanos, and then secured the material around each body with a length of rope, tying it around the feet and the chest area until it held the material fast and secure. With great effort, he slid each body into the hull and, using the bamboo poles and netting, Frank did his best to camouflage the caique as best he could. It had taken him two hours. It felt like a lifetime.

Frank opened his satchel and took out a small brown paper parcel. He sat down, placing the parcel in his lap, and unwrap it. Inside was a chunk of hard bread and some cheese. He ate with haste, even the left-over crumbs and washed it down with some tepid water from a canteen flask. His thoughts were awash with what he should do next. He frowned; he didn't know when he would eat again, but more pressingly, he needed to do the right thing for Fin and Stephanos.

The communications equipment would be safe for now, as he focused his gaze on the cave. Frank had noticed that the only indentations in the sand were from his feet. As far as he could tell, this was a good place to hide anything you didn't want others to find.

Four 5-gallon jerry cans stored in the hull of the boat were filled to the brim with diesel. He didn't know how many nautical miles this much fuel would provide. He didn't know where he would go or how he would get there. Stephanos knew these waters. Frank had never seen him use a map. The only map he saw was the one Stu had used. Despair engulfed his already depleted sense of survival.

Just then, his heart leapt. In the distance, he heard the faint but undeniable sound of pealing church bells. There was a town or a village nearby.

Chapter 19

Alexia Pouliou considered the old woman's request. She had known Mina since she was a child.

Mina fanned her wrinkled face in the sticky heat. 'Well, what do you think? Will you help an old woman whose back is bent and relies on a stick to walk?' Mina enquired, trying not to embarrass the girl, so she tried to sound inpatient.

It was a fair offer, but Alexia did not want to appear to be enthused about the extra money it would bring. She still had her pride. She brushed a stray hair from her face. 'Will you let me think about it?'

The church bell rang out. 'No, I won't. I need an answer now, as I'm going to church. You won't get a better offer. You either take it or leave it. And if we leave them too long, the Germans will take the lot.'

Alexia smiled. 'Then, I agree.'

'Good.' Mina crossed herself three times. 'I'll say a prayer and light a candle for you, Alexia.'

'Don't waste your prayers on me. Give them to someone who believes God is listening.'

'But he is, Alexia. Why do you think the Germans have not plundered my olive grove so far, unlike others? I have burnt enough candles to light the sky at night. He is listening, my dear.' Mina kissed Alexia on the forehead and leaning on her walking stick with an unsteady shuffle, she made her way to church.

Mina's olive grove was situated a few hundred yards from the village, sprawling over a piece of ground that had been in her family for generations.

Before the occupation, Mina's son, Ioannis, and his son had tended to the harvest, but Ioannis' unfortunate death from cardiac arrest and his son's departure to join the Greek People's Liberation Army left Mina with no one to tend her olive grove.

It would benefit them both, Mina knew. The sum of money she had offered Alexia to gather the olives was more than Alexia could ever hope to earn. What did Mina need the money for, anyway? It was worthless. Even a loaf of bread was out of her reach. It wouldn't always be like this, and once the war was over and Greece climbed from her knees, money would have value again. It pleased Mina, knowing Alexia would have the means to begin a new life. She had kept the drachma notes in an old, unassuming tin that she hid under the mattress of her bed.

Mina would have given Alexia the money without offering her the job, but knew Alexia would not have taken it. This way, both would benefit.

At twenty-three, Alexia was a widow. Two years previously, in 1941, the rumours spreading through Athens like wildfire became reality. Mussolini ordered an Italian advance from Albania. Italian troops failed to break the Greek defensive line. Like many young Greek men, Alexia's husband, Stathis, enlisted in the army. He was part of the Greek offensive that launched a counterattack and pushed the Italians back into Albanian territory. Before he enlisted, Stathis enthused that the whole of Greece had risen as one, they fought the common enemy, united in their cause, and it was every Greeks duty to fight Italian fascism and not allow one inch of their beloved Greece to be taken by Mussolini. It would be the legacy of every young Greek male to have played their part and influence the glorious victory and to have stood tall and firm to the threat of fascist tyranny. She feared his enthusiasm. The parliament in Athens, its politicians, the dictator Metaxas, and his regime were a government no better than the Italian fascists and German Nazis that the youth and young men of Greece would be dying for. A bitterness rose within her like bile in her throat.

Alexia was told Stathis died defending the honour of Greece. It was little consolation. In her mind, Stathis died for the Metaxas government, a regime that was anti-communist, anti-parliamentary state, a pro totalitarian state, committed to the very ideology of those that were now ransacking towns and villages and brutally murdering civilians.

She was left with a small one-bedroom house. A roof that leaked when it rained, and shutters that threatened to fall from their hinges every time they rattled in the wind, a goat and an orange tree.

Alexia felt a sense of elation and joy as she stood in her small kitchen. She had not felt like this for a long time and now savoured the experience. The work had worth and purpose, and she hoped it would be a harbour of activity to quell the debilitating loss of the life she once knew.

She ached to feel strong and whole again. It had been two years since Stathis left, and in that time, so much had changed. Her world was unrecognisable, it was one of resentment, of suspicion and a loss that surged in her heart.

Chapter 20

Frank had no choice. He needed to gain her attention, and he knew no other way of doing it. He had to minimise what would be a terrible shock. Frank peered at Stephanos' list of words, looking for the most appropriate. And then, to his immense relief, he found it. *British*. He thanked Stephanos and, taking a deep breath, he stepped out from behind the olive tree.

Before the woman could cry out, Frank raised his hand, and said gently, 'Vretanos.'

The woman's eyes darted around the grove, olives tumbling from her shaking hands. What if she screamed? Frank suddenly thought. She was startled, and he could sense her trepidation. The last thing Frank wanted was for her to turn around and run. If she did, he would not chase after her. The thought of alarming her more was detrimental to his purpose.

He cursed himself. What was he going to say now?

He glanced at the sheet of paper and frantically scanned the list, and after what seemed an age, he finally saw the word he hoped would defuse the woman's rising panic. When finally, he lifted his head, he froze, his throat tightened, and his heart sank. She was brandishing a small knife in her hand that was raised in front of her. She took a few steps backwards, her eyes wide, and it was as if something inside her had become callused.

Frank tapped his chest and again, in a gentle voice, he said the word he hoped would defuse the woman's hostility towards him. 'Voitheia!' (*Help*). There was a definite intimation of worry in his voice now. *Shit, don't run, please stay.* He thought about moving closer to her, but then thought better of it. She might see as a threatening gesture.

She could either sense his despondency, as his anguish was by now palpable, or something changed inside her.

'You are British?'

Frank drew in a sharp breath. He couldn't believe what he was hearing. 'You can speak English. Jesus. I can't believe it. That's just amazing. You can speak English.'

'And why should that surprise you?' Her face hardened again.

'Please don't take it the wrong way. I'm relieved, that's all. It makes it so much easier to be able to speak with you and be understood.'

'It will. Your Greek is terrible.' She didn't move her eyes from him. 'What are you doing here?'

'I need your help.' Frank explained how he had come to be on Corfu, about Fin and Stephanos, and the need to bury their bodies. He thought it prudent, not to mention the communication equipment.

'You are mercenaries.'

'No. No. My friends were part of the Special Operations Executive. They were British soldiers. They were on your side.'

'How do I know you are telling the truth? You do not look like a soldier to me.'

'I'm not.' He sensed she was beginning to doubt him. He sighed. 'It's a long story. I just want to bury my friends.'

'If what you are saying is true, then let me tie your hands and you can walk in front of me and take me to them. If you are telling me the truth, I will return with a spade.'

'You would do that?'

'Or I will run back to the village and come back with others who may not be as understanding as I am.'

'I prefer the first option.'

'Then get on your knees and put your hands behind your back.'

'Thank you.'

'Don't thank me just yet.'

'Why would you do this?'

'You have a kind face.'

She walked backwards, and then, beside a harvesting net, she scooped up a piece of rope, and swiftly moving behind Frank, she wrapped the rope several times around his wrists, pulling it tight as it dug into his skin, she expertly secured the rope in place.

She followed him down the steep track that was used to bring supplies and food to the village by mule. Beside them, a stream trickled with clear water and that and their breathing was the only sound to accompany them. Frank slipped and lost his balance, landing hard on his buttocks and jerking the muscles in his arms. The pain that shot through them was excruciating.

She waited. Embarrassed and in pain, he struggled to his feet, stumbled, but stayed standing this time. He sensed there was no enjoyment on her part at his predicament.

When he fell, Alexis saw his feet slide from under him and her heart missed a beat. Instinctively, her reaction was to break his fall and help him to his feet. She found it difficult not to do both; it was against her nature. She did not want to show weakness, after all, she had put herself in danger and she was now questioning if she had been too impulsive. Should she have run back to the village when she had the chance? It would have been the rational thing to do, but when had she ever followed convention? Her mother had been in the habit of chastising her that one day, her independent state of mind would land her in trouble. Alexia was now wondering if that day had now arrived.

What was she doing walking alone with this stranger, along a secluded trail, covered in a thicket of trees and undergrowth? She convinced herself his story was plausible. Otherwise, why would he agree to be bound in rope and marched at knife point if he wasn't telling the truth? There would be no possible logic to his actions that she could see. She could only surmise he was indeed taking her to a caique where the bodies of his friends lay. Alexia hoped he was the kind of man she could trust, and if not, was she prepared to use the knife that shook in her hand? She admired his sense of responsibility. He, too, was putting his faith in her and possibly his life.

He limped down the trail, gritting his teeth. It was only pain. His body felt the pain, not his mind. He wished she would speak. She had not spoken since they left the olive grove.

She could see he had small cuts and grazes on the back of his hand from the fall. She didn't know quite what to say, after all, she was the one who had tied his hands. He was her captive. 'Are you okay?'

She didn't expect him to answer, and it surprised her when he did. 'I've had better days.'

'If you are not a soldier, then why are you here?'

'I'm an artist.'

It was not the answer she expected. 'I do not understand.'

'I paint. I draw. It's my job, or at least it was.'

'That doesn't explain why you are here with a caique and two dead bodies. Why should I trust you?'

He stopped and turned. It was the first time he had looked at her properly since she bond his hands together. He felt the sting of her suspicion, but given the circumstance, he understood it.

Now that he was standing close to her, it was impossible not to view and regard her face. Her hair was dark and long and held up by a scarf tied around her head. Long tendrils had broken free and fell around her face in waves. Her eyes were dark and staring at him. She was sceptical of him. 'So, you have come to paint our beautiful countryside, capture the light in the trees and the blue of the sea.'

There was a silence between them. 'In another life, I would love to.'

'I am still not understanding.'

'No. I suppose I owe you an explanation.' Frank explained how he came to be on a ship that was torpedoed by a German submarine, then rescued by Fin and ending up in a small cove along the western coast of Corfu. He indulged in the detail, but did not reveal the boat's cargo or where it was concealed.

When Frank had finished, his story had plundered Alexia's harshness towards him. She felt sickened at the thought that he, too, had suffered grievously at the hands of the occupying German soldiers. There was something about this man and although she felt fear and anxiety, there was an undeniable impression that her apprehension was abating, and it left her momentarily wordless.

Alexia looked down at the knife in her hand, and suddenly overwhelmed and aware that she could come to harm, decided it would still be needed.

They came to a clearing, and the track headed off in two opposite directions. Frank glanced at Alexia. 'I can't remember which way it is.'

They were getting closer to the sea and Alexia smiled. She pointed to the left. 'It's this way.'

'You know where we're going.'

'I do now. I know this place. I used to swim there as a child. It's a good place to hide a boat.'

The track gave way to sand and the gentle sound of waves. On each side of the small beach, walls of white rock tapered to a narrow opening just wide enough to get a caique through. It was astonishing how well the boat merged with its surroundings. Alexia was not expecting to see nets drape the boat and deceive the naked eye. Even though he was bound, and his legs and arms ached, Frank gazed at the translucent water flushed in aqua blue and turquoise shades looking like some heavenly painter had dipped their brush in a pallet of colour and swept it along the surface of the sea.

'There is a boat,' Alexia said with heavy relief in her voice.

'Do you want to see the bodies?'

Alexia nods.

With effort, his hands still bond, Frank hauled himself onto the boat, Alexia following behind.

'They're in there.'

With an air of trepidation about her, Alexia craned her head so that she could get a view of the inside of the small hull. She turned to Frank with eyes sad and a look of resignation. 'It must have been difficult to do this. I'm sorry, I did not trust you.'

'I would've done the same if I were you.'

She slipped behind him and, with a few forceful thrusts, Frank's hands sprung from their confinement.

Frank rubbed the red marks on his skin. 'Thank you.'

'You will need to clean those cuts on your hands. You don't want them to get infected,' Alexia advised, with a trace of an apology in her voice.

'I'll do that. There's water in the flasks. I've got enough problems as it is.'

'I can bring you some antiseptic for them when I return. We will have to bury your friends near the boat.' She glanced towards some trees. 'Over there looks like a good spot. It is sheltered and out of the way. I'll bring you something to eat. It won't be much, I'm afraid.'

'You've done enough just coming here. I'm grateful for the courage you've shown.'

'We do what we must do. The war has changed us all.'

'Some more than others. I can't imagine what it must be like to be occupied by another country and the life you had suddenly not existing. Back home, they have no concept of that. The bombs have been dreadful, especially in the big cities, but people can still live in a country they can call their own.'

'As we still do. My country is in my heart and the Germans cannot touch that. I need to go, but I will be back tomorrow. The boat is well hidden. I think you should be safe.'

'There's a cave just over there. I'll shelter there during the night. You never told me your name... I'm Frank.'

'I am Alexia.' She flicked a strand of hair from her face.

Again, he could not help himself and as he contemplated her face, he could see she was attractive. At that moment, it was as if Frank's eyes were caught in a web. Self-consciously, he thought then, how he must look to her, tired and drawn looking, dishevelled, and unshaven, and even worse, how he must smell. The odour of stale sweat and his unwashed appearance left him ashamed and humiliated.

'Thank you, Alexia.'

She smiled. 'You can thank me once we have buried your friends.'

***

He stood on the sand, facing the pellucid and iridescent water of the enclosed bay. How could a place like this exist with such arresting colour, translucent water and wavering light amongst the turmoil and horror that had become the world around him? He felt concealed, and in that moment, he was conscious of a great weight elevating from him. His eyes welled. He unbuttoned his shirt and, like removing a second layer of skin, he peeled it from him his body. He slumped onto the sand, unlaced his boots, and slipped them from his feet. The relief was instant, and even better still, when he unwrapped his socks from his feet. He slid off his trousers and then his pants and stood up, naked and unbound from the filth and grime of the last few weeks. He took tentative steps forward and his heart lifted when seawater pearled between his toes and ebbed and flowed around his feet. He waded further, where the tepid water kissed his knees. Gradually, it lapped gently against his thighs, and he slid under, embracing the water sliding along the surface of his skin, in the muffled silence of a weightless universe.

Chapter 21

Alexia had spent the night tossing and turning, and the fleeting sleep she eventually managed only fed her active mind with nightmares and unrest.

Eventually, she rose at six in the morning. Still dark outside, she found that rising did not ease the feeling she had desperately tried to ignore throughout the night. The weight of her responsibility settled over her like a heavy winter coat.

Carrying a chamber pot, she went outside. Her neighbour's houses like the sky were still shrouded in darkness and a silence that was always peculiar to this hour of the day. A goat, tied to an orange tree, lifted its head and watched Alexia with searching eyes. Alexia stroked its head, and the goat nuzzled into her hand contentedly.

Once she had emptied the chamber pot, she lit an oil lamp and laid it on the kitchen table. Yesterday, she had drawn water from the village well and there was still plenty left to wash and cook. She filled a large, blackened pot with water and hung it over the fire, which she lit. As she sank into a chair, she sighed heavily and yawned.

She'd bathe, then after breakfast, wait for light and return to the little cove with the food and shovel she promised.

She knew this man could not remain hidden. His only hope was to take his chances on the caique and take to the sea. If he remained, he could easily be discovered. He did not speak Greek, and he certainly did not look like a local. Even his mannerisms gave him away. All she could do was to return with the promised food and shovel and once he had buried his friends... No, she could not have it on her conscience. She could not live with herself. He would never survive at sea. What was she thinking? She didn't even know if he could navigate. The man who got him here was now dead and about to be laid in the ground. As much as she hated to admit it, he was going to be a problem... her problem.

Frank awoke with a start and groaned at the sharp pain in his neck. He was lying on his back, staring at the roof of the cave. No longer dark, the morning sunlight illuminated the rock and sand in a yellow glow. He stretched his legs and rubbed the dull pain in his lower back. What he would give for a mattress and a roof over his head, he thought.

Hesitant, he ventured outside. The waves unfurled with their normal hushed, gentle crash. Frank marvelled at the sky adorned in lavender and pink and the sight reminded him of a recent painting, his last composition, before accepting the post as a war artist. He longed for the simplicity of that ordered life. A life that seemed so far. It was untouchable. It no longer existed. Overwhelmed by a sense of utter loss, nothing seemed normal anymore.

Now reliant on a woman he had stumbled upon, and in his desperation, he had put his life in her hands without knowing the first thing about her. For all he knew, she could be a collaborator, and the Germans could arrest him at any moment. It was too late to go back now.

It occurred to him that if she was not a collaborator, by helping him, he put her life in grave danger, and Frank knew, if caught, she faced imprisonment or death. She had already shown immense courage and compassion and he felt shamed even contemplating his endangerment while she risked her life to help him.

He had no option but to trust her and wait.

***

Alexia emerged from the trees. Frank saw her from the cave, and, to his relief, she carried a shovel in her hand.

He came out of the cave and walked towards her. As he drew close to her, Alexia stood, studying him. Her gaze slid from his face to his boots. It made Frank uncomfortable and embarrassed at how he must look to her, haggard and unwashed, but when he looked into her eyes, instead of seeing disdain, he saw pity.

'I've brought you some food. It's not much, but it's fresh, and this,' she raised the shovel and Frank took it from her.

Frank drew in a breath. 'Thank you for coming back. I wouldn't have blamed you if you hadn't. I know what you're risking and the consequences of that.'

'We are under the boot of the Nazis; every day brings its own dangers. That won't change, as long as they are here. They are pretending to be British soldiers, so they can get inside the resistance groups and learn their activities and movements. I had to be careful, that's why I tied your hands. I am sorry you fell and hurt yourself.'

'It was more my pride that was hurt.' He regarded the shovel. 'I'll start to dig the graves now, before it gets too hot.'

'Eat first.'

He followed her as she climbed aboard the caique. She flung a small satchel from her shoulder and dropped it onto the wooden beams. She opened the rucksack, took out a brown paper parcel which she unwrapped, 'There's bread, goats' cheese, and some olives. There is water too.'

As he ate, Frank could not help but think of Fin and Stephanos lying in the hull. It was a strange feeling. Back in Edinburgh, with Maggie and his paintings, such a thing would have been unthinkable. It would have been unfathomable to even imagine eating food, knowing that two dead bodies were only a few feet from him. Alexia must have sensed Frank's unease.

'If I thought about all the people who I know have died since the Germans came... Well, I try not to think about it. I would go mad if I did.'

'Nothing can prepare you for this. It feels like the world has gone mad. Maybe they are the lucky ones. At least Fin and Stephanos have escaped all of this.'

Once he had eaten, Frank entered the hull and, with an effort, eased the bodies out into the daylight. It was easier to slide each body into the shallow water and, with a struggle, Frank carried each one to the small clearing in the trees. It came as a relief that the shovel sliced through the ground with more ease than he had thought. The work was arduous, especially when he had to hack at roots. His eyes stung with sweat and his shirt stuck to his back, which ached with each shovel full of earth he extracted from the ground. After a while, Alexia offered to dig instead and let Frank rest, but he was adamant he alone would do the work. All the time he laboured, German troops could be in the vicinity, and it made it more imperative to accomplish his task.

Gradually, there was adequate width and depth to fit the two bodies into the makeshift grave. Frank placed Fin and Stephanos side by side and shovelled the mound of earth back to where it had come from.

Once Frank flattened the earth, Alexia said a prayer in Greek and crossed herself three times. 'I have not prayed for a long time, but it felt the right thing to do.'

Frank stood in silence, exhausted, flat, and devoid of emotion.

'You have done a good thing, Frank.'

'There should always be loved ones, family and friends to say goodbye, but there's just you and me.'

'You should feel glad that you were able to do this.'

'I'm not sure how I feel. I feel... flat and disconnected, I suppose.'

Alexia looked at him quizzically. 'I have seen people hanging from trees. Their bodies left to rot, food for birds and wild animals. Believe me, this is better. Before the Germans came, many young men left our village to join the army and fight the Italians in Albania. Only a few returned. Their mothers and wives mourned them, but they could not give them a burial, their traditions and beliefs expected of them, because their sons and husbands still lay where they died.'

Frank recoiled. 'I'm sorry.'

'For what? For being human. I won't judge you. We have all seen terrible things, some of which we should never witness in a lifetime. Some have done terrible things, even Greeks.'

They heard raised voices above the rumble of a truck, German voices. The surprise widened Alexia's eyes. Frank had been breathing heavily from his exertions, but now, he involuntarily held his breath, as if the sound would alert the Germans. He stared through the trees; he could hear the truck but could not see it.

Alexia raised her head. She drew in a deep breath and listened intently. 'It will be a patrol.' She smiled nervously. 'They have gone. You cannot stay here. It is too dangerous.'

The passing truck and the soldier's voices reminded Frank of the risk Alexia had taken returning to help him.

'I will leave with the boat tonight.'

'And go where?'

'Anywhere, but here. Every minute you spend with me puts your life in danger, too. I can't have that on my conscience.'

'Can you navigate?'

Frank looked away from her.

'It would be the same as walking into a German camp with your hands in the air.'

'How difficult can it be? I've seen Stephanos sail the caique. It looks easier than driving a car.'

'He knew where he was going and how to get there. No. You must come with me. The boat is well hidden, with luck, it will not be discovered.'

'No! I won't put you in any more danger. You have already risked too much for me.'

There was an intensity in her eyes. 'What choice do you have? We cannot take the main road to the village. This time, we will go up the mule trail, but at night, it will be pitch black. We would not see a thing in front of us. We will have to go now. It's not ideal, but we have no choice.'

He knew she was right. Even if he could sail the boat, he would still be vulnerable, and on foot, exposed. He had made a terrible, grievous mistake in getting Alexia involved, but he could not change what had happened, no matter how much he regretted it.

He managed a smile. 'I'll need to get my paints.'

By the time they had reached the caique, the air around them had grown silent again, with only the accompaniment of the ubiquitous waves in the foreground.

Frank clambered on board and disappeared inside the hull. He checked everything was in the holdall, his paintbrushes, pencils, paints, and sketch pads. Something caught his eye. He remembered then. It was Fin's pistol, lying amongst several small boxes of ammunition. Frank had taken the pistol from Fin's body, and not sure what to do with it, he left it in the hold.

He scooped it up, wrapped it in a rag and, along with some ammunition, stuffed them in his holdall.

Once outside, he staggered upright, his eyes squinted in the bright light. Alexia gazed at the holdall curiously.

'It's where I keep my paints, my brushes, and pencils. As well as my sketch pads, it's all I have.'

She smiled. 'You really are an artist.'

It was the first time he had seen her smile. 'I am. I draw and paint. I'm not a soldier. I prefer to preserve the living through art, rather than kill them.'

Alexia had no answer to that.

Frank followed Alexia through the thick woods before they came to a dirt track.

'This is the mule trail I took you down yesterday. Provisions are taken up this trail to the village by mule, it is quicker than going by road, and for us, it will be safer too.'

She felt something happening inside her. Seeing Frank with the bag slung around his shoulder had changed her. It was as if it confirmed what she had already known, but was too afraid to consider. He was the man he said he was, and in being so, she could unwrap the layers of doubt and suspicion she had about him that were instinctive in wartime and necessary in an occupied country.

It was a steep climb and Frank was thankful his hands were free this time. The higher they advanced, they became surrounded by olive and cypress trees and a thick forest of shrubs and bushes. The trail turned from dirt to rock and sometimes stone steps that the villagers had placed where the terrain was difficult to progress along. At one point, they traversed along the side of a steep cliff face, climbing higher towards the village with each turn and bend of the trail.

They stopped to rest for a while, and Frank was stunned at the view below him. A shelf of dense foliage and shrubbery spread out below him and continued to the sea. As far as he could see, stunning bays beautified the coastline in aquamarine and turquoise shades of the likes he had never seen. Alexia told Frank he was looking at the bay of Palaiokastritsa and there was no other place in Corfu that was as beautiful as what his eyes were now feasting upon. And he believed her, for he had never seen a landscape that had taken his breath from him like the view from the hill they had just climbed. Alexia pointed out a monastery, which dated back to 1225. It crowned a hill, like a jewel, and further to the left, beyond a heart-shaped bay, Alexia brought his attention to the village of Liapades, and with a sadness in her voice, told him her sister once lived there before dying in childbirth.

They continued on. Frank heard the trickle of a stream he remembered from yesterday, and now, when he thought of that time, strangely, it already felt another life. And at that moment, he realised he didn't recognise any aspect of his life anymore. Edinburgh, Maggie, the smell of paint and canvas in his studio, were all memories of another life, fragments of another time that with each step he took receded from him. A dull ache throbbed in his chest.

Alexia explained the trail ended at the opening of a narrow lane between two houses. There was a single road that travelled the length of the village. Once they crossed the road, they would disappear into another lane, and this would eventually lead them to her house.

He sensed a tension in her voice.

'It's still not too late.'

She stopped walking and turned to face him. 'What do you mean?'

'I could just disappear, and your life could continue as before. You don't have to do this, Alexia.'

'Don't you think I know this?'

It struck Frank then; he knew nothing of what it meant to suffer. Alexia, like many of her countrymen, had turned hardship, anger and uncertainty into honour and dignity. He wished then he could take back his words, for they shamed him, but most of all, they demeaned Alexia, and that was what hurt most of all.

When they reached the opening to the main road, Alexia paused and glanced both ways. It was quiet. Shutters were closed, and those that were open showed no sign of life behind them. She waved at Frank to follow her. They didn't look back. They reached the other side and entered a labyrinth of small, cobbled lanes. Frank's heart pounded as they hurried along narrow winding lanes that curved between limestone buildings where plaster cracked and peeled.

They heard two male voices, laughter spilling along the lane.

Alexia looked around her. 'In here,' she commanded.

She took hold of his arm and they slipped into a narrow lane, barely wide enough for one person to pass through. She drew in a deep breath as Frank tried not to press his body against hers. Her face rested against his chest and his sweat dampened shirt. She could smell the salt of the sea on his skin. He tried not to, but Frank breathed in deeply the sweet scent of her hair. Alexia took another deep breath. The voices grew closer. Louder. She closed her eyes.

When she opened them, Frank was staring at her. She exhaled, unaware that she had been holding it and Frank saw the fear that had flared in her eyes disappear.

'They've passed us.' Frank whispered, relieved. 'They were speaking Greek.'

'Do not take it for granted that everyone hates the Nazis, a few have done quite well out of the occupation. There are informers amongst us. We will need to be careful.'

'But I'm not a soldier.'

'No. You are not. But you are British. To the Nazis, you are still the enemy.'

Frank's stomach tensed.

She slid from him. 'Come. My house is not far.'

Finally, they stopped outside a small house with two blue wooden shutters on each side of a door. Alexia took Frank around the house to the small piece of land at the rear. The goat raised its head from sniffing the dirt, its nose coated in dust, and considered them before returning to explore the ground. To his surprise, Frank saw an orange tree with its bulbous fruit like little suns brightening the garden.

Alexia saw his astonishment. 'I know what you are thinking.' And with that, she plucked an orange from its branch. She turned it in her hands. 'In a few days, they will be ripe enough to eat. They are little miracles are they not, hidden from the Nazis in defiance?'

Once they were inside the house, Alexia filled a black pot with water and lit a fire.

'You need to wash and change your clothes. I have some soap. We can still get things on the black market. A man passes through the village once every two weeks, selling soap, oil, thread, meat, beans, chickpeas, and eggs. I have managed to keep a small stock of food and necessities. Even in times like these, some people still grow rich at the expense of their fellow countrymen. But it has saved many from going hungry.'

'I don't have fresh clothes. I'll need to put these ones back on.'

'That won't be necessary. I have clothes.'

He exchanged a look with her.

'They were my husband's. You are about the same build and same height he was.'

This new piece of information was unexpected. It startled him and Frank noted the past tense. 'I'm sorry if I seem surprised. It didn't dawn on me that you might be married.'

She corrected him. 'I'm not. I was... but he is dead now.'

'That was tactless of me. I'm sorry.' He would have liked to ask her how her husband had died, but feared it would upset her and he did not want to seem insensitive to her needs. In the end, she took that decision from him.

'Stathis joined the army, right after Mussolini thought it was a good idea to invade Greece. The Greek army held them on the Pindos mountains and, to everyone's surprise, forced the Italians back into Albania. The old men in the *kafenion* argued about Greece's chances when Hitler, fearing humiliation and an Italian defeat, came to Mussolini's aid. Most knew, as we all did, we were no match for the German military. The Royalist, Metaxas, who was the Greek Prime Minister, tried to persuade Hitler that he did not want to fight with the Italians and hoped that Hitler would end the hostilities by persuading Mussolini to end his attempts to invade Greece, and in doing so, Metaxas promised Greece would remain neutral. I had hoped for this outcome, too. Stathis had been gone for months by then, and without a word or letter, I was beside myself. When Hitler eventually attacked, Stathis and the Greek army were in between the Germans and the Italians.' Alexia clasped her hands in her lap. 'He never came home. That was two years ago.'

Frank shook his head, bewildered. 'I'm sorry, Alexia.' Words were inadequate, redundant even. How could Frank possibly relate to Alexia's suffering? He thought it better to remain silent.

'I still have some of his clothes. I don't know why I kept them. Maybe I thought he would still come home, that it had all been a mistake. It is lucky for you that I did.'

Alexia went upstairs and returned with a small pile of clothes, a towel, and a bar of soup. She placed them all on the table. She crossed the room and poured hot water from the pot above the fire into a basin and informed Frank she would feed the goat in the garden while he washed.

By the time he had washed and changed into his new clothes, Alexia had returned. She stood in the doorway. She swayed slightly and outstretched her hand to steady herself on the doorframe. The shirt was a perfect fit, but the trousers were slightly short and loose around the waist. The air in the house whirled with apprehension, and Frank's stomach churned with the knowledge he was wearing the clothes of her dead husband.

Alexia drew her hand through her hair. 'I'm sorry. For a second it could have been Stathis standing there.'

'Can I get you some water?' It was all he could think of saying, although it did not calm his nerves.

Sensing his unease, she tried to reassure him. 'I'll be fine. Honest,' she said, moving into the room.

'It feels strange wearing another man's clothes.'

'You can be honest with me. You mean it is strange wearing a dead man's clothes? I understand that. It is better to be honest with each other. That way, there is no misunderstanding, especially as this is an unusual arrangement.'

'You're right. I didn't want to cause you any more distress. I could see the way you reacted.'

'As I said, it was a momentary reaction.' Her attention was now on his trousers, and he felt her frown. 'You need a belt. I think I have one upstairs. I'll go and get it.' And with that, she disappeared.

Standing alone, he looked at his bare feet on the stone cladding floor. He would need socks, his were fraying and had holes at the heel. He would wear his own boots, at least they were salvageable. It felt like he was living inside another man's skin. It made the clothes feel acutely uncomfortable against him.

When Alexia looked at him, did she see the man standing in front of her, or was her mind consumed with thoughts of her husband? The peculiar feeling uneased him.

He heard her footsteps on the bare boards of the stairs. When she reached him, she handed Frank the belt. 'Try this.'

Frank buckled the belt around his waist and instinctively adjusted the trousers to his satisfaction. He drew his shoulders back and gave a slight grin. 'That's better. I won't have to walk around with one hand holding my trousers up now.'

Their eyes met, and Alexia smiled then, and Frank sensed something had changed between them.

They had both shared loss; Alexia's husband had died in action and the life Frank knew in Edinburgh with Maggie was also dead to him. At least they had this in common. It was something to hold on to.

Chapter 22

He saw in her deep brown eyes shame and as she ladled the watery soup with its few shreds of chicken and cabbage, an expression of embarrassment replaced it.

Frank took a spoonful of soup. 'Thank you. You have done so much for me. I'm indebted to you. I know this puts you in a grave situation and I will be gone soon, I promise. I'll go tonight. No one will know I've been here, and you won't have to live with the danger this puts you in.'

She looked down at the bowl with its watery soup where sunlight swept across the surface of the table. In the surrounding silence, he listened to her breath.

Questions gathered inside her, piling on top of each other, one after the other. But it was simple, really. There was no need to complicate the matter, so instead, she said, 'I would worry more about you if you were gone than if you stayed.'

'I feel trapped. I can't leave this island just yet, but I must. There is always the boat. I can take my chances on the boat. I don't want you to feel trapped, too, and that's how it will be if I stay. I couldn't bear to be here if you resented me.'

She looked at him steadily then and he could see that something, a thought, or a memory maybe, had darkened her face.

She let her spoon drop to the table. 'It's not about what I feel. Two nights ago, not far from here, a German truck was ambushed. All four of the soldiers in the truck were killed. This is terrible news for us. There is the fear that the Germans will come and seek revenge, for every German soldier killed, or truck blown up, ten Greeks will be shot, their houses burnt to the ground, sometimes entire villages are set on fire. Even if you wanted to leave, this is not the time to do so.'

Frank thought about the equipment in the cave. Should he have told Alexia? What benefit would have come of it? More worry and fear on her part, and that was something he was not prepared to add to. He tried to settle his mind, although it did not stop the ache of guilt crawl through his chest and the pulse of regret race through his veins.

Frank swallowed hard. 'I'll stay, but the first chance I have, I'll leave.' As an afterthought, he added, 'I'm grateful for your hospitality.'

Once they had eaten, Frank helped Alexia wash the plates and cutlery. Carrying out and sharing a basic routine of domestic activity, for a moment, defused the air of tension about them.

'I have to go back to the olive grove; I am behind in the work. You will have to be hidden when I'm gone.'

'Of course,' Frank agreed.

They made their way up the stairs that protested with every creek under their weight, crossed the landing and entered the bedroom. Frank could see a double bed with a headrest and a small mahogany dressing table with a standing mirror and two drawers with black handles. At the far end of the small bedroom, they stood before a vast wardrobe that loomed heavy, with dark wood and intricate carvings.

Alexia took hold of the handle and gently opened the door. Frank peered inside as she drew apart her dresses and blouses and slid open the panel at the back, revealing a hole in the wall, just big enough for someone to squeeze through.

One after the other, they entered the wardrobe and, crouching sideways, manoeuvred themselves into the space that opened up. Frank had to bend his head, as there was not enough head space to stand fully. The air was musty, and it caught his throat. He coughed into his hand. Pleasingly, it was cooler than the rest of the house. There was a mattress on the ground and nothing else. With no room to walk on either side of the mattress, the occupant of the room could only stand or sit, nothing more.

'It doesn't look much. I have only ever had to come in here once. The Germans searched every house in the village, and I stayed in here until they left. I could hear them downstairs and then I could almost smell them in my bedroom. They opened the wardrobe doors and then left.' She paused and Frank thought she wanted to add something, but stopped herself.

'I will be back as soon as I can. Stay here until I return. It is the safest place in the house. Promise me you will.'

He smiled. 'I will.'

She crept through the space and before she slid the panel shut, she smiled at him; it would be an image that would sustain his forced departure from the outside world.

He heard Alexia close the wardrobe doors, the creak of her footsteps on the stairs, and moments later she was gone, and his small world turned silent.

He sat on the mattress and leaned against the stone wall. His thoughts tumbled on top of each other.

He wondered what Alexia would be doing if he had not come across her in the olive grove and embroiled her in all of this. He didn't know it then. All he saw was a woman who could help him. Now he regretted even setting eyes on her, because in doing so, her life would not be the same as long as he was a part of it. For that very reason, if it had not been for Alexia's disclosure about the German reprisals, he would have left that night.

Chapter 23

Alexia returned to the olive grove. Before then, she called in on Mina, strapped the sacks she would need for collecting the olives onto Mina's ageing donkey and led it through the village.

She passed the usual gathering of old men. The daily congregation who sitting outside the *kafenion* under a cloud of blue cigarette smoke debated and argued. They sipped their black-market coffee, complaining about how weak it tasted. The daily buzz of chatter was a common activity amongst the older men of the village *kafenion*, where politics polarised vehement debates.

A shared theme was the terror of the German reprisal policy that was used to intimidate the local population. If armed men were found in villages, or shot at German soldiers, the male population of that village were shot or hanged, their houses and even churches burnt to the ground.

Doctors, teachers, priests, and other men of standing in the local communities were rounded up and taken to camps as hostages. Hostages were shot for any act of sabotage, attack on, or the death of German troops.

Some saw this as a deterrent, but others vigorously argued it was an enticement to support the resistance fighters. There was also the counter opinion that the resistance fighters deliberately incited the reprisals to provoke hatred amongst the local population towards the German troops and create nationalist sentimentalities. Others put the blame at the door of the puppet government of Georgios Tsolakoglou in Athens, sworn in to do the bidding of the occupying forces. It heralded the popular support in the villages and countryside that the EAM-The National Liberation Front was the only political party that could, after the war, transform Greece and bring about a democratic solution to the social and economic ruin of the country, while others bitterly viewed them as forcing the ideology of communism on the masses.

When rations were introduced, prices rose, and the drachma crashed. A quarter of a million people died of starvation. The black market replaced a failing economy. Tobacco, olive oil, fruit, crops, meat, and poultry were commandeered to feed the occupying army and sent to Germany to feed the German population.

As Alexia made her way through the village, leading the docile donkey behind her, she passed the baker's shop, whose ubiquitous aroma of fresh baked bread, pies, pastries, and cake had been extinguished by barren empty shelves.

She offered warm greetings to the women who sat and gossiped on the steps of their front doors, most dressed in black from head to foot.

She turned into a lane that led to the mule trail and the dappled sunlight from the trees that eventually engulfed her. Here, the smells of wild lavender, rosemary, basil, and oregano assailed Alexia, all combining to infuse the air with nature's garden. Alexia inhaled deeply, preparing herself for the work of harvesting Mina's olives.

The work was laborious and time consuming. She shook and struck the branches of the olive trees with a long wooden stick and as the olives fell; they rested on nets that covered the ground around the twisting trunks of the ancient olive trees. Alexia collected the olives and stored them in sacks, ready to be taken by the donkey through the steep terrain of olive groves, cypress trees and pine trees below the village.

As she worked, she wiped droplets of sweat from her brow and pressed her lips together, deep in thought. There was something about this man who had altered her life so unexpectedly she couldn't deny he intrigued her. She knew he was not a military man, but he was with soldiers who were now dead and lying in the ground. Was there an ulterior motive, a purpose for coming to Corfu with the pretence of a fishing boat as a smokescreen, or was he just a victim of circumstance? Her heart pounded with such thoughts.

Alexia wanted his story to be plausible. She bent to scoop up more olives and dispatched them in a sack.

There was a stranger hiding in her house. He wore her dead husband's clothes. A few days ago, this would have been unthinkable. Her life had shifted beyond comprehension, and it scared her to think about what may lie ahead.

Chapter 24

The moment Frank closed the panel between the wardrobe and the small space, the slither of light extinguished like a breeze across a candle flame. Frank sat with only his thoughts to give colour to and dispel the blackness around him. He thought of home as realms of memory played in his mind: his studio, flushed with sunlight, as his brush stroked canvas creating colour and depths, tones and shades, landscapes, and cityscapes.

Before the war, he established a profitable reputation as a portrait artist, taking commissions from those who could afford such luxuries to hang on the walls of their distinguished and elegant Georgian houses in the New Town of Edinburgh. He had been working on a portrait of Maggie, now covered in a white solitary sheet, unfinished and abandoned in the corner of his studio. Guilt colonised his thoughts like an advancing army. If only he could return to the last time he saw her, in that hot and smoke-filled pub in Leith Walk. How he would change the words he spoke before he vanished from her life. Those words reverberated in his mind.

He longed to hear the pounding of rain and smell the aroma it brought from the wet pavement. He yearned for the thunder of buses and the rumble of trams, the sounds and smells of packed cinemas, theatres, and pubs on a Saturday night. He would never again take for granted an aimless walk, a coffee at his favourite café, while scanning that day's news in The Scotsman or Times.

The concept of time, like the face of his watch, eluded him. Fatigue spread like oil into every pore and cell of his body.

After a while, his mind played tricks on him, and he saw shapes morph into ghostly faces and move in front of his eyes. His breathing amplified and punctured the silence and he strained to hear any sound, other than the occasional creak of beams and wood of the house settling around him.

In such a place, he thought it easy to succumb to madness if there was no prospect of leaving, like a prisoner in a cell.

He knew, at some point, Alexia would return, and it was just a case of waiting. He wished he had relieved his bladder beforehand as it tightened and burned in waves. His throat was dry and all he could do was stretch his legs to ease the stiffness of muscle and bone.

And then, he thought of the satchel still downstairs, propped up and leaning against a leg of the kitchen table. It struck him like a bolt of lightning. The handgun! How could he have been so careless? His heart raised as if he had run a marathon. Keep calm, he reminded himself. There was nothing he could do about it now. The more he considered the graveness of his error, the insalubrious possibilities presented themselves. Alexia may get caught up talking to neighbours, or worse still, what if she had injured herself and she was alone in the olive grove? Surely, someone would notice she had not returned. The chances of someone other than Alexia entering the house were slim and she would return soon. He was sure of it. But what if she didn't? Alexia had said herself, there will be reprisals for the killing of the German soldiers. The Germans could arrive and search every house in the village. If they found the gun, they would arrest Alexia. Worse still and unthinkable, she could be shot!

He remembered her words. *'I will be back as soon as I can. Stay here until I return. It is the safest place in the house. Promise me you will.'*

It would only take him a few minutes at most. It was decided. He slid open the panel and eased himself into the wardrobe. Alexia's clothes trailed across his face and arms as he reached out into the dark, his outstretched fingers seeking the solid wood of the doors. He pushed, and the doors opened with a creak. Piercing light flooded his eyes. Squinting and blinking, Frank unfolded himself from his confinement. It felt good to stand up straight. He moved quickly, out of the bedroom and down the stairs. He swooped his satchel from the table leg and instinctively he opened it and peered inside. And there it was, still wrapped in the oil-stained rag. Relieved, he pulled it out and sank into a chair. Frank unrolled the rag. He held the handgun in his hands, turning it over and feeling its weight. He wondered how many lives this gun had extinguished, how many men it had killed at the hands of Fin? It shocked Frank to think such a small thing that fitted neatly in his hand could have such destructive power.

He remembered seeing it in Fin's holster for the first time and it reminded him of the holstered guns he saw in the westerns movies he had watched in the cinema when he was younger. Fin had noticed Frank's intrigue, and he slid the handgun from its holster, thrusting it in Frank's face.

'You see this. This gun is my best friend. It has got me out of more scary situations than I care to imagine. Its official name is a Webley Mk VI, but I call it Conan, which means, 'Little warrior' in Irish. It fires the .455 Webley cartridge making Conan the most powerful handgun ever made. It has a Prideaux speed-loader, which means it's quicker to reload than most handguns. See, I'll show you.'

Fin pressed the thumb catch with his shooting hand, broke open the frame with his other, and pushed the complete loader into the cylinder. *'Now, all six rounds are in place and all I have to do is snap it shut and I'm ready to blow the face off another German's head.'*

Frank wrapped the handgun safely in the rag, when suddenly, he heard someone outside. He hoped it was Alexia, but he couldn't take the gamble. He gripped the handgun. His knuckles and fingers were bone white as he teared towards the door. Pressing his back against the wall, his spine splintered with the weight of trepidation. He held the handgun in both hands now, more to steady the involuntary tension that had spread through his arms and hands. He took a deep breath as the door opened, groaning on its hinges. It shielded him. He levelled the handgun, cocked the hammer, his heartbeat thudding in his ears, and it was at that precise moment, as the door swung closed, a thought entered his head. He did not know if the handgun was loaded.

She was small and bent over at the waist, leaning on a walking stick as she hobbled inside the house. Frank dropped his hands, the handgun almost crashing to the stone cladding, as his grip loosened, and the handgun dangled from his fingers.

For some reason Frank did not fully understand, he began to laugh. The old woman's head spun around to face him. Shock froze her as her jaw dropped in sheer horror, her eyes wide, as a shrill leaped from her throat. Panic-stricken; Frank raised his arms and thrusted his open palms in front of him, as he shuffled towards her, begging her to stop.

She screeched at him in Greek, raising her stick above her head and in a full arc brought it down like a whip, striking him on the shoulder. Before Frank could react, in an instant, she had raised her stick again and flashed it towards him. He threw up his forearm, shielding his face, as the stick cracked against bone.

'Please, stop,' he cried out.

'Mina!' Alexia stood in the doorway.

The old woman's head spun to the door. 'Alexia! Run! There is a thief in your house. He has a gun.' She raised her stick again.

'Mina! Stop hitting him.'

'Is he a German?' Alarm laced Mina's voice.

'No. He is British.'

'Thank you, Saint Spyridon.' She turned her gaze to Frank. 'And you know him?'

'Yes, I know him. Why do you think he is in my house?'

'Is she going to hit me again?' Frank asked, keeping his eye trained on Mina's walking stick.

Alexia glared at the handgun.

Mina lowered the walking stick. 'Who is this man and why is he in your house with a gun?'

Frank fumbled with the handgun and thrusted it deep inside the satchel.

'His name is Frank, and the gun is as much of a shock to me as it is to you.'

'I thought I was going to have a heart attack. In fact, in my condition, I'm surprised I didn't.'

'Sit down Mina.'

Alexia wrapped an arm around Mina's waist and guided her towards a chair at the kitchen table, which Mina sank into with a deep groan.

Alexia set herself into the chair opposite and explained the events of the last two days that led to Mina's unfortunate discovery.

None of this was intelligible to Frank, although he could feel Mina's scrutiny.

Their words jumped and danced in the air, like a rhythmic and warm melody. At times, their exchanges were fierce, and he thought the two women were arguing, but their body language and facial expressions told him otherwise. They both rolled their Rs, certain words sprung higher in pitch and others with clipped pronunciation. It occurred to Frank; this was the first time he had heard Alexia speak her own language. She looked different. She was more animated, more Greek. A feeling bore into the very depths of him. It scared him and enthralled him.

Then, suddenly, it was over.

Silence hung in the room as the two women considered him. Nothing was said for a long time and Frank wondered what their exchanged of words had led to.

Mina exhaled a deep sigh and flapped her hand in the air, as if waving away a fly.

Finally, Alexia said, 'It has been decided.'

Frank felt like a criminal waiting for his sentence to be passed.

'I have convinced Mina you are who you say you are. She is right to be sceptical. The Germans have tried to use their agents and even soldiers pretending to be deserters to infiltrate the resistance. The *andartes* have become suspicious of these kinds of contacts and will interrogate those who wish to join them, and if found out, they are shot. They take precautions now. They have passwords and ID cards. I have even heard of Italian soldiers joining the *andartes* after the treatment they received when the Germans arrived.

'What is, *andartes?*'

'The men and women of the resistance.'

'I see.' Frank glanced at Mina's walking stick and cringed at the recent memory of it. 'I'm glad she's so understanding. I wouldn't want to get on the wrong side of her again.'

'It is too dangerous for you to leave. Mina has told me the reprisals have already begun. In a neighbouring village, several men were taken by the Germans and shot. Their bodies have not been returned. We don't know if this will have satisfied the officers, and if now, the killing will stop.

'Mina is not happy about you being here, but she understands why you must stay. She has called it our duty to offer you protection and others in the village will feel the same.'

'You mean others will know about me?'

'You are not the first. Many allied soldiers and airmen have relied on the goodwill and courage of the people of Corfu, and you will not be the last.'

The time Frank had spent with Fin and his men, he had learned that the British Special Operations Executive (SOE) had deployed hundreds of British personnel by parachuting into occupied Greece to make contact and work with the Greek resistance. Fin had reminded Frank that they also had other goals to be met. Fin and his men were an example of that. Their purpose was not only to work alongside the various factions of the Greek resistance, but they also had other wartime objectives, such as sabotaging German supply lines, railways and viaducts, and military targets. It was a fine line to meet the needs of all the different Greek guerrilla groups. What Fin was aware of was that each act of sabotage would bring swift and violent reprisals against the Greek population from the Germans, and this often reduced the resistance fighter's involvement in engaging with their enemy. Fin also said that for the leaders of the various factions of resistance, their priorities were to increase their individual control and influence over as much territory and resources as they could without seeing to be directly involved in active combat and engagement in subversive acts against their German occupiers. If it was at all possible, they would avoid preventable losses and German retaliations.

'So, what is to happen to me now?'

'By day, you will stay in my house and at night sleep in the space behind my wardrobe. Mina has a spare room and has offered it to you. She does not think I should have a man in my house, especially one with a gun. I told Mina, her charity is welcomed, but not needed.'

'Thank you.'

'She has asked me about the gun, and I cannot explain why you have one. It was a shock to me just as much as it was to her.'

'I should have told you about it.'

'Yes. You should have. I invited you into my home.'

'I'm sorry. I didn't want to alarm you. It's Fin's gun.'

'One of the men you buried?'

'Yes. I saw the gun when I was leaving the boat with you, and given my circumstance and the possible dangers, I took it.'

'You should have told me. I need to be able to trust you, Frank.'

'You can... trust me.' Even to him, after what had happened, the sentiment was weak.

'I told you to stay hidden and here you are in my kitchen with a gun in your hand. How can I trust a man like you?'

Her indictment stung.

'For what it's worth, I remembered, I'd left my satchel in the kitchen. I panicked because of the gun. If your house was searched while you were away, and the gun found, that would implicate you in the soldier's killings. I couldn't allow that to happen. So, I came down here. I would have returned to the space behind the wardrobe... And, well. You know what happened next.'

'Have you ever used a gun?'

'No. That was the first time I've even held one.'

Alexia's eyes met his, beset with guilt.

Mina snorted something in Greek.

Frank's eyes stayed fastened on Alexia.

Alexia broke into a grin. 'Mina said. We argue like an old married couple.'

Chapter 25

He was sure Mina did not like him and that sat heavy on Frank, as he knew both she and Alexia were close. If Alexia was troubled by how the events of the day had transpired, she did not show it, or either, she was good at hiding it. Frank felt awkward and self-conscious for the rest of the day. The early evening light extended shadows across the walls and stone floor of the house as Alexia finished preparing a meal of potatoes, cabbage, olives, and beans. She plated it up and placed the food on the table.

'It doesn't look much, but it will be more filling than the soup.'

'There was nothing wrong with the soup and this looks just fine. I'm grateful for whatever you cook for me. I know this will cause you more hardship. I wish it was different.'

Alexia grinned. 'We won't starve. If we run out of food, there are always Mina's olives.' She chuckled and there was a sparkle in her eyes he hadn't seen before. It filled Frank's heart with joy. She was melting.

'How long have you known Mina?'

'She was my grandmother's best friend. They were more like sisters. I haven't known a time when Mina wasn't in my life.'

'I can see you are close to her and it's obvious she cares for you. I've got the marks to prove it,' Frank smiles, rubbing his bruised arm.

'Everyone I have loved. My parents, my sister, Stathis, they have all died. She is the only one who has always been there for me. She has been a constant presence in my life. When we were younger, my sister and I called her *Thee-a,* which means aunt. She, too, is on her own. Her son died several years ago, and her two grandsons joined the army. They have not returned.'

Frank exhaled deeply. 'I don't think there's a single person who hasn't suffered in this war.'

'What about you, Frank? Have you left someone behind in Edinburgh?'

He loved the way his name rolled off her tongue. He shifted in his chair. 'Her name is Maggie.'

Alexia straightened her back.

'We had been together for a while. Recently, things weren't going so well between us. In fact, the last time I saw her, we argued, and she left and the next day, I was on a ship that would take me thousands of miles from her.'

Alexia moved her food around on the plate and, without lifting her head, asked, 'This is something you regret?'

'In truth, it was probably over between us before then. I had the opportunity to tell her I was leaving, and I let it slip. I shouldn't have done that. She deserved more. It's something I'll always regret.'

She lifted her head, and their eyes met. 'Maybe, if you had told her, she might not have left you.'

'It doesn't matter now.'

'Are you sure? Your words say one thing, but your eyes say another.'

He sighed heavily. 'I've beaten myself up about it. Regret won't change what has happened. I hope by now, she's moved on and is getting on with her life. She deserves better. She deserves to be happy.'

Beneath their words, a tension simmered, and both were aware of it.

A nudge of anger coursed through him. 'At least, she has a life she recognises. There have been bombs and rationing, but nothing like this. There are no bodies filling the streets, hanging from trees, people going missing, being tortured, imprisoned, and murdered. Life back home has not changed beyond recognition. Not like this.'

'It must be difficult for you, too. How does it feel to be so far from home?'

'I think about Edinburgh all the time. It's weird how I took it for granted. It's not until now, I realise how much I miss it.'

'I have never been to a big city. Corfu Town is the biggest place on the island, and it only has several thousand people living there.'

'Have you been to the mainland?'

'Only once. It was for a wedding, and I was just nine or ten at the time. You have probably seen more of Greece than I have. What is Edinburgh like?'

He answered her with a question. 'What would you like to know?'

She thinks for a moment. 'Why would you call it your home?'

'That's a big question.'

'But surely it can be answered?'

'Okay. The first thoughts that come to mind are ... it's a city that has history, the most amazing architecture and it has a character all of its own. Compared to most cities, it's not overly populated, but it is the second biggest city in Scotland and it's the capital, so it's the most important. It has a long history and kings and queens have lived there. The most famous one was Mary Queen of Scots. Have you heard of her?'

Alexia shakes her head. 'No.'

'I think every woman should know of the struggles she had living in a male dominated world, even for a Queen.'

'Was she a strong woman?'

'She had to be.'

'I think I would have liked this...'

'Mary.'

'Yes. Mary. Maybe, one day, I will be able to learn about her life and learn from it.'

'I think we all should. She was a survivor.'

'We all need to be, especially now. Tell me more.'

'It has an extinct volcano called Arthur's Seat and a famous castle. There're several buildings that are influenced by the architecture of ancient Greece. It has a university. It is separated into the old town and the new town. Like every city, it has its areas where there's a lot of poverty and a lot of wealth, too. There are galleries, libraries, museums, theatres, and parks. You'd never get bored. There's so much to see and do. It sounds just like any other city, but it's not. It has its own character which is one of the many things I love about it. It's not just any city, it's my city.'

'Have you always lived in Edinburgh?'

'Yes. I have. I wouldn't want to live anywhere else.'

'I'd love to go there.'

'Maybe one day you will.'

She looked at a framed picture on the sideboard. 'I do not think so.'

'Is that your mum and dad?'

Alexia smiled weakly 'Yes. It was taken by a photographer in Corfu Town. It is the only photograph I have of them.'

'You look like your mum.'

'I miss them.' Alexia lifted the empty plates from the table and carried them to the sink.

'What happened?'

She turned to face him, and he could see the tears in her eyes.

'It was a terrible accident. They had just had this photograph taken, and they were on a bus coming home when it swerved to avoid hitting some goats. And the bus rolled several times and landed in an olive grove. My father was killed instantly, but my mother lived for some weeks after but died from her injuries.'

'I'm so sorry, Alexia.'

'It was ten years ago now. If it was not for Mina, I don't know what I would have done. She took my sister and I into her home and brought us up as if we were her own daughters. And then, I met

Stathis. Mina, being overprotective as usual, was not in favour of the marriage. She said it was too quick and just a reaction to my grief, as my heart was undoubtedly frozen with pain and loss. But, in the end, she gave her blessing. Which meant the world to me. We were married for two years. I've spent another two years in this house on my own.'

'What was Stathis like?

'He was a good worker. He provided for us. We did not have much, but what we had was enough. He was a serious man. He was a member of the Greek Communist Party and was always in an argument, or as he would say, a debate, concerning social liberation and the popular rule of workers and peasants. He was liked in the village. He was respected, and he respected others. He wanted to have four children, because it was his favourite number. Two boys and two girls. I never got pregnant.'

'I'm sorry.'

'Don't be. What kind of world is this to bring children into? The children do not go to school anymore. The school has closed.

'Why is that?'

'A few months ago, German soldiers came and took the teacher away. He never returned. His house is still empty. I heard rumours that someone saw him hanging from makeshift gallows outside Corfu Town with another six men. A German soldier had been shot and killed and this was the reprisal.

She stares at the meagre meal on her plate.

'We had fresh loaves of bread from the bakers. Most days, we were able to buy chicken and lamb, plenty of vegetables from the market. I always had lentils and beans. Even though it doesn't feel like it, we are more fortunate than a lot of others. At least I still have my orange tree. In some villages, the Germans have confiscated their whole harvest of olives and figs. Animals were taken away in trucks. I've heard that nearly all of Greece's livestock, fuel and tobacco have been taken to Germany. Shops in Corfu Town are empty. People are eating whatever they can. They are eating scraps of meat, the kind you wouldn't even throw to a hungry dog. If you need to see a doctor, you pay in an oke of corn, oil, or dried vegetables.'

'What is an oke?'

'It is a weight, like British... what is it you say?'

'Ounces and Pounds.'

'Yes.'

'So, the economy is in ruin.'

'Financial, economic, and political ruin. We do not exchange money anymore. It is worthless. We have become good at... I know this word... *battering*... Is this correct?

Frank smiled. 'I think you mean *bartering*.'

Alexia nodded. 'We barter. Money is useless now. Last week, Spyros, the shepherd, came into the village. He told the old men at the *kafenion*, some German soldiers gave him four hand grenades for a sheep. It was one of their birthdays and they wanted to celebrate. I have also heard it costs a gold sovereign for one hand grenade, and three eggs for a handful of bullets.'

Frank sets his cutlery on his empty plate. 'And it will be like this all over Greece?'

'In the cities and towns and the countryside, there is little food, only starvation. Corpses are gathered daily from the streets in carts. There are no mules, dogs or cats roaming the streets anymore. The people live of scraps.'

Frank grimaced. 'At home, the war has changed our lives, but nothing like this.'

Alexia glanced at him. 'In what way has it changed?'

'In Edinburgh, there have been bombings, air raids, houses and schools have been hit and people have died, not like Coventry and Clydebank. Those were devastating, but the air-raid siren is a common sound in Edinburgh. In the back gardens of houses and tenements, there are air-raid shelters. People have been fitted with gas masks. At one point, children were evacuated out of the city, but most have returned. There's been rationing, which means that families are only allowed a certain amount of food each week, but if they were to see what it's like here, they would count themselves lucky.'

He glanced at her left forearm, and for the first time saw three small identical circular scars, as pale as marble. Alexia caught his eye and stiffened. She stood abruptly, scraping her chair across the stone floor, and scooped the plates from the table.

'I'll help you with those.'

'They can stay in the sink for now. There's something I have to do. Something I should have done a long time ago.'

The plates clattered into the sink and, turning on her heels, Alexia took the stairs two at a time. Frank heard drawers opening and closing. Alexia appeared at the top of the landing; a pile of clothes cradled in her arms. She pounded down the stairs, her hair bouncing behind her. Her arms full, she crossed the floor, stopped at the door that led to the back of the house and the small piece of land where the goat grazed.

Without turning to him, she commanded. 'Open the door.'

Frank stood and did as she instructed. He watched as Alexia marched outside and dumped the clothes in the dirt. She spun around and still standing in the doorway, Frank moved to the side to let her pass. She yanked open a drawer, sending its contents clattering inside. Sifting through them, she snatched a box of matches, grabbed a jar of paraffin, her face flushed, and lips tightly set. With purposeful steps, she once again stood outside. Alexia poured the paraffin over the pile of clothes. She struck a match, threw it onto the soaked fabric and without flinching watched as it burst into flames. The goat sniffed the acrid air and strained on the rope around its neck.

Alexia stared into the fire with haunted eyes, her throat constricted so tightly that she struggled to speak.

'Sometimes, he was rough with me, especially at night, after he had been drinking. I hid my bruises with makeup or clothes, especially from Mina.' She swallowed her rage as she pressed her fingers into the scars on her forearm. 'He burnt me with cigarettes, hit me with his fists and afterwards, he was always beside himself, crying like a child, begging for forgiveness, and promising me it would never happen again. And each time, I believed him.

'I shed no tears for him when the letter came. I felt nothing but a release of torment that poured from me. I do not want his name mentioned in this house again.'

She turned from the flames and walked into the house.

Chapter 26

Two weeks passed. Frank awoke in the small space behind the wardrobe. To save any unwarranted embarrassment on both their parts, Frank waited until he was sure Alexia had woken and left the bedroom. His senses were now proficient in recognising the sounds and smells alerting him to when Alexia was downstairs, already preparing for the day ahead. It had become an unspoken routine between them.

Frank now had bedding, several sheets, and a pillow. He also had a candle, a box of matches, and a chamber pot. When he lay stretched on the mattress, his feet touched the stone wall.

At first, he found it difficult to sleep in such a restricted space, but now, he had grown used to it. It still felt awkward at night, knowing he was just a few feet from Alexia and sometimes he could hear her shout out whilst she slept, and he could only imagine the images that visited her in her dreams. He never spoke to her about this.

He yawned and ruffled his hair. Once he emerged into the bedroom, he washed from the basin Alexia left him each morning and shaved with Stathis' razor that Alexia found languishing under the kitchen sink.

He pulled his shirt over his head and, as he always did; he stood at the bedroom window, just out of sight and gently parted the net curtain, just enough to allow him to view the outside world.

Each morning, he was greeted by a refrain of songbirds, doves cooing, the chiming of the bell from the goat in the back garden and the garbage collector, who walked the lanes with an old donkey filling two bags strapped to the animals sore infested sides.

Downstairs, Alexia was filling two mugs with dark, strong-smelling coffee.

She lifted her head and smiled. 'KaIimera.'

154

Frank also greeted Alexia a good morning in Greek and as he sat at the table, he asked, 'Pos eisai simera to proi? (How are you this morning?)

Alexia replied in Greek. 'I'm well, thank you.

Frank leaned back in his chair, pleased with himself.

'You are learning fast.'

'It helps that you're a good teacher.'

'I think it is because you are speaking Greek every day and that helps you to remember the words.'

Every day, Mina would arrive at the house with a parcel of food. Alexia would always protest, but Mina, in her customary manner, waved away Alexia's remonstrations adding it didn't take much to feed an old woman and it wouldn't feel right letting food rot, especially when others were in more need than she was. Alexia always relented, grateful for the eggs, vegetables, and occasional slice of meat.

Frank always greeted Mina in Greek, and her stern and untrusting look melted with each daily visit.

That morning, there were the usual two wraps on the door and Mina entered the house with her usual hobble, but she stooped a little lower than normal and her face was the colour of marble.

Alexia's usual smile fell from her face and as Mila dropped her parcel on the table, she sank cumbersomely into a chair.

Alexia looked at Mina. 'Mina, what is it? Are you ill?'

Mina tried to speak but her words seemed to get stuck in her mouth.

'You're worrying me.'

Mina clutched her hands to her chest. 'I'm not ill. Theodora...'

'What has she done this time?'

'It's not what she has done, but what she has said.'

'Tell me.'

'Last night, her German officer paid her one of his visits. He had a bit too much to drink and let slip that there is to be house searches tonight here in Lakones, in Liapades, and Doukades. They have found the caique.'

Alexia froze for a moment. Mina spoke in Greek, but Frank caught the note of alarm in Mina's voice. He glanced at Alexia.

'Theodora is the local whore. As long as she is paid, she doesn't care who her customers are, even Germans. There is a particular German officer who visits her regularly. She sees only him now. He must pay her well. Last night, he was drunk and told her a fishing boat had been found. It had been hidden and camouflaged. They have found the boat, Frank. There are to be house searches tonight.'

Frank sucked in his breath. 'Did he mention anything else?'

'No. That's all Theodora said. Why?'

Frank trailed his fingers through his hair.

'Is there something I should know?'

'It was better not to tell you. If you didn't know, you couldn't be an accomplice if the radios were found.'

'What are you talking about? You are not making any sense. What radios?'

'Communications equipment... radios, transmitters, batteries. It was all on the boat. That's why we came to Corfu. Fin was to meet up with the resistance fighters on Corfu and deliver the communication equipment. It was part of the British military's efforts to support the resistance in Corfu. Only Fin knew the arrangements, how to contact the resistance fighters and the location where they were to meet.'

'But there was nothing on the boat.'

'I know. I moved it all into the cave. The one I slept in. We had got this far. It was not just Fin and Stephanos who died. Others had given their lives as well. I couldn't let their sacrifice be in vain. I didn't know what else to do, and then I found the cave, and it seemed to be the answer, until I could contact the resistance myself.'

'And how were you going to do that?'

'I didn't know. I still don't. But it might not matter now. If they have found the radio equipment, it's over. Every house will be searched. People will be taken. I can't stay. It's too dangerous for you.'

'You will be safe. Every night you have stayed has been a risk. Why is tonight different?'

'Because we know they are coming tonight. Because of me. And I'm responsible for what is about to happen. I am putting the whole village in danger just by being here. I can't take that risk.'

Suddenly, Mina spoke then, surprising both Frank and Alexia into silence.

When she had finished speaking, there was a pause and then, as if gathering herself, Alexia looked at Frank. 'There is a barn at the olive grove. Mina says it will be safe for you to stay there overnight. The Germans have already searched that area. Spyros, the shepherd, saw them yesterday.'

A silence descended upon them. Finally, Frank spoke. 'It is settled then.'

Alexia turned away from him.

Mina heaved herself from the chair with a grunt. She placed her bony hand on Frank's shoulder and nodded briefly. Alexia starred at her feet. Mina tilted Alexia's chin upwards with a finger and kissed Alexia on the forehead. She smiled. 'You could never hide your true feelings from me.'

Chapter 27

Frank felt a simultaneous buzz of relief and a bottomless pang of regret. He had anguished over telling Alexia about the communication equipment in the cave. In the beginning, he had kept it from her. He did not know her. She could have been an informer. He had no choice. As the days passed, and he became more acquainted with her, getting to know her better, it became a heavy weight around his shoulders that he constantly carried. He did not want to involve her. He persuaded himself it was for the best. What she did not know, she could not worry over. And now, he was finally relieved of this burdensome load, but it did not feel like it and he had spent the remainder of the day in low spirits.

He had spent enough time in her company to know the fluctuations in her mood. Since Frank had disclosed the existence and whereabouts of the communication equipment, Alexia had busied herself with domestic tasks. She cleaned the windows, swept, and washed the floor, scrubbed the stove, the pots, and pans, and normally, as she sat embroidering, which he grew to learn was a daily activity of hers, a contented glow normally accompanied her face, but today, it had darkened.

He knew what she was thinking because he was thinking it, too.

When the sky began to darken and the light fade, Frank secured the handgun in his jacket pocket. He smoked a last cigarette and turned to Alexia.

'Will they search every house?' he asked.

'I don't know.'

'If I could, I would stay. I don't want to leave you.'

'In war, we must do things we don't want to do. But that does not stop me wishing it was not so. Promise me you will be safe,' Alexia said.

'I promise. As long as I am not here, you have nothing to hide from the Germans. There is nothing for them to find. This will be over soon.'

She took a deep breath. 'I will come to the barn in the morning.'

'I'll be waiting.'

She gazed at where the gun was in his jacket. It filled her with fear. She tried to restrain every emotion, every want, and every need, but she could not stop the tears well in her eyes.

'I have to go,' he said it with an urgency that betrayed his desperation to stay with this woman, who in that moment, had become the centre of his world. This should be the start of something, instead it felt like the end. Words deserted him. What words could adequately define his feelings towards her? There was only the weight of silence around them, and the passing of each precious second.

She took his hand in hers and tightened her hold. 'Go, now.' She released her touch.

Chapter 28

He scrutinised the street as a dog barked and, for some reason it unsettled him even more. He waited. A donkey passed with an old man smoking a cigarette and sitting on its back. Frank crossed the street and then disappeared into the lane.

The gradient of the track was steep as he moved further into the thicket of trees and undergrowth. Soon, he passed a huddle of farm buildings not a hundred feet from him.

He stood motionless behind a tree and turned to look in the direction of the village. The darkness had fallen so rapidly, he could no longer see the houses, just outlines and the yellow glow of oil lamps in windows.

He heard the trucks, the groaning of engines, saw the beams of headlights, the screech of brakes, the crunch of boots, rasping voices. It had begun.

He was fleeing and abandoning Alexia. He could turn and run back to the village, give himself up, and stop the inevitable. He dropped his head in shame.

The track veered to the left and, pacing along its length, a quiver of uncertainty went through him. He tried to recall Alexia's directions, and then he saw the nets sprawled along the ground and the ancient olive trees.

The barn stood at the far end of the olive grove. As he drew closer, even in the dark, he could see it was no more than a small wooden structure, its roof covered in a fine layer of pine needles.

Inside, there was a bed of straw, probably used for feeding goats or donkeys, and several sacks, full to the brim with olives, leaned against the back wall.

He sat for a long time with his back leaning against the sacks, his satchel at his side, and a blanket around his shoulders and legs. He closed his eyes and tried to sleep. It was futile. His mind was too active with thoughts of Alexia. He prayed to the God he didn't believe in to protect her and keep her from harm. He tried to imagine the radios, transmitters, and batteries still packed into the recess of the cave. Had the Germans discovered them? He offered another prayer.

Abandoning sleep, thoughts flashed through him. He thought of Fin and the others, and what it took to eventually reach Corfu and the reason why he found himself in a wooden shed, hiding like a coward in the middle of the night while innocent people were at this very moment, being subjected to fear and brutality. This couldn't all be in vain. As horrific as it seemed, there needed to be a reason for this suffering. It struck him then. And like fog lifting, it became clear to him what he had to do.

The clear velvet night sky lit the track with blue moonshine, aiding his progress at a steady pace down the wooded sprawled hillside.

Around him, olive trees, ancient poplars and pine stood guard watching his progress. After a time, the track began to curve in easy loops, as it descended towards flatter ground and the placid shore of the Ionian Sea. On the hillside above him, Lakones with its white splash of houses looked tranquil and silent, yet Frank could only imagine what terror and fear must have befallen its inhabitants.

He turned back to the track, more anxious than ever. Before him, the track veered off in two directions. He glanced around, looking for something that would jog his memory. He heard the trickle of water from a stream and grinned; he remembered the very same sound when he and Alexia used this track to get to the caique.

Ahead of him, rising above the covering of trees, Frank saw a plume of smoke snake towards the sky. The Germans, or someone else, were close.

Through the trees, he saw the beach. A large formation of rocks skirted the shore and, using them as cover, Frank kept low and moved stealthily, but warily, unsure if there would be a guard of Germans near the caique.

He crouched, using the rocks to screen him. He scanned the beach towards the area he knew the caique was moored.

His heart sank. The caique was gliding towards the opening of the inlet. A German soldier stood at the wheel and Frank counted another three on board.

His ears snared the guttural spit of their voices. He looked in their direction. His eyes and ears straining, Frank watched nervously the dark shapes of the German soldiers, tension tightening his throat.

He saw several of the soldiers laboriously extracting heavy cloth sacks from the ground, while others looked on absentmindedly, smoking cigarettes and leaning against a truck.

A soldier dropped the tailgate as another two heaved one of the cloth sacks onto the truck. To his shock, it struck Frank with the realisation of what was happening; the defilement of Fin and Stephanos.

In his head, he heard the prayer Alexia spoke above the grave, and he recalled how fitting and pure it had sounded, sensuous, even. He swallowed hard and shut his mind to the memory. He withdrew the handgun from his jacket and, taking a deep breath; he tightened his grip around the handle.

A German sauntered along the beach and relieved himself in the sea. Frank had a clear shot. He raised the gun and cocked the hammer. The German turned then, looking over his shoulder. Frank could see the spray of urine emanate from the German, like a fountain, before Frank shrunk back against the rock.

Breathing hard, he held the gun to his chest. If he had to, he could kill another human being, he was sure of it.

His breathing grew faster. He gulped for air. He heard the German's boots kick up sand, closer and closer. Frank ached with fear. Steadily, he began to manoeuvre himself to turn round and aim the gun. If he shot the German, or if discovered, it would be the same outcome... He was already dead.

A shout rang out, more insistent this time. The heavy boots stopped, suddenly. The German was so close, Frank could hear him breathing. Another shout, and the truck's engine fired up. Frank squeezed his eyes closed and held his breath. When he opened them, expecting to see the German looming over him, he released his breath in relief. Above him was only the blackness of the night sky and hundreds of silver diamond stars as the sound of the truck's engine faded from him. There was nothing but the gentle slosh of the tide against the sand. Frank pressed his hand against his face. He wanted to laugh. He wanted to cry.

Frank clambered out from the rocks and looked about him. He was alone. He could see the fresh mound of earth that was Fin's grave. Frank turned away from it and walked towards the cave.

Chapter 29

Alexia sat at the table, pale and exhausted, her stomach churning, her coffee cold in its cup. She could hear the Germans move from house to house, shouting accusations, bellowing insults, barking like dogs. The uproar moved ever closer, leaving a wake of carnage, old women wailing, old men cowering and children weeping into their mother's chests. She knew she would be next. The heavy thudding, crunching of boots, and bellowing voices announced the inevitable.

Her door was already open to the night. She did not see the point in getting it ripped from its hinges if it could be avoided.

The first soldier to enter her house uninvited was a thin, angular man, with dark eyes and yellow teeth. The other, with disarrayed hair and acne scars across his cheeks, smiled at Alexia in a way that unsettled her.

The house search was merciless. The soldiers set about yanking drawers from their runners and scattering cutlery over the floor. They emptied every cupboard with ruthless efficiency, sifting through every sheet of paper, and flicking through every page of every book tossed across the room in disgust. Their rage seemed to grow with each passing second as they swept plates and bowls from the dresser, crunching the shattered pieces under their heavy boots.

When there was nothing left to search, the German she had christened *Scarface*, glared at her with contempt. They moved to the top floor of the house, bounding up the stairs two at a time. She heard the shattering of glass and objects being strewn across her bedroom. They hauled the mattress from the bed and when she heard the wardrobe doors being pulled open, her chest constricted, and her hands trembled. They hauled out her clothes, her dresses and skirts, her blouses, and cardigans. It felt like they were in her room for an age, and then they appeared at the top of the stairs, sweating with their exertions. To Alexia's horror, *Scarface* had a piece of underwear in his hand. He held it like a trophy in front of him. He bent to her face, his rank breath making her nauseous. He smothered his face in the crutch of the fabric and inhaled deeply, his eyes peering at her like daggers. He said something to the other German, who laughed and wiped the back of his hand across his mouth. *Scarface* grabbed Alexia by the hair and dragged her to the back door, which he forcefully kicked open, and although Alexia tried to free herself and claw at his grasp, she stumbled, and *Scarface* threw her, face first into the dirt of the ground.

He bent over Alexia and grabbed her chin, pushing her face inches from his. He snarled, 'I bet this isn't the first time you've had German steel inside you. You'll enjoy this, you Greek bitch.' He stood over her smirking, fumbling with his belt.

Suddenly, a vehicle screeched to a halt, and Alexia heard another voice. This one snapped with authority. 'What are you doing, soldier? May I remind you why you are here? Leave her. There are more important things to attend to.' It was the officer who visited Theodora, the one who had told her of the house searches.

The other German backed away, wanting nothing more to do with *Scarface* in fear of recrimination.

Scarface grimaced and reluctantly complied with the order. The vehicle drove off at speed, and scar face, driven into a frenzy, wielded his rifle like a bat through the branches of the orange tree, littering the ground with fruit. The goat, alerted to the prospect of food, stretched the rope around its neck and sniffed the ground with twitching nostrils. In a rage, *Scarface* trampled on the oranges, squashing them into a messy pulp. The goat sniffed the air and wagged its stump of a tail. *Scarface,* now engulfed with revenge, grabbed the goat by its head, yanked it backwards and, with a flash of steel, drew the blade of his knife along its throat. A gush of blood fell onto its chest, and in spurts, like water from a tap, it covered the ground in deep, red pools. The goat's legs buckled and crumpled, life draining from its staring eyes, like marbles inside its head.

'No!' Alexia screamed. She pulled herself onto her hands and knees, but then the force of *Scarface's* boot slamming into her rib cage forced the air from her burning lungs, and she tumbled onto her back. She braced herself for a further assault, but it never came. *Scarface* was dragged by the arm, away from her and Alexia knew the end of her degradation would just be the start of one of her neighbour's humiliations.

She glared at the stars flickering in the clear night sky and wondered if Frank was at this very moment gazing at them, too.

Chapter 30

He had waited since the first rays of the sun grazed the olive trees in a dappled silver light. He managed little sleep, overwhelmed with the events of the night before. His nerves were too strained. When he closed his eyes, it did not bring a slackening of limbs. It brought only tension in his tendons and muscles and the horror of Fin's desecrated grave, and the image of his corpse being tossed onto the truck, like a sack of potatoes.

He was not the same man who arrived as a war artist and blown off course by circumstance. It was not just others' war; it was his war, and it filled him with determination and resolve.

Alexia consumed his thoughts. His mind could not rest until he knew she was safe and well. He kept watch on the mule track that passed the olive grove; it was the only accessible route from the village.

Worse, he did not know what happened in the village last night. He had heard stories and rumours of the Nazi's cruelty and bloodthirst, and he could only hope they spared Alexia and the other villagers such violence and destruction. It eased him that no plumes of darkened smoke rose into the morning sky, but that was only one possibility of many. It was unbearable to contemplate the others.

Through the trees, he saw movement. His hand tightened around the handle of his handgun. Shards of white light danced through the trees. A figure disappeared behind a cluster of bushes and then reappeared again. It was a woman and this time he could see her. Alexia. A ripple of relief swam in his veins. He could not contain himself and ran towards her.

'You're here and safe, thank God.'

She smiled. 'And you are too.'

'Your house?' he asked, concerned.

'We have both survived.'

He released his breath in relief. 'That's good. And Mina?'

'She too is okay.'

'It must have been terrible.'

Alexia swallowed. 'I heard they took Stamatis and his wife.'

'Why would they do that?'

'He threatened the soldiers with his shotgun. It is as old as he is. They will use them as an example. I fear they will end up in one of the camps. The Germans ransacked their house, took what they wanted and destroyed every possession they had.'

'That's awful.'

'They don't need an excuse to steal whatever they want from us. No one has been untouched by them.'

'Did they take anything from you?'

Alexia shook her head.

'At least that's something. I'm sorry, Alexia. I'm sorry for everything. At least I can try to make it better.'

'What do you mean?'

'There's something I have to tell you, Alexia, about last night.'

Frank told her that the Germans had moved the caique, taken the corpses of his friends and about the moment he had readied himself to kill the German on the beach.

Alexia looked at him strangely, and Frank couldn't work out if she was stunned or amazed.

'You fool. What in God's name made you do that?'

'It was for a reason.'

She looked at him suspiciously. 'And are you going to tell me this reason?'

Frank pulled his hand through his hair. 'I have wanted to tell you, believe me I have, but I needed to be sure I could trust you.'

Her eyes widened. 'What do you mean, trust me?'

'You must admit, when you first saw me, you were suspicious of me. You tied me up and I let you, for God's sake. You didn't know if I was telling the truth or if I was a German spy. Trust needs to be earned.'

'And I have not earned your trust?'

This was not going the way he hoped. 'Now you have. Of course, you have. I trust you implicitly. That's why I can tell you these things.'

'Oh! Really?' Alexia said bitterly.

'That's what I'm trying to say. I trust you now. I have done since I've stayed in your house, and slept under your roof, and eaten the food you have shared with me. You have told me things that I'm grateful to have learnt about you. The time we have shared together has been special...' he felt awkward. 'It means a lot to me.'

A hot colour flushed her face. 'But you still have your secrets that you have kept from me.'

'If you would listen to what I'm trying to say, you might understand better.'

'Listen!' She gestured wildly with her hands. 'Is it not enough that I have taken you into my home, put myself and Mina in danger of being tortured and killed for you? I have had my home and my belongings ransacked by the Germans. I have been humiliated and treated like I was worthless.' Tears welled in her eyes.

'I know. I know, and I hate myself for being the cause of it.'

'You know nothing of my suffering.'

He reached out and held her arms. 'Alexia, please let me explain.'

She pulled away from him. 'There is nothing more to say.' Her words seemed to galvanise her, and she turned from him and hastened along the trail in the direction of the village.

'You can stay or come with me.' She cried over her shoulder.

Frank tapped his forehead forcefully with his fingers. He could not leave her, even though she was hurting, and he was the cause. Because of her, he would face whatever came his way. He would not give up on her. If there was anything this war had taught him, it was that his choices had consequences, and the choices he had made brought

Alexia into his life, and he was willing to face anything this war threw at him. There was nothing he was surer of.

Frank followed behind her, and he knew by the way she held her shoulders she was in no mood to talk. In that moment, words were extinct, and his heart felt like lead. He would be patient. He would pick the moment and tell her what needed to be said. Frank knew how she felt, and there was no need to intrude any further. Her silence was answer enough.

Their surroundings loomed close around them. The early morning light imbued a blue hue in the branches of the pine and olive trees. Cautiously they continued upwards until reaching the environs of the village. Alexia raised her hand for them to stop and waved it when it was safe to continue. Frank did as instructed, and they continued in this manner.

It still being early morning, there was little activity in the village, they kept to the cover and anonymity of the narrow lanes. Alexia brought Frank around to the back of the house, as not to alert others to their presence.

Seeing the ground littered in the trampled fruit, the naked branches and the pool of dark blood that stained the dirt, Frank stopped abruptly, alarmed, and fearful.

'Alexia! What has happened?'

Frank could see anguish flicker in Alexia's eyes. She opened the door and disappeared into her house. He followed her. Alexia was sitting at the table. She coughed and winced, holding her side.

Frank rushed to her. 'You're hurt.'

'It is nothing, just a bruise.'

'They hit you!' Frank was outraged.

'Just once.'

He shuddered to contemplate the reality of it.

'The bastards! Are you sure you are alright; do you need medicine?'

'No. It is just a bruise.'

'What happened outside?'

Her hair fell around her face. She spoke slowly. 'When they came, there were two Germans in my house. They were like madmen. Breaking and throwing anything they could lay their hands on. They continued upstairs but did not find the space behind the wardrobe. When they couldn't find anything, one of them dragged me to the garden.' She held her head in her hands. She took a deep breath. 'He was going to rape me in the garden. An officer stopped him, Theodora's German.

'The German could not have me, so instead, he killed my goat. I crawled back into my house, and the next thing I remember; it was getting light outside. I must have fallen asleep. The goat was gone in the morning. The Germans must have taken it.'

Frank's blood froze. He felt useless, unable to offer any words of comfort. Words would not change what had happened. He realised with sharp clarity the horrific ordeal Alexia had been put through, and now he understood her reaction in the olive grove.

He glanced around the house and saw where there was once the adornment of a home, crockery, plates, and bowls were now depleted on the shelves of the dresser. A chair lay at an angle, one of its legs broken in two. Pictures were absent from their hangings, ornaments cracked and chipped, drawers leaned at angles against cupboard doors hanging from hinges.

'I can mend most of the cupboards and doors.'

'I have some tools. Fortunately, the Germans did not find them.'

'How is Mina?'

'She is a strong woman. The Germans must have pitied her because of her age. One could speak a little Greek and he said his grandmother was Greek, although she lived in Germany now. Mina reminded him of his grandmother. She said he was very polite and apologetic. Her plates and bowls are whole. She said she only has a need for a few plates and cups, so I'm to replace what I have lost with hers.'

'That is good of her.'

'It is. She has wanted me to live with her. Not to look after her and care for her, she is too proud a woman to allow that. No, she said there was no need for me to be on my own when she had a house that she rattled in, that was too big for her. I think she also wanted the company.'

'She cares about you.'

'She is like a mother to me, but this is my home. This is where my memories are, good and bad. They are who I am.'

'I can understand that.'

She clutched her chest. 'You can?'

'Sure. It makes perfect sense to me.'

Her lips curled, and it was the first time she had smiled all day and he took comfort from it.

'What about you, Frank? Do you still know who you are? A lot has changed for you.'

Alexia's question caught him, and he was not sure how it made him feel. Was it a flicker of sadness, of pain, of regret, or all three?

His mind felt paralysed, and it took him a moment to gather his thoughts. Through it all, she was still smiling, and he sensed something had changed in her.

Eventually, he spoke. 'My experience of the war has changed who I am. I feel I'm having to put myself back together, but not all the pieces fit anymore. Does that make sense?

'You have changed.'

'I used to paint and sketch for a living in my spare room that became my studio. I'd get out of Edinburgh and spend the day in the countryside painting a landscape, have lunch in a pub and head back to Edinburgh. I was becoming known for my portraits. I'd paint scenes that I came across in Edinburgh, just ordinary folk... and there was Maggie and the life we dreamed of and planned for. Every couple tries to design the perfect life, don't they? Except that perfection may not always be shared, or in our case, that perfection can eventually lose its shine. So, my world was a million miles from the horror and death of Hitler's war, and I feel I've been dropped into a large ocean without a life jacket or a boat. I can either sink or swim and I've always been a good swimmer.'

'You are no different from everyone else. Everyone has the same story to tell.'

'You're right. I know that, but it is worse for you, for your neighbours, for Greece. The important thing is, how do we react as individuals, as a community?'

'It is already happening. Our country will not be liberated by the generals and their armies, or the strategies of kings and governments. It is already happening in the countryside, in the mountains, on the islands, in the villages and towns and in the cities. Inch by inch, foot by foot, every second, every minute and every day, Greece is being liberated.'

Frank nodded. 'And I want to be part of that. I want to play my part.'

She met his eyes with a look of curiosity. 'In what way?'

'I have a chance to do something. I thought it might have slipped from me, but thank God it hasn't.'

Alexia's eyes widened. 'This was what you were talking about earlier. When you spoke of trust.'

The spike of regret that pierced him that morning continued to trouble him as he nodded. He wished now he had told her sooner.

Frank tried to justify himself. 'I owe it to them, to Fin and Stephanos and the others that gave their lives. It's because of them I'm here in Corfu. It's because of them that we met. I will not do nothing. I've been a bystander in this bloody war for far too long.' He took a deep breath. 'It was a stroke of luck really that Fin found our lifeboat. Normally, their operations were in and around the Aegean Sea, but they were returning from a reconnaissance mission in Kythira, an island that lies opposite the south-eastern tip of the Peloponnese.

'We spent some time with Fin and his men. I knew I didn't want to go to Athens with the others. I thought I could be of more use still being a war artist but capturing the day-to-day exploits and missions of soldiers like Fin. Their missions were secret. The British public had no idea that soldiers like these were fighting a different kind of war on a daily basis, and in my head, I wanted to put that right. To my amazement, Fin had no objections to me joining them, and as it turned out, it was a decision that saved my life. I can still see the sergeants face, as he looked at me before he left Fin's boat, it was a look of pity, and in less than a minute, he and all the others I had been with since our ship sank were dead, killed by the Germans.'

Frank paused and collected himself. 'A few days later, Fin had been given orders for a new mission. We were about to head up to Paxos. It was unusual, as they had not been that far north, especially in the Ionian Sea. Anyway, the Germans had established a communications base in a building that used to be a bank in the capital. It was strategically important. Fin's briefing was to take it out of action and strip it of all its communication equipment, radios, transmitters, batteries, and generators. From there, we were to rendezvous with the leaders of the resistance in Corfu and offload our special cargo. Only Fin knew the details of when and where the meeting would take place.'

Alexia crossed her arms, intrigued.

Frank continued. 'When Fin and Stephanos died, I moved everything from the hull of the boat.'

'That's why there were just the two bodies in the hull.' Alexia was overcome with remorse at how she had judged him that morning in the olive grove.

Frank nodded. 'I found a cave, deep enough to hide everything and keep it hidden.

'I had to know if the Germans had found the radio equipment. Too many people have died, and their deaths can't be a meaningless waste. It has to be for something, and it still can be... It's all still there, Alexia. Everything is exactly where I put it. It's my guess, the Germans will be looking for men, for soldiers, not radios and transmitters. I need to get in touch with the resistance.'

In the midst of all the horror and death he had witnessed, Frank felt compelled to do what was the right thing.

Chapter 31

Continuous thoughts swept through Alexia as she walked the short distance to Mina's house. It amazed her how Frank had gotten under her skin, and she could think of nothing else but him. He consumed every wakened moment. He engulfed every sense and seized her every thought. The need to touch him was an ever-present impulse. To gaze upon every pore and to inhale his very essence was life-sustaining.

The air was turning cooler, and out towards the sea a sombre-looking sky sagged heavily with steely clouds. She wrapped her cardigan around herself when she heard her name being called. It was Theodora. She had just passed the *kafenion* to the mixed looks of disgust and curiosity from the thin gathering of old men who sat outside, on green wooden chairs, wrapped in their coats, drinking coffee, and putting the world to right.

Theodora eyed Alexia curiously. 'How are you today, Alexia?'

'I've been better.' Alexia bit her lip and wrapped her cardigan tightly around herself.

'I hope last night was not too much of an inconvenience.'

Alexia gritted her teeth. 'An inconvenience!' She stopped herself and tugged at her cardigan. 'More so than for others, I would imagine.'

'I heard old Stamatis and his wife were detained. They must have had something to hide.'

'He was protecting his home.'

'And his old bitch of a wife had it coming to her. Always gossiping and making up stories. That's how rumours start, and the truth and lies can often blur.'

A shiver ran down Alexia's spine. 'She was just an old woman.'

Theodora shrugged.

Alexia brushed her hair from her face.

'You're looking tired, Alexia. All that work in the olive grove must be taking its toll.'

'I've had a cold, that's all.' Inwardly, she chastised herself, but if she had to lie to Theodora, it was a small price to pay.

'It's a shame you have been doing the German's work for them. They will be requisitioning all the olive and fig crops within the next few days, by the way.' She lifted the hem of her skirt. 'Do you like my new stockings? They're silk. Can you imagine how that feels against my skin? Oh! Silly me, of course you won't know. Walter bought them for me on his recent trip to Berlin and some makeup, too. I particularly like this lipstick. It emphasises my lips, don't you think?'

Theodora's lips were coated bright red. 'It's all the rage in Berlin, seemingly.' She wiped the corner of her mouth with a fingertip.

As much as she wanted to, Alexia did not rise to Theodora's petty mind games.

She had known Theodora since they were children, though was a few years older. As a young woman, Theodora learnt that she could use her sexuality to get what she needed from men. They were always willing to oblige her with the promise she would make it worth their while. When the Italians invaded, she exploited their Latin temperament, their taste for alcohol and female companionship and, because of this Theodora did not go without. When the Germans invaded, her reputation met the ears of a Senior Officer, Captain Walter Waldheim, who let it be known in no uncertain terms that Theodora was now exclusive to his company and pleasure.

'Walter tells me that his men are having roasted goat tonight. The spoils of war, I imagine.'

Alexia frowned. 'Let's hope they don't choke on it.' Her face flushed red and her composure thinning, she made her excuses, brushing past Theodora.

Chapter 32

'I swear she knows something,' Alexia frowned, pacing up and down Mina's kitchen.

'She's just a stupid girl whose status is superficial. Once this is over, I'd hate to be in her shoes. Her German officer won't be interested in her then.' Mina poured dark coffee into two cups. 'What if she goes sniffing around your house?'

'She won't. And anyway, Frank is in the space behind the wardrobe. We are careful, Mina, and I need to be seen in the village, doing the things I've always done. I need to pretend everything is still normal.'

Mina nodded, knowing she was right.

'There was one thing Theodora said that was helpful.'

'What was that?'

'I'm sorry, Mina. It's about the olive harvest.'

'Don't concern yourself with that. It was expected. It has been arranged. Theodora is not the only one who has visits from Captain Walter Waldheim. Did you know that back in Germany he was a businessman, owning his own factory that sold agricultural goods?'

Alexia looked at her, wide eyed.

'Many producers of olive oil, me included, hid our harvest from the authorities. We formed a secret co-operative and charted a boat to smuggle the olive oil to the mainland where it was sold, albeit at a lower price than we would normally get. The marketeers started to get greedy and charged higher prices. What they were doing was illegal and expensive as well. They had to charter boats, and it was also dangerous from attacks in the open sea. So, Captain Waldheim, being the businessman he is, forced the olive farmers, under the threat of violence, to tell him about our expected harvest on the basis of the number of olive trees we had. Then, after the harvest, he would give us a certain quota and took what was left at a cheap price. I heard he is selling to olive oil merchants at six times the normal price.'

'He's a crook.'

'He is, as are all the black marketeers. The difference is, he wouldn't think twice about killing those who did not co- operate with him. He is a Nazi. We have no choice.'

It incensed Alexia. Mina stroked her cheek. 'Keep that anger for another time. This way, I still get paid. It's better than nothing, and it puts food on the table and as you know, I don't need to eat much these days. I am better off than most. Because of the olive grove, I have been able to put a little money away and with this year's harvest, there will be a little more.'

She stood and hobbled over to her dresser. She opened a drawer and pulled out an old tin. She sat back down, and with her arthritic fingers, she opened the lid and removed a bundle of drachma notes, carefully rolled up and secured with an elastic band.

Mina smiled. 'Your payment for the work you've done.'

'No. This is not what we agreed. This is too much. Far too much.' She pushed Mina's hand from her. 'I will not accept it.'

Mina shook her head.

'What?'

'Just like your mother.'

'Then she taught me well.'

'This is not about your pride. It's about surviving. Take the money, Alexia.'

Alexia knew she was not going to win this argument. 'Okay. I'll take it.'

'Good. I worry about you, Alexia.'

'I know you do, and it is not good for you.'

'These are unusual times. Nothing is normal anymore. Life has changed for all of us. It is unrecognisable, but more so for others. You have gone through a tough few years, Alexia. You're still young, you have a lifetime ahead of you. At my age, each day is a blessing.'

'Mina! Don't talk like that.'

'It's true, Alexia. Nothing would make me happier than to know you will be cared for when I'm gone.'

'You mean a husband?'

'It's been two years.'

'I'm not exactly spoiled for choice.'

'That's my point. The war hasn't helped, but if you wait much longer, you will always be a widow.'

'Times are different now, Mina. It's not like it was when you were young. Getting married and having children isn't a life decision that has to be made when you're young anymore. Women want much more than that.'

'What is wrong with having a family and a husband to care for you?'

'Women are educated. In the cities, they want jobs and careers that will not only benefit their families but also society as well. Aren't you sick of being treated like an animal? We need to fight against the conventions of what is expected from Greek woman. I'm talking about woman's education, emancipation, resistance, reform, and an improvement in the life Greek woman have been shackled too for generations. I read an EAM pamphlet, which praised women who were running food kitchens, taking part in demonstrations. Some have even joined the *andartes* as fighters and as nurses. We are equal to men. Hasn't this war shown you that? Don't you think that if woman were educated and were valuable contributors to the village, the town or city they lived in, then the concept of *family* would be stronger? You, of all people, should know that.'

'All I'm saying is that it would put my mind at ease.'

'Well, let me put your mind at ease. I'm happy the way I am.'

'How can you be?'

'If I were to marry again, it would be because of love, not necessity.'

'There's no chance of that happening. You have a man, a stranger living in your house and if the Germans find out, well, the less said about that, the better. I'd say your chances of finding love are zero now, and that's not even taking into account the lack of young men around here.'

'There are more important things to be worrying about.' An air of steel entered her voice. 'And anyway, he's not a stranger, not anymore.'

Mina stared at her.

'You can't be constantly in each other's company from morning until night without getting to know one another. We do talk, you know.'

'Is that all you mean?'

'Yes. He is no longer a stranger to me.'

'Do you like him?'

'He is not unlikable.'

'I didn't mean it in that way.'

Alexia turned and stared out of the window.

'Do you have feelings for him?'

'I tried not to. I really did.'

'Oh, my girl. This will only complicate an already complicated situation. And what about him? Are these feelings reciprocated?'

'Yes. I believe they are.'

'You do know nothing good will come of this, if anything, there will be just heartache. He's British, Alexia. There's no future in it.'

'Of all the days I would have appreciated some understanding, it would have been today.'

Then it dawned on Mina. 'Oh! Alexia. It's your wedding anniversary.'

'Not that I'm celebrating it.'

'No, I don't suppose you will be.'

'It's just a reminder of a time in my life that should have been happy, not the worst time.'

'I'm sorry. Listen to me going on and on. On a day like today as well.'

Alexia rubbed the finger where her wedding ring should have been. 'So, what if it only lasts a few days, a week, a month? I just want to feel happy for once. Is that too much to ask?'

'No. It isn't. If anyone deserves to be happy, it's you.'

Alexia stared into her coffee.

'I'm sorry for being an old fool.'

'You are anything but an old fool. You are the most level-headed and wisest person I know.'

'Nonsense. You need to widen your social circle.'

'I mean it, Mina. I don't think I could have coped with these last few years if it was not for you.'

'You do yourself a disservice, my girl. Beneath all your words, you're the most determined woman I know. You are a force of nature, a woman of courage, and I wouldn't envy anyone, man or woman who tries to contain you. I wish I had half the spirit you have.'

'Are you sure you're talking about me? I don't feel any of those things, that's for sure.'

'And that's what makes you who you are. Look at what you are doing. How many people would put themselves in the way of such danger?'

'Others would have done the same.'

'A few, if you're lucky. I just want what's best for you. I might be old and have old ways, but I'm not that insensitive to know that there are times I could be wrong. It's just that if anything was to happen to me, I would want you to know that all I have ever wanted is for you to be happy, to find your happiness, whatever that may be.'

'Mina! Nothing is going to happen to you. You are not ill, are you?'

Mina took Alexia's hand in hers and looked into her eyes.

'You're beginning to worry me now.'

Mina shook her head. 'No. I'm not ill. Well, not that I know of. I want you to know that if you have feelings for this man then, I suppose what I am saying is, follow your heart. You are like a daughter to me, Alexia. I just want what is best for you and I don't want you to have regrets in life. I know you're not looking for it, but if he makes you happy, you have my blessing.'

'That means so much to me.'

Alexia had been biding her time. She needed to pick the right moment, and she felt now was as good a time as any. She took a deep breath. 'Mina, there is something else I need to tell you. Frank and I have spoken about it, and he agrees you should know.'

'Know what?'

By the time Alexia had finished, she felt she had not drawn a breath. She looked at Mina, unsure what reaction her words would manifest.

'The *andartes* already know about this. They have been waiting for word from this man, Fin. They know about the caique and that it has been taken away by the Germans and what was previously arranged has not gone to plan.'.

Alexia cocked her head, bemused at Mina's words.

Mina thought for a moment. 'And talking of plans, does Frank have one?'

Alexia shrugged. 'Not in any detail. He wants to finish what was started and to do that, he needs to contact the right people.'

'So, not much of a plan. He doesn't even know who he should be talking to. There are informers even inside the ranks of the *andartes*. He could be just as easily signing his own death warrant.'

'How do you know all of this? What is going on, Mina?'

'The *andartes* have eyes and ears, even here in Lakones. There are a few trusted individuals who would be able to get this information to the appropriate people.'

Alexia was stunned. 'How do you know such things?'

'Just because I'm old and my eyes and ears are not as good as they were when I was your age, they haven't completely failed me yet.'

Disbelief swept through Alexia, replaced by a pang of guilt.

'You let me rant on about the untapped potential of women and our place being no better than animals and here you are, all this time working for the resistance.' Alexia was dumfounded. She did not know what to think. 'How long has this been going on?'

'I'm just an old cog in a larger machine. I'm not that important. When my boys left to fight, I made it known to the appropriate people I wanted to be of use and offer my assistance in any way I could. I don't do much. I watch and I listen.'

'Would you have told me?'

'Probably not. There was no need.'

'And what about Frank? Have you told them about Frank?'

'Yes, they know. It was delicate. And it is now a developing situation.'

'What do you mean?'

'There was a boat expected, and it arrived at the location agreed, but the man called Fin was the contact, and when it was known he was dead and the only other person alive was Frank, naturally there was suspicion. The options were Frank was who he said he was, he was a German informer or a German working under cover, if it was either of the latter two, the resistance and their operations would be compromised, and they needed time to gather the information that would either confirm or negate that.'

'So, they used me. You used me.'

'No, no Alexia. It was you who took Frank into your house of your own free will. It just made it easier, that's all. Either way, I was still worried, and what was I to do? You had made up your mind that you were protecting him. How could I have changed that?'

'I see. So, what has changed?'

'The *andartes* could have searched the boat for the radios and transmitters, but that would have been risky. If Frank was working for the Germans, they would be expecting just that, so they waited.

'Then there were the house searches. Why would the Germans search for one of their own? A scouting party had been watching the boat that night. The Germans were seen removing the caique and the bodies. Another person was observed at the beach too. He wasn't with the Germans. In fact, he was doing his best not to be seen, and he fitted the description of Frank. When Frank told you that the equipment was in the cave and that he needed to contact the resistance, this means everything has changed.'

Chapter 33

In her bedroom, Alexia knelt, and with a kitchen knife, prised open a floorboard. She reached inside and retrieved an old jewellery box. Alexia had been overcome with relief that the Germans did not discover it on the night of the house searches.

She sat on the bed and opened the lid, then, reaching into the box, she drew out a smaller compartment lined in purple velvet material. In the centre sat a gold ring. A mixture of emotions caught her breath as it always did, the weight of sorrow, the warmth of affection and hollowness of grief. It was the only tangible and physical connection this world had to offer to her mother. She ran a finger over the smooth surface and her eyes glazed with tears.

The ring signified the love and bond between her parents and the promise they had made on their wedding day to love each other no matter what this world hurled at them. They had brought Alexia and her sister up in a loving and secure family and so it was with shame and brutality she lived her life with Stathis, unable to tell her parents the stark reality of her marriage. In a perverse sort of way, Alexia felt a failure every time she was in the presence of her mother and father, for it was a constant reminder of what her union with Stathis was not. She would not have brought that kind of worry onto her mother, so she suffered in silence and perfected the persona of a dutiful wife, who flourished in the perfect marriage.

She wiped the tears from her cheeks and swallowed the boulder lodged in her throat.

She had no wedding ring of her own. With each new day of Stathis being missing, her wedding ring burned her finger, until finally she felt strong enough within herself to remove the symbol of her suffering and degradation. She took it to a Jewellery shop in Corfu Town and, with the money; she bought the goat that she brought home and tied up in the garden. It sustained and nourished her more than her marriage ever did, until it, too, was taken from her by the Germans.

She managed a warm smile at the memory of the story behind her mother's wedding ring. Her father had bought the ring at a jeweller in Corfu Town owned by a Jewish family and her father knew the owner, Isaac Nehamas. They were guests at her parents' wedding and attended Alexia and her sister's baptisms. Alexia's memories of Isaac, Hadassa his wife, and their daughter, Eliora, were still clear. They visited several times, and they had all gone to the beach and had lunch at a local taverna. Alexia could still remember swimming in the warm sea and playing on the beach with Eliora.

She had heard stories from the mainland that the Germans had closed Jewish shops, cafes and tavernas. They had thrown families out of their homes, apartments, and places of work. Their homes looted, there had been stories of daily public humiliation, synagogues ransacked, and Jewish cemeteries destroyed, the tombstones used to build roads and buildings. It horrified her to read in the Nazi controlled press that the entire Jewish population in the city of Salonika were deported to camps, their existence eradicated from the city.

Under the Italian occupation, the small Jewish community in Corfu Town had lived in comparative safety. Alexia had heard this had dramatically altered once the Germans had taken control of the Ionian Islands. Even in Corfu Town, Alexia had been told that Jewish citizens suffered daily humiliations under German rule. These people were Greeks. Some had fought in the war in Albania. It was incomprehensible to her that such atrocities had been committed against people because of their religion.

The thought of what might have befallen the Nehamas family made her nauseous. She hoped they were safe and well but feared the worst.

Downstairs. Frank had set the table and although the bowls were chipped and cracked, it sent a flutter through her stomach. In all her married life, Stathis had never set the table, not even once. In the middle of the table, Frank had lit a candle and Alexia noticed fresh logs and a fire set, which crackled and glowed warm and seductive. Her heart felt lighter, more than it had done for months, and as she neared the table, her eyes met Franks.

'The soup is warming in the pot and there's bread and some cheese.'

She grinned. 'It is a banquet.'

'Why don't you take a seat and I'll serve up the food.'

Alexia waved her hand over the table. 'Why all of this?'

'It's my way of saying thank you.'

He ladled the soup into the two bowls and sat opposite Alexia. With the kitchen knife donated by Mina, he sliced the bread and even the crumbs flaking onto the chopping board looked too delicious to waste.

'Spyros, the shepherd is due to come down from the hills tomorrow. He is Mina's contact; I couldn't believe it when she told me what she had been doing. Who would have guessed?'

'A perfect contact then.'

'Yes. I suppose so. Mina will relay the information to Spyros, who has his own contact. He will be the one who tells the *andartes*. A date will be arranged for a meeting. Spyros thinks it will take only a few days to organise.'

'Good. A few more days won't make any difference.' He broke some bread and dipped it in the soup before placing it in his mouth. 'Mm, the soup tastes lovely.'

'Mina paid me today, far too much, more than we had agreed, so I was able to buy potatoes, a cabbage, and ham. Some salt too.'

'You deserve it.'

She smiled sadly. 'Look what we have been reduced to, grateful that we can afford watery soup, some bread and cheese.'

Frank sat back in his chair. 'We're living like kings.'

'I think we should celebrate that you will finally achieve handing over the communication equipment to the resistance. Because of you, the *andartes* will be better prepared and organised in liberating our country. It will also save lives. You should be proud of that.'

Alexia rose from her chair, and striding across the room purposefully, she plucked from the dresser a bottle of wine. She smiled satisfyingly. 'We can drink like kings, too.'

'Where did you get that?'

'Mina gave it to me. She has a small cellar; her husband loved wine and collected it before the war. She hates the stuff; she thinks it tastes like cat's piss.'

'How did she hide it from the Germans?'

She pointed to the writing scrawled on the bottle. Frank glanced at it.

'It says arsenic. She said it was for the rats, as all her cats were dead now. The young German could speak Greek, remember? It was just as well he could read Greek to.'

'It's a vintage year then.'

Alexia poured some wine into two cups and handing one to Frank. She raised her cup, 'Yeia mas.'

Frank smiled. 'Yeia mas.' He took a sip. 'I wasn't expecting it to taste like that. That's an excellent wine.'

'You know your wines?'

'I'm no expert, but I've drunk enough to know the difference between a good wine and a bad one.'

They ate the food and drank the wine, and Alexia could feel her head feeling slightly fuzzy. She lifted the bottle of wine and, tilting it, poured the remainder into Frank's cup.'

'Don't give me all of it, save some for yourself,' he protested.

'I've had plenty. I can feel it going to my head already.'

With the shutters closed and it already dark outside, the candle flickered a yellow light that settled over the table. Alexia rose. 'I'll put the lamp on.'

'No. Leave it. This feels cosy.' He wanted to say, *this feels romantic* but held back.

She glanced at him oddly. 'I don't know this word... cosy.'

Deep inside him, something lightened. 'It means warm and homey.'

Alexia's face lit up. 'I like this word.'

He studied her as a subtle shadow fell across her face. Over him crashed a flood of such intense desire. It left him fearful of wanting too much. Light exploded where there had only been darkness and hope flared where there had only been dread. She was responsible for the change in him, although she would be too self-doubting to believe it. She was beautiful and she would be the last to think so, and that was part of her beauty, too. She had a frankness that he admired; she allured him with her sense of justice and defiance.

One of the few objects left intact and untouched after the German search was a radiogram that sat in the corner of the room. At night, they huddled around it and listened to the BBC, whenever there was a decent reception, catching up on the progress of the war. Whether it was the wine or that Frank had a sudden surge of bravado, he drank the wine from his cup and wiping his lips, he reached the radiogram and switched it on. It crackled into life. He turned the tuner knob, scanning the frequencies, static hissing, like a piercing scream. He turned it again, this time, slower, more precise, and then, the unmistakable sound of an orchestra. The silvery and velvet violins, the deep and layered voices of the cellos and the resonating woodwind instruments, filled the silence around them with rich, majestic melodies.

Frank turned to Alexia with an outstretched hand.

'Would you dance with me?'

'I don't dance.'

'You either can't or you won't?'

'I have not danced for a long time.' She looked away from him. He pondered if it brought her uncomfortable memories.

'I'm sorry if I've upset you.'

'It is fine.'

'We can just listen to the music. I haven't heard music since I was back in Edinburgh.'

'Did you dance then?'

He smiled. 'Sometimes. At the weekends, people would go to the dance halls and dance to the latest hit songs. The men would go to the pub first and have a few drinks before they met their girlfriends as there was no alcohol sold at the dancing.'

'Did you go dancing with Maggie?' Alexia asked.

'I did.'

The music ended and there was a silence between them.

'I will dance with you, Frank.'

Alexia stood up and stepped towards him. The slow meandering beat with a melancholic trumpet intro started up and Jo Stafford sang, *Blue Moon.'* Frank reached out and gently placed his hand on Alexia's hip and, with the other, curled his fingers around hers. They swayed slowly and tentatively, clumsily to begin with, until eventually, they fell into a timely rhythm. She averted her eyes and stared at his chest. He could feel her breath against his shirt. She made a tiny movement with her palm, pressing gently against his side and then, fragile at first, she lay the side of her face against him, before letting its weight rest on his chest.

In the dim light, the warmth of her body radiated through the fabric of his shirt, and all he could do was look in wonderment and inhale the sweet fragrance of her hair.

It amazed him that in such a short time, every detail of her face, every gesture of her hand, every expression she made, were as familiar to him as if they were his own. He felt he had known her all his life.

Hesitation had lodged itself in his mind. He swallowed it. It didn't matter to him now if she rebuked him. He could no longer abandon the urge to show her how he truly felt. His heart thumped, and he wondered if she could feel and hear it against her ear. He reached with his hand at the back of her neck and entwined tendrils of her hair in his fingers, feeling its weight. Instinctively, she looked up at him, her brown eyes pulling him like magnets.

He traced the tip of his finger along her cheek, the curve of her lips, her skin warm and smooth to his touch, and it infused him with what he already knew; nothing else mattered, but this time, there was nothing more important than her.

Their eyes locked. Her lips moved slightly, but no words parted from them. He moved his hand along the length of her back, knowing he had dreamt of such a moment every night in her company.

Then, with the music slowing in the last refrain of Jo Stafford's voice holding a final seductive note, it faded from them.

Alexia pulled away from him and stepped back, dropping her hands at her side. She cleared her throat as if to say something, and he sensed her slipping from him.

As they cleared and washed the dishes, Frank's thoughts tumbled one after the other. It was sheer madness to think they could be anything other than what they were. His feelings were irrational and nonsensical given that he could not even walk with her along the street in daylight without fearing being discovered.

Alexia pressed the palm of her hand to her forehead. 'Soon you will be thinking of leaving.'

Frank was unsure if this was a question or a statement.

She continued. 'It is important that you think this way. The war could last for many more years.'

'Yes,' he said quickly.

'The *andartes* have helped Allied men in this way.'

'Have you known many?'

'Some. One stayed for a few days until it was safe for him to move on.'

'Was he British?'

'Yes. Most are. He was from York. I remember, because it reminded me of New York. His name was Tom.'

Frank felt a slither of jealousy.

'He was young and scared. He spoke about his mother and family a lot. At night, I would hear him cry. I hope he is safe and well.'

Frank recoiled inside, regretting his initial reaction. Poor bastard, he thought. He was probably just out of school or university.

For some time, they don't speak, instead they sit with their own thoughts for company.

Frank rose from his chair. 'It's getting late.'

Alexia did not look at him. 'I will lock up.'

At night, Frank always filled a bowl with water and went upstairs to wash. Then, he would move into the space behind the wardrobe and slide the panel shut. Alexia would retrieve the bowl and empty it, then she would wash herself, and in her bedroom, she would undress for bed.

She had just stepped into the bedroom to take the washing bowl back downstairs when, startled she caught her breath and saw Frank still standing amongst the dim shadows of the room.

'I couldn't leave you for the night without saying something. If I don't, I'll go mad.'

His eyes fixed on her and as he moved closer to her, there was a gleam of determination that would not be dissuaded.

'I can't help the way I feel about you, Alexia. I've tried not to feel like this. I really have. It doesn't make sense. We're two people who have been thrown together. We live in different worlds, but none of that matters. What does matter is how I feel, and I can't change that, just like I can't stop the sun rising each morning. With you, I feel complete. I feel whole. You have made me like this. I can't imagine wakening without you being the first person I see, the first I talk to and being the first to see you smile. I can't contemplate having a life that you are not a part of, one in which I can't share my joy, my sadness, my thoughts and my dreams with you. I can't go back to a life that does not have you in it.'

She reached for his hands and held them in hers. 'I'm afraid.' Her voice trembled. 'For two years, I have been on my own. I swore to myself that was all I needed. I did not need anyone else, except Mina. I'm scared to let people get close to me. I thought I could live that way.' Alexia tightened her grip on Frank's hand. 'I was wrong.'

He wanted to take her sadness and expel it from her world, but something ingrained it in her memories, Stathis' violence and mind games, the deaths of her sister and parents. These were beyond his capabilities. He would be here for her; she would no longer be alone. She could share her thoughts and her dreams with him, and he with her. He felt soaked in what he could only describe as love.

Frank reached over and slid Alexia's hair from her face. She tilted her head, and he leaned towards her, their eyes locked. His hands rose to her face, and ever so lightly, he traced his thumb over her lips. His breath, like a warm soft breeze, drifted along her skin that tingled with a longing to be touched by him. And when he kissed her deep and with such passion, it affirmed the love her heart denied.

He turned to the wardrobe, but she held his arm steadfastly. He turned back to face her, and she raised her hand to his face, tracing his cheekbones, the angle of his jaw, and then, she slid her hand around the nape of his neck along the curve of his throat where she released a button from his shirt, and then another and another. She tugged the tails of the shirt from his trousers, and slid it from him, discarding the garment onto the floorboards. She put her mouth on his chest and peppered his skin in light, delicate kisses, the touch of her lips exhilarating and stirring him.

She sat on the bed and, pulling him towards her, she leaned back and enveloped him in her arms.

He didn't know how long he had been looking at her. Time had no significance. He sat enthralled in the moment. When he slept in the space behind the wardrobe, he had ached to be with her. He listened to the muffled sounds. The distance between them, so close yet so far, but still audible. The padding of her feet, as she climbed the stairs, and the creak of the floorboards, as she entered her bedroom. The splash of water, as she washed herself, and the creak of springs, as she lay on the bed to sleep.

He tried to imagine what she might be thinking, as she lay only a few feet from him. He was present, yet he was not. It was an unusual arrangement. He lay in the darkness, his ears acute to the faintest sound. He never slept until he was sure she had succumbed to sleep herself.

And now there was no barrier between them, only a calmness about her as he watched her sleep. Her body enveloped in a stillness and quietness that seemed to protect her from the harshness of the world.

He could not shake loose the images that were forced upon him when she told him what her husband did to her. It was the bed where he, whose name he would not mention, even in his mind, forced himself upon her, used her and tortured her mind. He recoiled at what must have taken place in the bed in which they had laid together last night. And even as she was unbuttoning his shirt, it was another man's; it was the shirt of her abuser, a reminder of the pain he inflicted upon her. Even with this before them, her touch was delicate, and it was as if she was exorcising the room and the clothes of the memories and pain.

He tried to brand on his memory every minute detail of her. He had luxuriated in exploring every inch of her with his fingertips, his hands, his tongue, and his mouth, seeking a union, not only physical, but a sense of oneness, a fusion of sorts, a thousand nerves on fire.

She awoke to a slice of golden sunlight seeping into the bedroom. She turned onto her side. Frank sat on the chair at the dresser, facing her and wearing only the shirt, unbuttoned. She propped herself up on her elbow.

'Did you sleep well?' Frank asked.

'I did. What are you doing?'

'Looking at you.'

'How long have you been sitting there?'

'It was still dark when I got up.'

'And you've been watching me all that time?'

'It was better than dreaming about you.'

Alexia smiled and, in doing so, it radiated her face in light.

'I would like to draw you. Would you let me?'

'If you want to.'

'I'll get my pencils and pad.'

'You want to draw me now, in bed?'

'Don't move. The light is perfect.'

Frank went downstairs and returned with an assortment of pencils and his sketch pad.

He sat back down and scraped the chair a few inches towards her. The bedsheet had fallen from her and exposed the curve of a breast. She tried to adjust it, but Frank dissuaded her not to.

His gaze flitted from pencil to Alexia, back and forth, the pencil sliding and flicking in strokes. He used his finger like a brush, rubbing areas of his drawing to shade and highlight. He lit a cigarette and continued to sketch with it clamped between his teeth.

'Your complexion is flawless in this light.'

'My head is itchy,' her nose creased as she spoke.

'It's okay to move. You can scratch it if you want.'

She raised her hand and scratched her scalp, and he observed long tendrils of hair falling across her shoulders, licking her skin that stretched taut over her clavicle, and he knew he had to depict the detail precisely as he saw it to translate an aura of intimacy, and of connection that he desperately wanted to capture.

When he had finished, he studied his work. To his satisfaction, he had captured her likeness, but most importantly there was a soul in her eyes. She was alive on the sheet of paper, and it prickled his skin.

'Have you finished?'

After a moment's consideration, he replied. 'I have.'

She leaned forward, and he handed her the sketchbook. She studied it for what seemed an age and Frank tried but failed to decipher her reaction. Eventually, he asked her. 'Well, what do you think? Do you like it?

Bewilderment settled in her face. 'Is this how you see me?'

His heart sank. 'You don't like it.'

'It is a beautiful drawing. I see someone, but I don't see me. You have drawn someone I do not recognise.'

Her criticism stung. Then he realised what she meant. She seemed to deflate before him.

'I do not feel how this woman looks. He took my self-worth from me. He made me feel I was nothing. He shamed me. I was dirt underneath his boots.'

He reached out and held her hands. 'Alexia, you are none of these things. This is who you are, a beautiful, strong, and dignified woman. He cannot harm you anymore. He is dead, he is dust, and you are alive, and each day moves him further from you. You are a flower that has bloomed, and he is a weed that has withered and died.'

Suddenly, something rose inside her. She put her hand to her mouth, and, like an eruption, it flowed from her, all the anger, the shame and pain and when it started, it would not stop until she lay exhausted, aching, and drained. Sensing a change in her, he lay beside her and curled his arms around her. He kissed her shoulder and put his lips to her neck.

She murmured, 'I feel so much lighter, I could float into the sky.' Her breathing sank deeper, and she fell into a sleep.

Chapter 34

Several days passed. They did not speak of what happened. They expressed it in the way they touched one another whenever their lips met and in the intimacy of the love they made.

They lived in a world of their own making, cocooned within the walls and rooms of the house. Alexa only left to buy food: meagre scraps of meat, cabbage, onions, peppers, and even, to Frank's surprise, the luxury of soap.

Frank would wait anxiously for her return, a strange mix of fear, that something might happen to her, and elation, that they were together. They talked a lot, exploring each other's past lives and sharing memories. It welded them together, creating links on a chain that defined them as people that shared their innermost thoughts and feelings, giving themselves to one another unconditionally. The lenses of her past gradually blurred, her trauma and pain slowly melted, replaced by a soft glow that kindled within her. They spent most of their time under the sheets, keeping warm, making memories to last a lifetime. He sketched her several more times, and he luxuriated in every aspect of her, every detail, every pore of her skin.

They spent hours speaking only in Greek, and to his satisfaction, his competency progressed at a rate where he could hold a simple conversation with her.

Gradually and tentatively, she gave herself to him. Her hesitancy abated, and she expressed her needs and desires. And the gulf that had been between them like a wall crumbled with each new touch and sensation.

Hours passed and days fell away and something vivid ignited in her abdomen.

One afternoon, they set a fire, the days now growing shorter and colder. With a knock at the door, Mina limped into the house, a headscarf covering her hair, and wrapped in a long black coat, the cold still stubbornly clinging to it. She warmed her hands at the fire and Alexia brought her a chair so she could sit beside it and feel its heat. Mina rested her weary self and rubbed her vein-streaked hands together.

'It is getting that cold, I can feel the blood freeze in my veins,' Mina complained and sipped the hot coffee Alexia had brought her and placed in her hands.

Frank hoped Mina's visit would bring the news he had been waiting for. He sat in silent anticipation.

Mina met his eyes steadily and wiped a dribble of coffee from her chin with the back of her hand. 'I've informed Spyros of the information he needed to know, and he assured me it would take only a few days to get the news to the *andartes* and then he would return with their instructions.' She shook her head sorrowfully. 'There has been no word from him, no news. And there have been rumours that he is already being interrogated by the Germans. I fear someone is leaking information to the Nazis, which means even I could be compromised, and it may only be a matter of time before they come looking for you, Frank.'

Although Frank could only decipher a few keywords, he understood by Alexia's sad eyes that the news was not what he had wanted to hear. Frank's heart thumped as he met Mina's stare.

'What do we do now?' Alexia asked.

'It is possible that we are being watched right at this very moment. Our movements, and comings and goings observed only to be reported back tonight or tomorrow. Whatever we decide, we act now.'

Alexia translated Mina's words and Frank nodded, knowing Mina was right, even though he wished he could carry on indulging himself in precious time spent with Alexia. He felt an overwhelming longing to finish what had brought him to this island, and Alexia.

'I don't see any other option.'

Alexia turned to look at Mina then, as if to say, tell him how stupid that would be.

Mina shot a glance at Alexia. 'There is no other way.'

'He can't go. I've been hiding him for weeks.' She felt his eyes on her.

'I can't be invisible forever,' he said calmly.

'You can't just walk around unnoticed; you will be seen. I will go with you.'

He placed a finger to her lips. 'No. I can't allow that. I wouldn't be able to live with myself if anything happened to you.'

Alexia turned to Mina. 'Tell him, Mina. This is madness.' And even as she was remonstrating, she knew it had already been decided.

Mina had already worked out what was to happen next. In the village of Liapades, a few kilometres from Lakones lived Mina's counterpart. He owned the café in the square. Mina told Frank he would know who it was because he would be recognisable as he only had one eye, a result of a freak accident when he was a child. A password system operated between the *andartes,* who also increased their security by issuing ID cards to their agents. Mina wrote her password in Greek and an overview of the purpose of Frank's visit and his need to speak with someone of authority within the island's resistance movement. She handed the sheet of paper to Frank and warned him to destroy it if captured by the Germans.

Although Liapades could be reached by road, it would be safer and less obvious to reach the village by rowboat. This would entail a short distance of two bays away. He would hide the rowboat in a cave at Rovinia Bay and then the village was less than half a kilometre climb, along a track that cut through the thickly wooded hillside.

They agreed he should go the next day. He would take one of the rowboats that was moored in the bay across from where the mule trail ended. Frank knew the geography by now, and he was confident he could reach the boat undetected.

Chapter 35

He left a few hours before sunrise. He and Alexia had lain in her bed, but sleep was hard to come by. When he finally submitted to its pull, it was just below the surface and he submerged restless, even in his sleep, his mind raced with images of the day to come.

After Mina had left them, Alexia was uncustomarily reserved. She busied herself with tasks around the house, and Frank thought she had pulled away from him and retreated into her thoughts, a form of protection he was unwilling to challenge.

When she spoke, she turned to him, her eyes wide, her mouth set. 'I knew this time would come. Nothing, especially this, can last forever.'

'I will return. After this is done, I will come back to you.'

She put her hand to her chest. 'It is better for me to think you are leaving. That way, there is an end to this, to us. Life will go back to how it was, and hopefully you will be able to leave Corfu and...'

Frank reached out and touched her face. 'If this is how you want to think, that's fine. If by convincing yourself that I'm not coming back helps you cope, then that's fine too, but I will do everything possible to come back to you, believe me. If I don't, it's because I can't, and I'll be either dead or captured.'

Her big brown eyes burned into him with their sadness. Tears glistened and fell onto her cheeks, and Frank wiped them away with his thumb.

'I've never felt like this about anyone in my life. I love you so much it hurts.' He wove his fingers through her hair, and leaning into her, kissed her soft lips.

He could feel the heat from her body seep into him as she slept beside him and every inch of him memorised her touch upon his skin. He ached to make love to her one more time. She shifted slightly, and in the darkness, her hair brushed his arm, and drifted across his skin. He took a deep, melancholic breath. Time had caught up with him. It was time to leave.

Reluctantly, he eased himself from her and, taking his clothes, he went downstairs to dress, as not to wake her. He slung on his jacket and secured the handgun in a pocket and shoved the sheet of paper Mina had given him, with the password and instructions, in another.

He sensed her behind him, and as he turned to face her, he could hardly see her in the dark. She wrapped her arms around him and nestled into his chest. Her redolent hair riveted him to the spot, and he knew if he didn't leave now, he never would.

Into the stillness, her voice came. 'I love you.' And like some strange form of osmosis, his skin absorbed her words that melted into his heart.

She stepped back from him, and taking a deep breath, he opened the door. He did not look at her one last time. It was the most difficult thing he had done, the cruellest of departures.

And when he was gone, she wanted to scream. Instead, the darkness took her voice. The heaviness bored into her, like grief, a bereavement of a kind.

He found the rowboat just as Mina had said. He pushed it out into the shallow water. He climbed inside and began to row. At first it was easy, but as soon as he was in deep open water, the swell of the sea fought against him. His arms burned and his back strained. Behind him, high up in the hill, the pinprick lights of Lakones shimmered like stars, and at the horizon, the first light of the sun, illuminated the sky in yellow and orange streaks, tinging the edges of low-lying cloud in halo light.

He kept a steady course, hugging the shore as safely as possible, whilst keeping a respectable distance between himself and the perpendicular rock of the sand blushed cliffs.

Rovinia beach was sheltered with shingle sand underfoot. Frank manoeuvred the rowboat into a cave tucked into the cliff. When in-

side, he jumped into the shallow water and dragged the boat deeper, sliding its bulk out of the sea onto shingled ground, as far as he
could, until it satisfied him it was well hidden.

Scuttling along the beach, he saw a hollow in the vegetation
where a track emerged. Sand turned to dirt as the track curved up the
hill.

The area was dense with trees and scrubland. Above him, a high
canopy of branches filtered the soft twilight glow, illuminating his
progress. The track skirted the coast and steepened. To his left, the
cobalt sea frothed and cascaded on the smooth shine of black rocks
below, sweeping spray wildly into the air.

After walking for several minutes, his eyes darted from side to
side, tree to tree, bush to bush. When nearing an olive grove, he saw
a rifle slung around a broad shoulder.

Two men eyed him suspiciously. One had a thick dark moustache, his hair long and greasy, swept back over his head that lay in
straggles down his neck. They wore thick black coats and trousers
tucked into mud-stained boots that rose to just below their knee.

The men watched him warily. As Frank approached, one man's
hand curled around the pistol tucked in his belt, the other swung
his rifle from his shoulder and raised it, the barrel pointing towards
Frank. Frank raised both arms in the air.

'Who are you and where are you going?' One asked, his pistol
cocked and pointed at Frank.

He could just make out the first part of the man's question.

In his rudimentary Greek, Frank replied, 'My name is Frank.'

The men stepped closer. The one with the pistol spoke again, but
Frank could not understand him this time, the words rolling off his
tongue too quickly.

'I'm sorry, I don't understand.'

Frank raised his hands higher in supplication. 'I need help,
please.'

The one with the rifle gestured with it, and this time, Frank understood. He dropped to his knees, his breathing coming quick and heavy.

In desperation, Frank pleaded, 'Do you speak English?'

They ignored him. The one with the rifle pressed it against Frank's forehead, while the other opened Frank's coat with the barrel of his pistol and grinned.

He said something to the other, who chuckled in return, and then removed the handgun from Frank's inside pocket and slid it under his belt. He rummaged through the other pockets and pulled out Mina's piece of paper. He unfolded the sheet and read. When he finished, he cocked his head and the other peered at the sheet. They spoke amongst themselves, and Frank knew they were debating the authenticity of his note. Then, the Greek with the rifle gestured for Frank to stand.

'You will come with us,' he commanded in perfect English, to Frank's surprise and relief.

'There is only one person who will know if this is genuine. Until then, if you try to run, we will shoot you.'

Frank nodded. He was a step closer, and that was all that mattered. Hope interweaved with anguish.

They walked in silence. Frank could see the lay of the land, a flat verdant plain, intersected with the occasional house, and then, further, he saw wooded rolling hills. The track grew wider as they headed inland now, passed olive groves, crumbling stone walls and the occasional outlying house and farm building. The two Greeks smoked cigarettes without offering one to Frank and engaged each other in conversation, but Frank could only detect a word or two. Then, suddenly, three short sharp whistles rang out.

Initially, Frank thought it a bird, but when the Greeks stopped abruptly and, one placed a finger to his lips for Frank's benefit. One of the Greeks murmured to the other. Another three short sharp whistles. To the right of them, a stone wall bordered an olive grove. The Greek with the pistol gestured for Frank to follow them and they leapt the wall, hunching behind it. Frank felt the pressure of a sharp blade against his neck and slowly, the Greek placed a finger to his lips once more.

Frank heard them then, the crunch of boots on the dirt, the unmistakable and distinct German accents. The Greek with the rifle pressed his eye against a crack in the wall. He raised five fingers. The other nodded. A patrol, Frank thought. He could feel the frantic thudding of his heart and a throbbing travelled from the base of his neck up and over his skull. The two men's faces were tight with tension. When they were sure the Germans had passed, they hesitantly lifted their heads above the cover of the wall. Two short, sharp whistles could be heard somewhere in the trees.

'We go now.' It was a cautious whisper, and the knife left his throat.

They proceeded along the track, and soon, Frank could see the slated roofs. Liapades was near. Once they reached the village, the pace quickened, along narrow lanes, some only wide enough for a mule to pass. Around another bend and a square opened with several buildings, a taverna, and a church. Two mules were tethered to a tree that dominated the centre of the square and several men sat at tables observing the newcomer's approach.

They stopped outside the taverna and the Greek with the pistol went inside. When he reappeared, an older man with thinning silver hair and badger toned stubble came out of the taverna behind him. One eye was closed and scarred.

'What is your name?' The voice was deep and gravelly.

'Frank.'

'My name is Georgios. Come with me Frank, we can talk inside.'

Frank followed Georgios inside the taverna. Georgios went behind the counter, 'Are you hungry? It's breakfast time. I can't offer you my usual menu, and there isn't a choice, but it will be filling, and right now, that's all we can hope for. We still have nice coffee. The Germans are useful for some things. Would you like one?'

'A coffee would be nice.'

'I'm sorry about the reception you received. As you will know, there are spies everywhere, who have their motives, mainly grudges, revenge, money, food...' Georgios tutted. 'The list goes on. Here's that coffee and something to eat.'

Georgios placed a plate of bread, cheese, two boiled eggs, and some grapes on the table in front of Frank. He sat opposite Frank and, plucking a grape from its stem, he placed it in his mouth.

Frank explained the details and ate as he talked: the mission on Paxos, the journey by sea to Corfu and burying Fin and Stephanos. As he spoke, his heart sank at the memory, but he mustered himself and continued. He told Georgios; he knew it was imperative to find a safe storage for the equipment as he knew the Germans could discover the caique at any moment. Fortuitously, he found a cave nearby, one deep enough to hide the radio equipment. He told Georgios he had been staying in a house in Lakones for several weeks. The woman whose house this was knew Mina, who wrote the note that was now lying in front of him. He then spoke with a matter of urgency.

'The equipment is still in the cave. I know this because I went back, and I've seen it. You have to get this information to the hierarchy of the resistance in this part of Corfu, or whoever it is you speak to.'

When Frank was finished, Georgios offered him a cigarette from a packet, then lit his own. Drawing a long drag on it, Georgios did not speak. His silence made Frank edgy, and he shifted in his chair, returning a grape to the plate.

Georgios spoke with an edge of authority. 'Everything you have just said has been verified in Mina's note. When we heard a caique had been found by the Germans, I sent several men to gather information. When the bodies were removed, we assumed the worst, that the Germans had also found the communication equipment on the caique. It had been arranged that Captain Fin would contact us once he was in a position to do so. That contact never came, so it was assumed the mission had failed, until now.'

Frank looked at him 'What's going on?'

'You have achieved what you set out to do. You have informed the *andartes* that the mission was a success, although with regrettable losses.' For the first time, Georgios smiled. 'Thank you, Frank. You have done a good thing, and in doing so, your friends will not have died for nothing, and because of this, Greek lives will be saved. You have furthered our struggle against the occupation.'

It suddenly struck him. 'Mina doesn't know who you really are, does she? She thinks you are just like her, the resistances eyes, and ears on the ground. You are a *kapetan,* an officer for ELAS'

He shook his head. 'It is better this way, and it helps me to really know who to trust and who not to trust. Only a few individuals know my real identity. Not everything is as it seems and that is the way it has to be.'

Growing in confidence, Frank asked. 'What happens now?'

'Since the caique was taken from the cove, there has been little German activity around that area. The sooner we have the radio equipment, the quicker we can put it to use. We will do it tonight.'

Frank looked puzzled. 'You have that authority?'

'To the Nazis who come to my taverna and drink my coffee and eat my food, I'm just the one-eyed owner of a taverna. So far, it has been the perfect cover. You are privileged, Frank, to know of this, but with such knowledge comes responsibility and trust. You have proven you can be trusted, and you have risked your life. I am indebted to you.'

Chapter 36

Alexia tried to ignore the gnawing in her stomach by spending the morning painstakingly scrubbing iron pots and pans, mopping the downstairs floor and the wooden floor of her bedroom.

Alexia washed the bed linen and hung it out to dry in the morning sun that slanted over the village roofs. She chopped firewood and stacked it in piles, only stopping when her back ached and her mouth grew dry. Inside, she drank some water, and washed her hands. After scrubbing the kitchen table, she sat down and sewed the hem of a dress she had been putting off for weeks. Then the needlepoint pricked the soft skin of her finger, and she flinched as a spot of deep red blood appeared. Alexia stared at her hands. Her throat burned. She was exhausted, and powerless to prevent spirals of thoughts that scramble her mind with endless worry. Beneath the industrious bustle, her composure wavered, and a torrent of fear breached the wall she had erected around herself.

Alexia had tried not to think of Frank, but he kept slipping into her mind, and every time, her stomach spasmed and her mind raced, saturated in tormented thoughts. *The Germans had captured him. They had shot him. The rowing boat had capsized, and he had drowned.* On and on it went. She felt she was balancing on the edge of a razor, until there was no more, just the kindling of a fire in her stomach.

It hurt so much to love. It drained her.

The moon shone a silver cone of light over a placid Ionian Sea as the caique motored towards the small cove where Frank had once landed. That now seemed a lifetime ago.

'You can still change your mind,' Georgios had told Frank before they set off for the cave. 'You have done well. It is not necessary for you to put yourself in more danger.

'I have to see it finished.'

209

'I understand. I would do the same.'

There were six *andartes*. Each man was armed, and Frank now had his handgun again.

The *putt, putt, putt* of the pistons from the diesel engine amplified against the enclosed surroundings of the cove, sending nerve ends on alert.

Darting eyes scanned the thick vegetation, sweeping the beach, and treeline further beyond. Georgios pressed a set of binoculars to his eyes, adjusted the lenses and muttered to himself.

When satisfied, he instructed his men. 'Stavros and Nikos, stay on the boat and load the equipment in the hull as we pass it on board, the rest come with me. We keep it silent. No talking.'

Tension followed their footsteps across the sand towards the cave. A feeling of extreme uneasiness lay heavy on Frank. He prayed the Germans had not returned and found the radios and transmitters? The thought tortured him. After what he had been through, it would be too much. By the time they had reached the entrance to the cave, he could even detect the apprehension in every breath Georgios took. They entered the dark cave and lit a lantern.

To Frank's immense relief, everything looked the same as when he was last there, and he eased the tarpaulin aside. Georgios stood for a moment, his eyes wide, and then he slapped Frank on the back, grinning widely. He reached into his pocket and took out a miniature bottle of brandy. He unscrewed the lid and drank a generous amount.

He passed the bottle to Frank. 'Take it. You deserve it.' Frank knew if he didn't, it would be viewed as an insult, so he took the bottle, set it to his lips, and took a drink.

Georgios took the bottle from him and turned to his men. 'Let's get this lot on the boat as quickly as possible.'

They moved the equipment in silence. As they worked, a stillness settled over them, accompanied by gentle waves that casted themselves against the sand. Above them, the night sky glittered in tiny stars, like lanterns hanging in the sky. The cave empty, Frank felt an elation build inside him, just like a finished painting. It was a sensation of closure, of self-satisfaction and absolution.

Something was wrong.

Georgios looked past Frank, along the beach and into the darkness and around them the tide continued to whisper. Then they saw it, out in the trees. Lights flashed, soldiers hastened, and dogs barked. A collective breath of alarm spread amongst them, raised rifles flashed in the moonlight as the rush began to make it back to the caique.

An insistent command to '*Halt*' was ignored, and a flurry of bullets whizzed past Frank and struck the water like miniature torpedoes. From the deck of the caique, Nikos' rifle flashed, and Stavros turned the engine that spluttered into life.

Georgios and his men waded through the water. Frank heard a thud and the man next to him propelled forward and smacked into the water. Frank grabbed the arm of the man and heaved it out of the water. To his horror, a dark pool of blood seeped from where the top of the head used to be. Frank dropped the arm, as if it had burned him, and frantically pushed through the water with leaded legs. Around him, the world turned ear-splitting and terrifying.

With frantic effort, he made it into the caique and kept as low as his body would allow. His hands trembled.

It was an eternity. Frank lay on his back and peered at the sky. How serene and still it looked while all around him hell had broken out.

By now, the caique had gained a steady pace and had reached the open sea. The men around him were eerily quiet, contemplating the loss of one of their numbers, a fellow resistance fighter, a friend, and possibly a brother, even. How many more lives would be taken for the acquisition of radios, transmitters, and batteries? But Frank knew it was more than just the physical ownership of this equipment that was imperative. The *andartes* now had the ability to be more effective. Their operations of sabotage, and their organisation would be coordinated, and information relayed within seconds. It was a major boost to the *andartes* capabilities and morale. Many lives would now be saved. It was a sacrifice these men were prepared to take, as had Fin and Stephanos and the others before them.

Once they reached land, they unloaded the equipment and transferred it onto a truck. When the tailgate was closed and bolted, a weight lifted from Frank. It was finally over.

'Where are you taking the radios?' Frank asked.

Georgios looked at him sternly. 'It is not your concern and best you don't know.'

Frank knew he was right.

Chapter 37

When they returned to Liapades, and entered the village square, some customers sat at the tables outside the taverna. Frank looked around the square. No one paid much attention to them. Frank had the impression they were being ignored, and he was sure everyone had their part to play. Like actors, this scene had been played out many times before. Georgios tied his apron around his waist and mingled amongst his customers, as if the last few hours had never happened. The guiding hand of Stavros, who was the only *andarte* left with them, ushered Frank inside the taverna. He gave him a glass of wine and a piece of bread and cheese to eat.

Once the last of the customers had left, Georgios pulled up a chair and offered Frank a cigarette.

'We must make plans to get you off, Corfu. It will take a little time, but it can be arranged.'

'And what if I don't want to go?'

Georgios' expression changed immediately. 'What do you mean?'

'I'm not ready to leave. I can't. I love her.' It was the first person he had disclosed his feelings to, other than Alexia, and he would never have envisaged it being like this.

Georgios scratched the stubble on his chin. 'Who is this person you love?'

'Alexia. The woman I've been staying with.'

'Ah, these things happen, I suppose. You have been through a difficult time, your life has changed, it is not the life you knew. You have seen things most men your age never witness in a lifetime, and a woman has given you understanding and cared for you, and no doubt, she is pretty. People have desires. It is understandable, but it is not love, not life-changing love. It is a meeting of mutual need, that is all.'

Frank stared at Georgios. 'You're wrong. It's nothing like that,' Frank insisted indignantly.

'You are shocked at my response. We are under occupation, Frank. We are at war. The devil, with all his angels, has descended upon our island and is spreading his evil. People turn to what they know. When they have lost everything, they will hold on to any scrap that offers a glimpse of what they have lost. It is not love, Frank, it is survival.'

'How can you possibly know what I feel, what she feels?'

Georgios sighed. 'You can stay here until we can arrange a time for you to leave. It will be safer than staying with this woman. She has risked her life for you. Don't ask her to continue to do so. What she has done is punishable by death. You do understand this. You have completed what you set out to do. It is time to leave.'

'And if I don't, what then?'

'You must not have much to return to, is all I can say. Was your life that bad that it is now better to risk it every single day?'

Frank's heart plummeted. Without her, he couldn't imagine a life. He had never felt like this about another. He was sure he could not breathe without knowing her touch, hearing her voice, and seeing her face every day. In return, he could offer her a life of constant worry, of looking over her shoulder, of waking each day with the knowledge it could be her last. How could he live with himself if he was the reason for her suffering, her pain? He could not imagine such things.

'I couldn't leave without seeing Alexia. I couldn't do that to her.'

Georgios was insistent that it was now too dangerous for Frank to return to Lakones, instead he would now have to wait until dawn and two of his men would escort him back to the village, using well-trodden tracks that the Germans did not know. And, Although Frank was desperate to return to Alexia, he knew Georgios words made sense.

Later that night, in the room above Georgios' taverna, Frank slept little. His mind a constant buzz of activity, he ruminated on the dreadful things he had witnessed. They visited him like an unwanted and intrusive visitor. As he peered into the darkness of the night, he saw a bright light. Alexia. When he awoke, she was the first thing to enter his head.

Chapter 38

The trek back to Lakones was uneventful. The two *andartes* said their goodbye on the outskirts of the village. The route to Alexia's house, now well known to him, Frank kept to the narrow lanes to keep himself from being seen.

When he entered her house, Alexia looked up from her breakfast and dropped the chunk of bread from her hand. He crossed the room, and she stood. She threw her arms around him. He pressed his lips to hers. He had longed to taste her lips on his and be so close. The beat of her heart pressed against him. He wanted it to last forever. When their lips parted, he stared into her dark, tear-brightened eyes, and she mesmerised him. After all, he had been through, this was the only thing that mattered, and he felt ashamed that he had even contemplated following Georgios' advice.

'I'll never leave you again, I promise.'

'Don't make promises you cannot keep.'

He peppered her forehead in light kisses. The scent from her hair caught his breath as it always did, and he breathed it, as if it were life giving air. 'I love you, Alexia.'

'You only think you do.'

He smothered her words with his lips and whispered,

'I've never been surer of anything in my life.'

'You have a life. Your life is not here.'

'I will make it here, with you.'

'You are not speaking what is the truth.'

'I will make it true.'

'You will leave and return home.'

'I am home. Wherever you are is my home.'

She smiled. 'I think you are drunk.'

'I'm drunk on you.' He placed both hands gently on her thighs. 'And I want to drink more of you.'

Later, Frank told Alexia about meeting the *andartes*, the decision to retrieve the communications equipment from the cave, and the run in with the German soldiers.

Alexia listened intently, and then she placed her hand on Frank's forearm. 'You did it, Frank. How does it feel?'

He shrugged. 'I don't know, really. I suppose I feel... empty.'

Alexia frowned. 'I don't understand. This was all you wanted. It was the reason you came to Corfu.'

'You're right, it was.'

'So, why do you feel like this, as you say, empty?'

His heart thudded inside his chest. Alexia's hair had fallen over her face and she brushed it aside with a flick, as if it was an irritant fly.

'Something has changed in me, Alexia. It flies in the face of common sense and has no trace of rationality about it, but I can't deny how I feel. I just can't.'

Alexia stared at him. 'I don't understand your words. What does this mean?'

He had to tell her. It lingered over him like a virus. If earlier he had been drunk with his feelings for her, he was now facing sobriety.

'The man I told you about, the one who owns the taverna, the one who decides what the *andartes* do and don't do in this part of Corfu, well, he wants me to leave as soon as it is possible, he wants me to leave Corfu, to leave you, but I can't. I know what he said makes sense, and it's the right thing to do. If I was caught, you would be interrogated. We would both be interrogated and probably killed, but the thought of leaving you and never seeing you again would make my life worthless. Does it make me a terrible person that I would put you at risk, so that I could be with you? Who knows how long?'

Her fingers tightened around his arm and her mouth tightened. 'I can choose to be loved, and to love, and I have chosen these things, because I want to be loved by you and I want to love you. We deserve to be happy, and if that happiness has a limited time, it is something I am prepared for. At least, I will have given the best of me to you, and anyway, there is always hope that this war will end and where there is hope, there is life.'

He touched her face and traced his finger along her cheek. 'I have nothing to offer you. I have no money, no job. I can only give you uncertainty and the prospect of never being able to live a normal life.'

'What do you think we have been doing since the Italians came and now the Germans? I can't remember what normal is anymore.'

He ran his hand through her thick hair. 'I'm sorry. It was the man in me speaking. I didn't mean to belittle what your life is like now.'

'I know you didn't.' She stroked his arm. 'All I want and all I need is here with me right now. Nothing else matters if we have each other.'

'You can speak Greek now,' she said, wide eyed. 'Although you would struggle to have a conversation that relied on detail in the language, most Germans do not speak Greek. They would not know if you were speaking it correctly or not. And your face and hands have weathered in the weeks you spent in the sun. We Greeks all look different. A German does not know a Greek from an Albanian or Italian. It is not impossible for you to pass as Greek. Each day, we will practise speaking Greek and soon you will be speaking much better.'

'I never thought of leaving the house, but what you're saying makes sense.' Frank looked hopeful. 'It would be risky, but it would mean I could escape these four walls and we could be together, just like any couple.' Then his eyes clouded. 'But what about the others in the village? They would not want me openly living amongst them. Could you imagine the consequences if I was caught by the Germans?'

'You do not understand. The sacrifices you have already made will be enough to win their silence and acceptance. Mina will also speak for you, and people know she has favour with the *andartes*. Her word will be all we need, and you will be one of us.'

It crossed Frank's mind that not everyone would be as accommodating as most of the villagers. 'The woman who has relations with the German officer, she would be a problem. I'm not sure if this is such a good idea after all. By what you have told me about her, I wouldn't remain a secret long. Maybe this is too good to be true and we're getting too far ahead of ourselves.' Frank's stomach sank.

'It is true, Theodora would be a problem, but not one that could not be persuaded to keep her silence. I hear she is opening her legs to more than one German and her affections for her officer are not as exclusive as he thinks. I'm sure she would not want him to know that not only is she doing this without his knowledge and blessing, but she is also not doing it for nothing either.'

'A German Officer would never believe you, Alexia. If anything, he would turn on you.'

'I'm not talking about me. It is true what you say. My accusations would be met with punishment first before they were investigated, but not if it were to come from someone who he already had dealings with and agreements, someone that makes him money.'

'You mean, Mina.'

Alexia smiled and nodded. 'What could Mina gain from such an accusation when there would be no reward asked for, no financial gain? In the Officer's eyes, she would be doing him a favour and lessening his embarrassment in the long run. I'm sure he would end up thanking her.'

'Mina would do this?'

'If she had to, she would do it for me, but it need not go that far.'

'What do you mean?'

'I will give Theodora the option. She can either promise her silence, or her secret will be exposed, and she knows what the outcome of that would be for her.'

Frank looked worried. 'It's not without its risk to you, as well.' He shook his head adamantly. 'No. It would be like putting yourself in front of a firing squad. We can't do this; you can't do this.'

'I am not frightened.'

'Perhaps you should be.'

'I have known Theodora all my life. We went to school together; we grew up together. If she thinks that by buying her silence, she can continue to make money, or exposing her deceit towards her officer and having everything he gives her stop and taken from her, I know which one she will choose.'

Frank looked less assured. 'It's a gamble, Alexia, and once again, you are facing the real prospect of putting yourself in danger for me. If we were to go through with this, this wouldn't be the last time you would have to put yourself in such a dreadful position.'

Alexia looked at him with determined eyes. 'Then nothing will have changed, because this is what I have done the second you set your foot over my doorway.'

'And I am reminded of that every time I look into your eyes, each and every day.

She smiled. 'So, it is agreed then.'

Chapter 39

Days passed, then finally, after Alexia had observed that several German soldiers had visited Theodora during the dark hours of several nights, Alexia slipped on her coat.

'Once I have finished with Theodora, I will see if the baker has any pies today,' Alexia said.

Frank licked his lips. 'I haven't had a pie for, oh, I don't know how long, not since I've been in Greece.'

'Before the war, the baker sold many different types of pies. They made so many delicious varieties. I used to make my own as well. My favourite is Kreatopita. It can be made with a meat filling, some leaks, feta cheese, béchamel sauce, and various herbs and seasonings, parsley, oregano, thyme.'

Frank leant back in his chair. 'My mouth is watering.'

She smiled. 'Maybe, one day, I will make you one.'

He considered this and what it meant. 'You will, I'm sure of it. When the Germans lose the war and have been chased out of Greece, we will sit at this table and have a feast.'

She grew quiet for a moment. 'Sometimes, I let myself think of such times and I'm frightened those days will never return and it will never be the same again. If and when the Germans leave, who will lead Greece out of the ruined country it has become? The Communists? The Liberals? or God forbid, the Royalists? Some say that the exiled government in Cairo will return, a puppet government under the influence of Churchill and the British.'

'Even the worst of them have to be better than fascism,' Frank said.

'None of them are without their sins. They have all committed atrocities, murdered innocent civilians and those who do not agree with their political views. Some of their followers are almost as bad as the Germans. How is that different from fascism?'

221

Frank heaved a sigh. Alexia was right. It would take more than Greece's freedom from Nazi occupation to quell the hatred and evil of the ideological factions that would fill the political vacuum this would create.

He touched Alexia's hand. Her face was drawn and tired looking. 'Be careful.'

***

The morning was cold and grey. A watery sun hung in the milk sky and as Alexia walked with her back straight and her shoulders back, she wrapped a woollen scarf around her head and neck and hoped Theodora would invite her indoors.

A jeep with two German soldiers inside trundled past her. It reminded Alexia to remain alert, but the sight of the jeep unnerved her. She was being foolish. They had become so insulated in their own thoughts and feelings towards each other that they were now blind to what was around them. She should turn around and walk back home. Regret and guilt would surely shroud her as she explained her return to Frank. And Theodora would continue to use her prestige and privilege under all their noses, safe in the protection of her officer, while Alexia's life would remain caged and tethered to chains.

As she drew closer to Theodora's house, Alexia struggled to hide the hatred in her eyes. She was asking Theodora not to let her hideaway, but to let her live and to let her love. It stuck in her throat like a rock, but for Frank's sake, she needed to be strong.

Before she knew it, she stood at Theodora's green wooden door. She drew in a deep breath and released it, then she wrapped her knuckles on the door. She waited. Part of her wanted the door to stay firmly closed and her grief and loss demanded it to open. She knocked again, harder this time. Four knocks in rapid succession.

'Who is it? I'm not expecting anyone.'

'Theodora, it's me, Alexia.'

Silence. Alexia lifted her chin. 'I need to speak with you.'

Again, a deafening silence.

'I'll keep knocking on this door until you open it. I'd like a few minutes of your time. If it is inconvenient, tell me a time when it is not, and I'll come back.'

A key turned in the lock and the door opened, just enough for Alexia to see Theodora's surprise widen her eyes.

Theodora stared at her. 'This is unusual, to say the least. I get very few uninvited visitors these days, but you!'

'Is it a wonder?' Alexia regretted the words the second they left her mouth. 'I'm sorry. There was no need for that. I apologise.'

'Well, there's another thing I wasn't expecting, an apology. Two surprises in the space of a minute. My reputation must be improving amongst the high and mighty.'

'I've not come to argue or pick a fight with you.'

'Then why have you come?'

Alexia shuffled on her feet, rubbing her hands together. Someone might see her.

She detected movement behind Theodora, a man buttoning his tunic, a soldier. Alexia flinched at the sound of his voice. He said something in German and Theodora replied. Alexia heard a door open and then close at the rear of the house.

Throughout it all, Theodora's eyes did not leave Alexia's face. 'You haven't answered my question.'

'Aren't you going to ask me in, since your gentleman has left?'

Theodora opened the door and waved her inside. 'You'd better come in.'

Alexia glanced left and right, then entered the house. Theodora closed the door firmly, turning the key.

Alexia stared at the lock.

'Don't worry, it's a habit of mine,' Theodora said as she directed her inside.

Alexia was unsure what she felt, apprehensive or relieved now that she was inside.

Compared to her house, this was a palace decorated with Nazi money and the best furniture from the grandest shops in Corfu town.

'Can I get you a drink?'

'I'm fine.' Alexia removed her scarf.

'Then you won't mind if I do.'

'It's your house.'

The beginnings of a smile appeared at the corner of Theodora's mouth as she poured a large brandy into a crystal glass. Alexia imagined the German officer drinking from the same glass. Her stomach soured.

An unspoken tension sat between them. Theodora offered Alexia a cigarette, and she accepted it.

'Please, sit. Take the weight of your feet, although there's not much left of you these days, Alexia.'

It took all her resolve to ignore the remark. Instead, she peered past Theodora to a door half opened, enough for Alexia to see an unmade bed.

Alexia sat in a chair, sinking into its fine leather upholstery. Across from her, Theodora sat crossed legged, then sipped her drink. Her lips pursed as she peered suspiciously at Alexia from over the rim.

'How is Mina these days?' Theodora asked.

'She is fine.'

'I know she has dealings with Walter. He doesn't disclose much, but she profits from him. We are similar in that respect.'

'I don't think so.'

'Stop the pretence!'

'What you do and what Mina is forced to do are two completely different things. Mina has no choice in the matter. Your German Officer takes her profit for himself and gives her the scraps that are left. He is a gangster in a uniform.'

'I don't want to argue with you, Alexia. My point is, we both benefit financially from the Germans. It is a business arrangement, nothing else.'

'Listen to yourself. You talk as if you are in control of all of this.' She waved her hand. 'What you seem to forget is that it can be taken from you at any time. If your officer gets tired of you, or if you displease him, you would be in the same position as the rest of us. Your world is like mine; it is not a safe place to be. All of this is a charade. It's not real. You are vulnerable, Theodora. You are his puppet on a string, and your Walter can cut the string whenever he pleases.' *God, I've gone too far. I need to learn to shut my mouth.*

'Well, this is very civilised.' Theodora sniffed. 'You could never hold that tongue of yours, could you, Alexia?'

'You always seemed to bring out the worst in me. Even as children, we never agreed on much.'

'I always thought that was the attraction between us. Opposites attract and all of that. We always remained friends.'

'Until we grew up. We're nothing like each other, Theodora.' It should have sounded impartial, but it came out as an allegation.

'We are survivors, both of us. That makes us allies in a way. I'd say we've more in common than you'd like to think or would admit.'

Alexia shifted in her chair. Theodora's hair shined and curled in ringlets around her face and high cheekbones, falling effortlessly down her delicate neck and along her shoulders. And it was not a play of light that made her skin glow healthfully, her painted lips shimmer. When Theodora drew on her cigarette, Alexia could not help but notice the slender wrist, the manicured fingernails, unblemished and long. Her dress was not worn nor threaded at the seams. It hung on her like a second layer of skin, perfectly cut with fine, precise stitching accentuating her curves and the quality of the fabric.

There was a world of a difference between them, but despite Theodora's refinery, Alexia did not feel inadequate or intimidated. Instead, she felt sorry for Theodora, and her initial dislike retreated. Theodora was lonely. She was a pawn to be used and discarded; she was a plaything for the Germans.

At that moment, she sensed a warm glow inside her. The difference between them was she was loved, and she loved Frank. She was doing this for him, as well as for herself.

'Now that the pleasantries are over, what do you want, Alexia?'

Alexia swallowed and lifted her shoulders. 'Your silence. I need your silence.'

Theodora drew heavily on her cigarette and blew a cloud of smoke towards Alexia. 'For once, I'm lost for words, but intrigued all the same.' She took a sip of her brandy.

'If I could, I wouldn't have you involved in this, but I have no choice.'

'Involved in what?' For the first time, Theodora's confidence deserted her.

The seed of doubt stirred inside Alexia, but she could not turn back now. She had committed herself. She had gone too far.

Once Alexia explained the reason for her visit, she could hear her heartbeat inside her chest and feel the dampness of her palms.

Theodora smiled. 'I knew you were hiding something... someone. And now you want to have your cake and eat it. I can understand why. You are lonely since your husband died. Is it love, Alexia? Or is it just infatuation? It's a gamble, definitely. A very dangerous one. You have guts, I'll give you that, and I admire your loyalty towards this man.' She took a sip of her drink. 'But it's not enough?' Theodora said dryly.

Alexia felt intimidated, but she expected this.

'He is a stranger no more to me. I love him. Everyone deserves to be happy, even you, Theodora.'

Theodora smiled at the desperation in Alexia's voice. 'What's in it for me? I won't give my silence for nothing; you'll have to buy it. Oh, wait a minute, let me rephrase that. I know you can't, so Mina will have to buy it.'

If she was gambling, then Alexia was about to play her trump card. The weight of her responsibility bared down on her.

'I don't think that's an option, especially for Mina. You see, Theodora, you've been reckless. You've slept with any German that would pay you for the pleasure. It is very short-sighted of you.'

'What do you mean?'

'Mina might be old, but her olive harvests have been very profitable for your German Officer.'

'His name is Walter.'

'You see, Mina makes him money, where you, well look around you, you drain him of money, with your clothes, your makeup, and your fine furnishings. You are dispensable, where Mina isn't. So, who is he going to believe, someone he has to pay for pleasure or someone who makes him money?'

'He is not a man you can convince very easily.'

'He won't need convincing. I'm surprised he hasn't already found out what you've been doing behind his back.'

'What if I tell Walter you're harbouring an enemy of Germany? That's punishable by death.'

'You could, but your officer will still be told that you are not as exclusive as he thought you were. Imagine his embarrassment. He would have to set an example.'

'That's blackmail, you bitch.'

Theodora sprung to her feet. She grabbed Alexia by the arm and wrenched her from the chair. Alexia screamed as Theodora grabbed a handful of hair, dragging Alexia across the tiled floor. Alexia clawed

Theodora's arms, as her hair yanked from its roots, tore a searing pain across her scalp.

The air rushed from her lungs. Theodora's foot thumped into her again and again. Alexia crawled into a ball and pleaded for Theodora to stop.

Possessed with rage, and deaf to Alexia's pleas, another barrage of kicks followed.

Desperately, Alexia's hand clawed and grasped, finally clamping around Theodora's ankle. With an adrenalin fuelled effort, she twisted and pulled. Tumbling backwards, Theodora cried out in frustration, releasing tendrils of hair from a weakening grip. She collapsed in an awkward heap.

Alexia crawled to her hands and knees, staggering to her feet, gasping painfully, a piercing pain shooting along her ribs. When Alexia turned, to her horror, Theodora was already on her feet and lunging at her, a flash of silver in her hand. The blade from a kitchen knife sliced through the air, millimetres from Alexia's face.

Alexia's heart pumped wildly, the blood in her veins a torrential river. Theodora lunged forward again. Alexia stumbled backwards and toppled to the floor, hitting it hard. Theodora jumped on top of Alexia, her legs straddling her. With two hands gripping the handle, Theodora plunged the knife towards Alexia's face. Alexia whipped her head sideways. The blade stabbed the tiled floor.

The knife thrusted towards Alexia again. She grabbed Theodora's wrists, the point of the blade scraping her eyelashes.

Her eyes wide, Theodora leaned her weight into Alexia's grip. Her hands trembling and weakening, Alexia screeched, the point of the blade so close it blurred in her vision.

Theodora drove her weight through the handle of the knife, grunting with exertion, a slither of saliva dangling from her mouth.

She was losing her grip. She would not let this happen. This was not how it would end. She would not die here.

With a summoning strength from deep within her, she dug her nails into Theodora's forearm. Warm, wet blood trailed between her fingers.

Theodora howled in pain and released Alexia's hands.

Alexia heaved her hips, twisting her body, and with all the force she could muster, yanked Theodora's arms from her. Theodora collapsed onto the tiles. A sickening thud gored the air.

With Theodora lying on her back motionless, a sticky dark mass oozed from her hair and staining the tiles. Alexia covered her mouth with a trembling hand as Theodora moaned, a whisper that faded and stopped deep in her throat. Alexia scrambled to her. Frantically, she felt for a pulse, and with widened eyes, she urged it to beat, but there was none.

Suddenly doused in fragility and fear, Alexia lay the lifeless hand over Theodora's chest. She sat slumped and terrified within the stillness and silence that fell around her.

***

She could make no sense of what had just happened. Her hands trembled, her mind froze, and eventually shut down. She had no idea how long she had been sitting with her knees to her chin, her arms wrapped around her legs, staring, she registered nothing.

Eventually, Alexia hauled herself to her feet.

She was weak at the knees. Her brain seemed to float and hit the sides of her skull. She thought she was going to faint. She leaned on the table and closed her eyes to stop the relentless spinning of the kitchen around her. She inhaled deeply, wishing the weightlessness in her head to stop.

When she opened her eyes, she turned her head and looked at Theodora's body. A shiver ran through her. Theodora's eyes stared at the ceiling and her blood seeped over the floor like a river.

'Why, Theodora? Why did you do this?'

She sudden anger took shape in her stomach. She had to get out of this house.

Chapter 40

'Thank God you're back. I've been worried sick. I thought something had happened to you.'

Alexia slipped off her coat and let it fall to the floor. In the light, Frank could see her eyes flushed red and glazed with tears. Alexia buried her face in her hands and her shoulders heaved. Her sobs filled the house.

'What is it? What's happened?' Then he saw the dried blood on her fingers. 'My God! You're bleeding.'

'She's dead.'

'Theodora?'

'She tried to kill me with a knife. I can't believe it. I killed her. She's lying dead on the floor.'

'Did anyone see you?'

'I don't know.'

He looked at her intently and squeezed her hand. 'Think, Alexia.'

'There was a soldier when I arrived, but he left before I went in the house. He did not see me.'

'Are you sure?'

'I think so.'

'You need to be sure.'

'He did not see me.'

'Good. You need to wash your hands.'

He guided her to the kitchen, where a pot was heating over the fire. He poured the water into a basin and with a brush, scrubbed her hands.

Alexia starred at her hands as if they were not her own as Frank dried them with a towel.

'She will be found soon. Either by her next customer, a soldier, or worse still, her German officer.'

231

'I killed her.' She stumbled over her words. 'She came at me with a knife.'

It was like a bomb had detonated in her mind, and she was shell-shocked. Frank took her hand and gently wrapped his around her shoulder. He guided her upstairs to the bedroom. They crossed the room. Her shoes scuffed the floorboards. Frank slid back the sheets and as he gently laid her on the bed, Alexia flinched and held her side. He ran his hand along her ribs, applying a little pressure with his fingertips. She flinched again at his touch. He apologised.

'I think you've broken some ribs.'

Carefully, he removed each shoe. He lay beside her, and the bed creaked with his weight. He ran his fingers through her thick hair. Her long, dark eyelashes blinked twice. Her eyes closed, welcoming the darkness.

He brushed Alexia's hair from her face. There were two faint wrinkles at the corner of her eye, only visible when close to her face.

How close he had come to losing her. He could not imagine life without her.

Frank couldn't be sure, but he assumed Theodora was dead. What would happen now? He was unsure. If Alexia was seen leaving Theodora's house, she would be implicated in her death. It was common knowledge soldiers visited Theodora, anyone of them could be a suspect. Either way, a storm was coming, and they had no shelter. He was tired of running.

Alexia slept late in the afternoon. When she awoke, she refused to eat. She had little appetite, and the thought of eating made her stomach wrench. She complained of a headache. Her scalp was raw, burning, and the pain from her ribs was sharp and jagged whenever she moved.

'If you feel a sneeze coming on, you'll have to pinch your nose to stop it, otherwise those ribs will hurt even more.'

Alexia whispered. 'I don't know about my nose, but I could do with a cigarette.'

Frank reached for the packet, took one out, lit it and handed it to her. The end of the cigarette glowed red as she drew on it heavily and blew smoke into the air, satisfying her craving.

Frank looked at her, concerned. 'A doctor friend of mine said it was better to let broken ribs heal on their own without binding them up in a bandage. Though you'll need pain relief.'

'I'm sure Mina will have something.'

The mention of her name felt like Mina was already in the room with them.

'We'll have to tell her.'

Alexia nodded in agreement. She stubbed out her cigarette with a long, slow sigh. 'I only have myself to blame. You warned me and I did not listen. What have I done?'

Frank leaned towards her and put his lips to hers. She flinched slightly, a little whimper escaping her.

'I'm sorry. I didn't mean to hurt you.'

She placed her hand on the nape of his neck and kissed him back, a slow, lingering kiss. When their lips parted, Frank sighed and nestled his forehead against hers, looking longingly into her eyes. 'I'm never going to let you out of my sight again.'

There was a slight hesitation. 'Don't make promises you cannot keep.'

Chapter 41

Instead of his usual driver, discretely parked out of sight, Captain Waldheim's personal car screeched to an abrupt stop in front of Theodora's house. Captain Waldheim and two studious SS officers were greeted by a soldier with the familiar Nazi salute and stomped into the house.

Mina observed their arrival as she hobbled past the *Kafenion* on her way to Alexia's house. It did not escape the attention of the old men, coffee in one hand and a cigarette in the other, strategizing and contemplating their next move on the backgammon board.

Mina grunted. 'I saw SS officers and Waldheim going into Theodora's house. I wonder what's going on?'

Alexia felt a jolt in her stomach.

Frank got up and pulled a chair from the table. Mina leaned her hand on the table and lowered herself with a sigh without removing her coat. 'What's that stupid girl got herself involved with now?'

'She's dead,' Alexia said bluntly.

'What!'

Alexia's eyes stung. 'I killed her.'

Mina's mouth fell open.

Alexia bit her lip. 'She knew I was hiding someone. She wanted money to keep quiet. I threatened her by saying we'd tell her officer half of his men had been in her bed. She went crazy, like an animal. I was only trying to stop her. She had a knife... she tried to kill me. When she hit her head, I knew she was dead. There was so much blood.'

Mina reached over and squeezed Alexia's hand. 'Ahh, Panagia mou!' Mina crossed herself. 'If there was ever a time to be strong, it's now. It was an accident. You can't change what has happened.'

Mina scratched her head. 'Did anyone see you?'

'I don't think so.'

'That's not good enough. You could have been seen.' Mina removed her headscarf.

A fire started in Alexia's stomach.

Mina looked at Alexia. 'What is it?'

'My scarf! I left my scarf.'

'Waldheim will know it's not Theodora's scarf.' Mina frowned.

Frank could not understand every word, but he got the gist of it, and he knew by their reaction's events had taken a turn for the worst.

'What is it, Alexia?'

'I can't believe I've been so careless. My scarf is still in Theodora's house. They will find it.'

Frank's stomach sank. 'But it's just a scarf.'

'Theodora wouldn't be seen dead in one like that.' Her choice of word was not lost on her.

'It doesn't implicate you.'

'It does if I was seen wearing it.'

'Who would come forward with that kind of information?'

'No one, maybe. But two soldiers passed me when I was walking to her house.'

'Speak Greek,' Mina requested.

Once Alexia told Mina about the possibility of being seen by the soldiers, Mina's mouth dropped.

'If they did see you and this information got back to Waldheim, it would only be a matter of time before you were arrested. You can't stay. You'll have to leave.' Her eyes were hard.

'It would only prove my guilt.'

'What choice do you have?'

'Where would I go?'

'I have a friend in Corfu Town. There is a small apartment above her shop that hasn't been lived in for some time. If I offer her rent, I'm sure she would be happy for you to stay there. She is discrete. She won't ask any questions.'

Alexia shook her head. 'No. It's unthinkable.'

'It won't be forever, but you'll have to go tonight.'

'This is my home. I won't be forced to leave.'

'And it will still be here when you return. Don't worry, I will check the house every day,' she assured Alexia in a gentle voice.

Frank tried to guess the meaning of their words. He had detected a trace of panic in Alexia's voice. Her hands arched and sliced through the air as if electricity ran through them. Alexia looked at Mina and then Frank.

'We have to leave,' she told him.

Chapter 42

Alexia packed her only suitcase. It didn't take long to pack clothes for both of them in the small bag. She wore her brown winter coat that fell to just below her knees, and black leather shoes she had polished the night before. Frank's jacket hung on him loosely. He tied a belt around his trousers to stop them from sagging and falling from his waist. He was grateful he and Stathis shared similar sized feet as the boots slipped on perfectly. Alexia suggested he wear a cap to deflect attention from his face. It made him look older and when she reached out and tipped the peak over his forehead; she managed a small smile despite her heavy heart.

'Are you ready?'

Alexia sighed heavily. 'No, but if I don't go now, I never will.'

Frank checked his watch. 'The truck should arrive in ten minutes. It will only stop for a minute, then move off again. We should get going.'

Alexia took one last look around her house. 'I have many memories within these walls, recently more good ones than bad. It has finally started to feel a real home.'

'This place is just four walls with a roof. It's the memories you've made inside it that make it a home, and you can take those memories with you wherever you go.'

Alexia touched his face with her hand. She felt a sadness around her, but also relief. She was not doing this on her own. She remembered what it used to be like, alone and guarded, lost in her own mind, in her fear and loneliness and the turmoil of her thoughts. All that had changed now. Frank had given her hope. She never thought she would ever have the capacity to love again, to connect intimately with another, not just physical, but a connection of minds that were not afraid to expose their innermost thoughts and feelings. In such a brief space of time, he had made her laugh again. She found she could smile at him and even experience a joy in sharing the little pleasures and orientations of her life. It was a marvel to her. His presence sustained her in a newfound happiness in a fragile world.

They hurried along one lane and down another as far as they could go and waited. Alexia touched his hand, and Frank wrapped his fingers around hers and tightened his hold as he stared along the main road through the village.

'Here it comes.' There was a tension in his voice that he failed to hide. 'We'll wait here until it stops.'

Alexia moved from one foot to the other, staring at the truck as it progressed towards them. The truck squealed to a stop, its engine still running. Frank scanned around the street, along the row of houses and shopfronts with their closed shutters. The *kafenion* tables sat empty except for a scruffy dog that lay sleeping spread legged under one.

The truck stopped and the driver bit into an apple, the signal they awaited. When Frank and Alexia approached him, they were to whisper the agreed password.

Still holding her hand and with the suitcase in the other, and his satchel with his sketchpads and pencils slung around his neck, they left the relative safety of the lane and walked steadily towards the truck.

Although it was cold, under his jacket, Frank's shirt was damp with sweat. He looked up towards the driver, who had a prodigious walrus moustache and thick beard.

'Niki.'

'Victory is at hand,' the driver replied encouragingly. 'Throw the suitcase in the back and get in.'

They did as instructed.

As the driver shifted gears, Frank noticed a rifle balancing between his legs. Still munching on his apple, the driver said, 'Georgios was going to personally drive you, but he has other business to take care of.'

'He has done enough already. Thank him for me, would you?'

Mina had gotten word to Georgios about the urgency of the situation, and to Frank's relief, Georgios agreed to help them travel to Corfu Town

Soon, the truck hurtled down the narrow road, its steep bends and turns, demanded the full attention of the driver.

'I'm Frank and this is Alexia.'

The driver nodded. 'Thalássios íppos.'

Alexia grinned.

'It's not my real name. When we join the resistance, we pick a *nom de guerre*. I'm called the walrus.'

Frank smiled. 'Ah, the moustache.'

'Before the war, I lived in America, but came back to liberate us from the fascists. First the Italians and now the Nazis.'

'That's why your English is so good.'

'It is helpful. I can interpret for British agents when needed. It is like a gun. It is a weapon in our struggle.'

'And Georgios, that is not his real name,' Frank asked.

'Saint George, England's patron saint, the slayer of dragons,' the driver said. 'The Nazis being the dragon.'

'How far will you take us?' Alexia asked, as the streets in the Corfu Town were narrow and unsuitable for traffic.

'I can drop you off just outside the town. Any further could raise unwanted attention.'

'We're grateful.'

'Do you have an address?'

'I do.' She told him the address.

'Ah! It is in the Spilia district of the town. I will take you to the port. From there, it's only a short walk.'

The old area of Corfu Town was a warren of cobbled lanes, narrow streets, and squares. It had the presence of a neo-classical town with mainly a Venetian influence, although French and British architecture were also prevalent due to its history of occupation. Shops and cafes traded their wares at street level. Above, another two floors, sometimes three, were situated apartments and homes decorated with shutters and iron railing balconies.

On 14 September 1943, the Luftwaffe bombed and extensively damaged the Corfu Town. The bombing raids destroyed buildings, houses, churches, the Ionian Parliament, the market, the hotel Bella Venezia, the municipal theatre and library, buildings in the old Citadel and the Jewish quarter Evraiki. They reduced almost a quarter of the town to rubble. Many residents had died, and the living continued to suffer daily humiliation under German occupation.

At the port, Frank and Alexia said their farewells to the walrus and then cautiously made their way along arterial lanes, bustling with townsfolk and soldiers, relaxing and sitting outside cafes.

Frank was exposed and vulnerable. Both were also etched on Alexia's face. They'd entered a different universe than the one they had inhabited. Being so close to the soldiers unnerved Frank. They had left Lakones to escape the attention of the Nazis, and here they were just a few feet from soldiers, sitting outside, enjoying drinks, conversing, and laughing. Frank was entrapped, like he had unknowingly wandered into the lion's den. His eyes darted from one group of soldiers to the next, but the more he looked around, he realised he was not the object of their attention. In fact, he was invisible to them; he passed them without even a turn of a head, a curious glance, or even a note of interest. He released his breath. Maybe this was going to work after all. Here they could live inconspicuously, unseen in the shadows and fade into obscurity.

'Here it is,' Alexia announced, glancing at the address scribbled by Mina on the piece of paper she held in her hand.

An awning shaded wooden boxes sparsely filled with fruit and vegetables, tomatoes, melons, pulses, and oil. A yellow light emitted from inside the shop, and it was like a beacon as they both entered it.

An older woman, in her fifties and fair-haired, sat behind the counter reading a paper. She looked up from her reading and grinned at them, and Frank found himself smiling slightly, too.

Alexia spoke to the woman in Greek and Frank could detect by her relaxed demeanour she was expecting them.

She stood up and walked around the counter, gesturing for them to follow. She took them into the rear of the shop, through a door, and up a flight of stairs. She unlocked a green wooden door that led into a narrow hallway and opened into a spacious room with a small kitchen area, a sturdy wooden table with two chairs, and a bed and wardrobe at the far end. Two large windows bathed the room in vivid sunlight.

Frank placed the suitcase that held all they had on the wooden floorboards and took in his surroundings while Alexia and the woman spoke some more, and as she left; she handed Alexia a door key.

Alexia glanced around the room. She opened drawers and cupboards, checked their contents with a critical eye, bounced gently on the bed mattress, testing the springs, and looked out of the window to the view of the street below.

Frank came over to her slowly and wrapped his arms gently around her shrinking waist, trying not to startle her or disturb her from her contemplation. She turned to look at him and her eyes searched his. He, in turn watched her avidly. She deserved so much more than this life. He wished with all his heart he could take her from this room, this country, this war, to Edinburgh, and his home. He recognised the pangs of homesickness stabbing him, but beneath it all, it was with a fervent consolation that his time spent in this room and in this town would be precious to him.

Chapter 43

In the weeks and months that passed, winter sucked the light from the sky and the sun hung behind watery clouds. Fear had loomed over them, a constant presence whenever there was an unexpected knock at the door, when they went outside to buy food or sit in a café. In an unexpected way, their exile had brought them freedom. Unlike the confines of Lakones, there were no restrictions to their expression and expectations of a couple in love.

Mina continued to send them money and although he was grateful, and both Frank and Alexia relied on her benevolence, it dented his sense of worth. Alexia helped their landlady, Melina, in her shop most mornings. At first, she was the subject of curiosity amongst the regular customers. Alexia prepared a short speech she repeated each time a customer asked about her.

She had come to live in the apartment above the shop as her house and village on the mainland had been razed by the Nazi and Melina, an old friend of the family, offered her refuge.

It was successful in haltering further enquiries and Melina was happy to support the protective pretence.

One day, they left the apartment and sauntered along crisscrossed alleyways in the Jewish Quarter. Heading along Réale Street towards Solomou Street and Palaiologou Street. They came into Velisariou Street, where La Scuola Greca, the only surviving synagogue of four, remained. The others bombed by the Germans. Along the way, the heart-warming smells of cooked food drifting from the opened windows of faded multistorey houses tantalised their taste buds.

'This is it,' Alexia said, surveying the houses. 'I think it's on the third floor.'

They climbed the stairwell, stepping over children playing, and a dog stretched out asleep across an entire step.

Alexia stopped at a door and turned to Frank. 'I hope they are home.'

'You should have warned them we were coming.'

'I wanted it to be a surprise.'

Alexia knocked on the door. When it finally opened, a bearded middle-aged man, wearing a black waistcoat and white shirt, stared at them with small, rounded eyes.

'Can I help you?' He glanced over Alexia's shoulder towards the children.

'You don't recognise me, do you?'

A hint of bewilderment crossed his face. 'No, I'm afraid I don't. should I?'

'Isaac, it's me, Alexia.'

He stared at her and as if a light had suddenly been switched on. His face brightened.

His hands covered his mouth. 'Alexia, it's you. My God, I can't believe it. Look at you, you're a woman.'

'I am,' she confirmed with a grin.

With opened arms Isaac hugged her so tightly, she thought she might need to gasp for air. When he finally stepped back, he had tears in his eyes.

'Where are my manners? Come in, please come in?' Isaac ushered them inside. He regarded her with a wide smile on his face. 'I can't believe you are standing in my house. This calls for a celebration. I have some wine in the kitchen. Please sit.'

When he returned, he placed three glasses on a table and poured the wine.

'Psalms 104:15 talks of wine as *"Gladdening the human heart,"* and my heart has never been this happy for a very long time.' Isaac raised his glass and, smiling broadly, proclaimed, 'L'chaim.' (*To life*).

He sat opposite them. 'And who is this young man?'

'His name is Frank. He's Scottish. It is a long story, but we've had to leave Lakones for a while.'

Isaac glanced at Frank. A look of fear started to grow over Isaac's face. She had seen it many times on the faces of others.

'If you feel uncomfortable, we can leave.'

Isaac raised his hand in protest. 'Not at all. Everyone is welcome in my house.'

They had been speaking in Greek, and Isaac turned to Frank and asked in English. 'Do you speak Greek, Frank?'

'A little. I get by, but my Greek is not as good as Alexia's English.'

'Then I'll speak in English, that way it will be less complicated.'

He sat back in his chair. Behind him, a vast array of books sat on a bookshelf, running from wall to wall. Isaac saw Frank gaze at them. 'It's my life's collection. Some of my books are very rare, while others are precious just to me. Do you read Frank?'

'I'm afraid it's been a long time since I read a book.'

Alexia placed her hand over Frank's. 'Frank is an artist.'

'That's wonderful.' Isaac said in admiration. 'I've always wanted to paint, but unfortunately, what I envisaged in my mind never translated to the canvas. It was never going to be my forte, I'm afraid.' He took a sip of wine. 'How long has it been since we saw each other?'

'At my mother and father's funeral.'

'How time slips by so quickly. I miss them both.'

A display of family photographs sat neatly on a dark wooden cabinet. Alexia saw a particular one that looked quite recent, a family portrait of Isaac, his wife Hadassa, and daughter,

Isaac caught her eye, and his face tightened. 'Hadassa passed away four years ago.'

Alexia's heart sank. 'I'm sorry.'

'She had been ill for some time. In the end, it was quick, which was a blessing. At least she did not have to witness the terrible things that have happened to us... to us all.'

'I know. And Eliora. How is she?'

Isaac smiled sadly. 'As far as I know, she is still in Athens. She is married now and has a child, a daughter. You will have passed her on the stairs outside.'

'Her daughter?' Alexia asked, perplexed.

Suddenly, Isaac looked tired. 'Athens is not safe for anyone, but especially in you are Jewish. Eliora thought they had escaped the worse. They had heard of the deportations from Salonika. Then it all changed.' Isaac scratched his hands. 'The Jewish community in Athens was forced, under the threat of being shot, to register with the authorities and report every day to them. Many refused to register, their properties were taken from them, and their belongings and furniture sold. Hundreds, maybe even a thousand, have already been deported at gunpoint and taken by trains to camps.' His lips trembled. 'Eliora sent her daughter, Amalia, to me, thinking it would be safer here than to stay in Athens. I have had no contact with her since then. I have heard terrible stories of what has happened. It is not just in Athens, this is happening. All over the mainland, we are being persecuted and taken from our homes to these camps. The Nazis want to extinguish us like flies. These people are not human. Even here, in Corfu Town, there has been a change. We must register as well. We have lost our jobs. I am not allowed to teach anymore, and our children are not allowed to go to school. I fear the worst.' As he spoke, Isaac's face turned pale.

'I don't know what to say,' Alexia gasped.

'You don't have to say anything. We are all suffering. Greece is suffering.'

They sat in solemn silence, staring at their feet.

Then finally, Isaac said. 'Enough of me. Tell me about you two.'

Apprehensively, Frank glanced at Alexia.

'It is alright. Isaac is practically family.'

Frank began at the beginning and described the events that led him to his encounter with the mistrusting and interrogative Alexia. Isaac, smiling at that part, raised his eyebrows and sipped his wine. He could hear the tenderness in Frank's voice whenever he mentioned Alexia's name. And then his face took on a more serious look. He listened intently, his eyes saddened, his mouth set.

As Frank spoke, Alexia tugged at the material of her dress.

When Frank had finished, Isaac tried to formulate a response, but in the end, he said simply, 'When will it end?'

Frank noticed a scruffy boy he had never seen before appear in their street, almost daily. At first, Frank paid little attention to him, but as the days progressed, his intuition bothered him, like an itch he had to scratch. He began to pay attention to the boy and watch him closely whenever he appeared. He couldn't put his finger on it, but it felt like he was being watched. The boy would wander from shop to shop, always close to their apartment. At times, he would sit on steps and offer passers-by a begging bowl. Other times, when Frank passed him, he discerned the boy's eyes burn into him, but when Frank turned towards him, the boy always averted his eyes. Frank had considered approaching him, but feared his Greek, although much improved, would hinder any positive results from what would need to be a mild but probing interrogation.

One morning, he decided to mention the boy to Alexia when she was getting ready to work in the shop.

'He will just be a boy like many others who need to beg for money,' she said while combing her hair. 'For all you know, his parents could be dead or ill. Who's to say he even has a roof over his head?'

'I would have thought the same, but there's something different about him,' Frank said. 'I can't put my finger on it. He definitely has an agenda.'

'Why don't I ask Melina if she knows him? If he turns up this morning, you can point him out to her.'

Frank went to the window and gazed down into the narrow street. 'That's a good idea.'

She stood then. 'She might know who he is.'

'Yes. That would be helpful.'

'I better go.'

Frank crossed the room and circled her in his arms. He traced his finger up and down her spine and felt the weight of her hair in his hand. Frank kissed her forehead, and they parted reluctantly.

'I should go.'

'What if I don't want you to go?'

'I'm only downstairs.'

'I know, but you wouldn't be with me.'

'True, but I'd be earning a handful of Drachma to feed us.'

'Be careful.'

Alexia waved him away. 'I always am.'

Frank observed him from the protection of his apartment. He watched the boy sit on the stone steps next to the haberdashery shop. His posture bent, resting elbows on knees, his chin cradled in the cup of his hands. The boy looked disinterested in his surroundings, staring into space. But every now and again, he twiddled his thumbs, and his eyes darted back and forth.

Suddenly, the boy glanced up towards the window. Instinctively, Frank sank into the room, a dark figure in the shadows.

He still had a good view of the boy. The boy's gaze slid from the apartment. Something was different about the boy today. It nudged at Frank like an impatient child. His face was older, more serious looking. No, it was more than that... apprehension, anguish even. Frank's stomach curdled as he stroked the bristles on his chin.

Alexia peered from behind the counter, out of the window and into the narrow street. 'I think that's him there, Melina, the boy I told you about.'

Melina tore herself from packing a shelf and looked over Alexia's shoulder.'

'Where?'

'Sitting on the steps. Look, the one without shoes.'

'Ah, I see him now.'

'Well, do you know him? Have you seen him before?' Alexia said impatiently.

Melina shook her head. 'He doesn't look familiar.' Her expression changed. 'Oh! He's pointing towards the apartment and look, soldiers are coming.'

Alexia's hands shot to her mouth, and she cried out in horror. She always feared this day could come, but recently, as time slipped by, she'd let herself believe they were finally safe, camouflaged in a coat of ordinariness, and conceived by a simple existence.

The talons of panic grabbed her. She brushed past Melina and clutching a bread knife from the countertop; she barred the door to the stairs.

'Alexia! What are you doing?' dread cracked Melina's voice.

When the soldiers entered the shop, Alexia raised the knife in front of her. The soldier who entered the shop first stopped abruptly. His eyes narrowed, his smile like a grimace. 'Get out of the way, or I will walk through you.'

Alexia peered at him defiantly, every inch of her body rising to fill the door.

'Have it your way.' He raised his rifle and struck her with the butt. Alexia screamed as she crashed into the counter. Melina covered her mouth with her hands as the soldiers bypassed them, their boots heavy on the stairs.

Alexia heard the crack of splintered wood and imagined the door to the apartment dangling from its hinges. A trail of blood stain her skin from her forehead and down the curve of her eye socket. Her eyes blurred with the searing pain across her skull, and when the darkness fell, she tried to concentrate on the pinprick of light, but like quicksand, it engulfed her.

It happened so fast. He saw the group of German soldiers round the corner, where the church of Saint Anthony and Andrew stood. Locals looked on, sensing the air had changed. It was not unusual to see soldiers in the streets, but these soldiers were studious in their manner, their hands fixed around rifles, their expressions intent and purposeful. When they reached the boy, still sitting, there was a fleeting exchange of looks. The boy raised his hand, pointing upwards towards the apartment.

Frank cursed out loud, scampering from the window. He was trapped and there was only one exit. His heart pounded. He scurried across the room, and reaching for the bed, he lifted the corner of the mattress, grasping the handle of the handgun.

For a frantic second, he thought of jumping from the window. He would surely injure himself, or at worse, break an ankle, maybe both, and anyway, there would be a sentry outside the shop on the street.

From downstairs, Frank heard an anguished cry and then the thudding of boots echoing in the stairwell. He swivelled, his hands raised, clasping the gun, his eyes burning into the door.

He could kill one or two before the inevitable, but with the gun in his hand, he was already dead.

His hands trembled and his arms ached. He swallowed. Frank knew what awaited him. He had heard the stories of the brutality and horror of the interrogations and torture.

If he stayed alive, there would always be hope. If he could still breathe, he would find his way back to Alexia. Her face would sustain him, even in the darkest moments. He opened his hands, and the handgun fell from his grasp, clattering to the floor.

Chapter 44

He sat on a chair in the middle of a windowless room that reeked of stale urine and sweat. Around him, the stone walls secreted water like droplets of rain. His hands and feet were bound with rope that tore into his flesh and burned in searing pain with the slightest movement. The previous occupant's blood and bodily fluids pooled at Frank's feet in puddles of death. Outside in the corridor, the stamp of boot heels echoed sharply on the stone floor. The metallic creak of an opening door brought piercing screams and terrified cries.

An officer, his Gestapo uniform immaculate and his hair swept back from his forehead, took a cigarette from a silver case, and lit it, blowing the smoke over Frank's face.

He grinned. 'I would offer you one, but you seem to have your hands tied.' The officer said in English.

The soldier behind Frank yanked his hair, forcing Frank's head back so that he looked at the officer.

'Your name?' the officer asked.

Frank remained silent.

The soldier released the handful of hair from his grasp, and as he moved around to face Frank, his fist whipped Frank's head sideways. The bitter metallic taste of blood saturated his mouth.

'It will be less painful if you answer my questions. Let's start again. What is your name?'

Frank knew it would be futile to resist. 'Frank Hart.'

'Tell me your regiment, rank and serial number.'

'I'm not a soldier.'

The knuckles smacked into Frank's face, blood spurting from his mouth and oozing down his chin.

'It's simple. You tell me what I want to know, and the pain stops. Tell me what your regiment and rank are?'

'I've told you, I'm not a soldier.' Frank braced himself.

It felt like a hammer. The blow smashed into his jaw.

'Then you are a spy?'

Frank shook his head. 'No.' He spat blood from his mouth.

The officer stared at Frank, and he took a long thoughtful draw on his cigarette. 'So, if you are not a soldier, or a spy, then why are you in Corfu?'

Frank closed his eyes. His heart pounded in his chest. He tried to summon an image of Alexia, the shape and colour of her eyes, the curve of her lips, the sound of her voice and the touch of her hand. Each blow had been a brick that built a wall in his mind, and now she was lost to him.

His stomach was hollow, and he swallowed hard to stop from heaving. He could not give the officer the answers he demanded.

His chin fell to his chest. His breath came in fast gasps. 'I told you, I'm not a soldier and I'm not a spy.'

He met Frank's gaze with a renewed interest. 'We have reliable information you were working for the Greek resistance. We captured a few of them and before they were shot, they were loose with their tongues.'

He is bluffing, Frank was sure. He would have mentioned the radio equipment. 'I don't have the answers to your questions.'

The officer gave a slight nod of the head, and the strike was hard, sending the chair toppling sideways. Frank's head cracked the stone floor and the full weight of the soldier's boots, again and again, pummelled his arms and his legs, his stomach, and head. The blows rained on him relentlessly.

The officer said something in German, and the strain of the rope loosening around Frank's wrists and ankles. He welcomed the numbness and then he was being dragged by the hands. Weightless. Floating. Darkness.

***

It was the shivering and coughing that woke him. He lay on the stone floor in a damp, wet, and freezing cell. No light penetrated the walls except for a thin strip under the metal door. His head throbbed incessantly, and his body ached from bruised muscle, broken bone, and opened wounds. There was no bed or sheets, no running water or toilet, just a bucket in a corner. The basics of human comfort denied. He had no idea how long he had slept, or if it was day or night.

Frank shivered convulsively. He touched with his tongue a space where a tooth should have been. His bladder was burning. He needed to urinate. He tried to move, but pain thundered through him. He closed his eyes and with a sigh; he relieved himself.

Time fell in on itself. The interrogations followed the same lines of questioning, the same beatings. At times, Frank lost consciousness. It was then, freezing water was poured over his head to wake him so that the beatings and the same questions could be asked again. There was no medical attention offered.

Each day, they gave him a watery broth that tasted like foul and filthy water, enough just to keep him alive. At some point, the officer asked Frank about his accent, saying it sounded unlike the other English prisoners he had interrogated. When Frank said he was Scottish, the officer told him he had visited Edinburgh before the war and was enthralled with its Greek Neo Classic and Georgian architecture. The officer's voice changed; it was less hostile, gentler, friendly even. He asked Frank about his life in Edinburgh. Frank gave little away, and then, as quick as he had started, he returned to the same line of questions.

In his cell, the only sound Frank heard was the constant dripping of the water seeping through the stone walls. When he slept and then drifted into consciousness, he had no idea if it had been for one, two, or eight hours. The time that passed had no measure or sequence.

Had Alexia been arrested? The very thought tortured his wakened hours. The officer had not mentioned her. Was this a psychological tactic that Frank now understood the questions about Edinburgh had been?

If she had been arrested, the Gestapo would have used her to get to Frank, perhaps parading her in front of him, or worse, torturing her in front of him, but they had done neither. It meant only two things; she had not been arrested, which gave him a sliver of possibility of hanging his hope to, or she was already dead.

The familiar rattle of keys in the lock signified only one thing: more beatings and the same questions that brought forth the same answers. He was sure he was going to die in this place and each day that passed brought the same thought.

The heavy cell door opened and one of the guards who always escorted him to the interrogation cell ordered Frank to get to his feet. There was something different in the guard's posture. He held himself differently, but Frank couldn't put his finger on it. The guard ordered him to stand and kicked Frank in the back.

'Hurry, get up,' he shrieked.

Using the wall to steady himself, Frank eased himself to his feet. His legs shook with a tremor and his head spun, distorting his vision. He heard other cell doors open and orders barked.

He saw the rifle come towards him and Frank flinched as it whipped the back of his legs. 'Move. Hurry. Get out.'

Frank stumbled forwards, and the rifle pushed painfully into his spine, guiding him down the corridor, and not as usual, towards the interrogation cell. If this was the end, he welcomed death.

A door swung open, and light steamed into the corridor. Frank was shoved out into the daylight, his eyes pierced and blinded with the sudden brightness. A truck, its engine labouring, stood with its tailgate open. Frank heaved himself up, and the guard pushed him in the back, and he tumbled forwards, every inch of his body screaming in pain. He crouched into a sitting position and leaned his back against the truck's sides. It was then he became aware of two other men, their clothes ragged and torn and stained with blood. Their heads hung low as they sat in the far corner of the truck. He heard one whisper to the other. Italians, Frank thought. Two soldiers jumped into the truck and unfolded the canvas flaps, swallowing the sky and sunlight, and as the truck jolted forwards, they lit cigarettes that glowed yellow in the dimmed light.

The truck rattled through the streets and Frank's muscles and bones felt every pothole and ever judder that the brakes made. His mind tumbled and spun. If they were going to kill him, it would have been easier to do it in the interrogation cell. He had heard stories of mass executions where the detainees were taken to secluded spots, ordered to dig trenches, and while doing so were shot, then the trench filled with dirt again concealing the bodies.

The truck began to slow, and eventually it stopped. The soldiers dropped the tailgate, and Frank and the Italians squinted in the sunlight as they eased themselves from the truck. Instead of some secluded wood and a firing squad, Frank found himself standing at the harbour below the old fortress where lines of bedraggled men were being herded onto gangplanks of a waiting ship.

Chapter 45

The ship took over a day to arrive at the island of Lefkada where a makeshift detention centre had been erected. A week later, the ship had docked at Patras. On the dockside hundreds of men, women, and children, some hysterical, whaling and crying, others numb with shock, stood in long lines. Frank turned and stared at the Italians, his gaunt expression asking a question. One of the Italians answered him by simply murmuring, 'Jews.'

When the trains arrived, they were herded and crammed into cattle carriages, verbally abused, and beaten with whips, truncheons, and rifle butts. Even the children and elderly were not spared the German soldier's brutality and vile insults. Dogs barked and strained on their leads, saliva dripping from jagged and bared teeth.

They crammed into every available space, holding onto each other in desperation and fear.

When the doors were slid and rumbled shut, extinguishing daylight, mothers clung to their inconsolable children and others screamed and cried out in fearful madness. Whistles screeched and the train lethargically crawled forwards, the only light, a soft glow pushing through the slats of the carriages.

Before long, the carriage was stifling and suffocating, the stench of sweat clung to skin, a swirl of urine and faeces filled the only two buckets in a pungent smell that infested each intake of breath. Every second moved him further from Alexia. He did not know where he was, or where he was going, but there was one thing he was sure of; if this was living, they would all be better off dead.

Several Kilometres outside Athens stood the SS-run prison at Haidari. It was situated on a rocky hillside, just beyond the Byzantine church at Daphni.

It had a notorious reputation. Originally built as a Greek army barracks, it had never been finished, lacked appropriate accommodation and sanitation. There were few beds and blankets and no running water, which had to be transported from Athens. The drains constantly blocked, and the prisoner's diet consisted mainly of bread, beans, and water. Prisoners defecated and urinated in the corridors and stairwells. Their bodies were malnourished, lice infected, and the ill and injured given minimal medical treatment.

Haidari was also a transit camp for Italian soldiers, Jews, and for those awaiting interrogation by the Gestapo. Haidari was feared and tantamount to death and torture, not only for those within its walls, but those outside as well.

For those that were not transported to Germany to work in the labour camps, life expectancy at the prison was perilously short. There was the constant fear of execution, being killed by the guards or shot as hostages.

Prisoners taken to the notorious Block 15 were fated for execution, while others, destined for Block 21, were used as human shields in steel cages attached to the front of trains to deter the *andartes* from blowing them up.

It was through the western gate of this perdition that the trucks entered. The prisoners were exhausted, hungry and thirsty, their bodies filthy and fragile, their minds traumatised and shocked.

They were surrounded by a triple wired fence with guard towers every 200 metres and two-storey barrack style buildings had been constructed in alternating lines.

Truncheons cracked bones, and whips sliced skin even as they vacated the trucks. The guards screamed at them to form lines in the square. They grouped the prisoners into political prisoners, Italian and allied soldiers, and Jewish men, women, and children.

Frank's body ached with bruises, cuts, and several broken ribs. He staggered, almost falling, when a hand reached out and caught his arm. It was one of the Italians who had been in the truck with him. Frank thanked him as they were carried along with the surge of bodies, like debris in a flowing river.

A group of uniformed men appeared. Frank could tell within the order of the prison hierarchy they were senior. One, a stocky individual with a brutal face, cracked a whip, sending the bedraggled newcomers into an eerie silence.

When satisfied, the stocky officer, his eyes peering in disgust at the new arrivals, passed a sheet of paper to the man next to him, his interpreter.

The interpreter held the sheet in his hands, and with a bellowing voice read. 'Mayor Radomski welcomes you to Haidari. He would like to personally demonstrate to you how worthless your lives are and what little value it holds. Any infringement of the rules and regulations will be met with severe punishment. Today, The Governor of Haidari, Major Radomski, will personally execute before you the prisoner named Errikos for attempting to escape on the day of his arrest. Beware! The same fate awaits you in such a case.'

Two guards dragged a man, his face blooded, in front of Major Radomski. Clutching the whip, Radomski cracked it across Errikos' face, slicing the flesh in two as he screamed in pain. The guards released him from their grasp, and Errikos slumped to his knees. Calmly and purposefully, Radomski unbuttoned his holster and withdrew a revolver. He pressed it to Errikos' forehead and, looking into his eyes, Radomski pulled the trigger. The back of Errikos' head exploded in a mass of blood, skin, and bone. He collapsed to the ground, lifeless and still. A communal gasp of horror and panic reverberated through the prisoners. Screams, whimpers, and weeping impregnated the air. Frank sucked in his breath and stared ahead, his mind exhausted, closed, and numb.

Radomski turned to the interpreter. 'Take off his shoes. They look new and expensive.'

Every day, except Sundays, Frank and a hundred other inmates were forced to dig holes and then immediately fill them up again, the backbreaking work did not stop, they built brick walls, and then, brick by brick, they were instructed to dismantle them.

'Why are we doing this? What is the point?' an exasperated prisoner asked Frank as the last spade full of dirt was thrown back onto the filled hole.

'They want to humiliate us and degrade us, make us feel we're worthless and that they have total control over every detail of our lives.'

On one particular day, for no reason other than they could, the guards raided Frank's block, throwing the prisoners' meagre possessions out of the windows, stealing anything of value and burning what they did not want.

As the weeks passed, Frank learned the impoverished living conditions, the constant beatings and whippings, and the threat of death were premeditated to send a wave of fear and terror through the prisoners to terminate their will and subdue their imagination.

At any second, minute, or hour of the day, the terror system was far-reaching. Death awaited every prisoner. Frank had seen men crumble into the depths of madness, and others take their own lives as the only solution to escape the inescapable.

Each morning, there was a roll call. A list of names called out. Each man was dragged from the line and shot. Sometimes, an extra roll call took place. Those on the list were chosen to be released that day. When the men, rarely women, stepped forward, they cried in disbelief and euphoria at the mention of their names, and they were taken away.

Frank had been placed in the storerooms, packing stolen possessions, furniture and items raided from Greek homes and families. Part of his duties was to sort out the clothes of the individuals who had been shot. There were rumours that those who had been called out on the second roll calls had also been shot. To his sadness, Frank learnt it was true. He often came across their clothes and personal items.

Frank experienced and witnessed the brutality and the sadistic behaviour of the guards daily. He raked the depths of his mind about what could make others treat their fellow humans in such a torturous and humiliating manner. It was abhorrent to him and as hard as he tried, he could not navigate the evil that infested the minds of such men.

Were they just following the policing methods of the Third Reich and the orders of their superior SS officers, or had their minds become so dark and fallen into the depths of depravity that a human life was of less significance and had less worth than a fly?

Alexia was a constant presence in his mind, from the moment he woke to the last thing at night, lying in the darkness with a sheet pulled to his ears. She was the only reason he was living.

It was a constant source of heartache that Alexia had no knowledge of what happened to him. Often, he wondered if Alexia believed him to be dead, in some way, he welcomed such thoughts and an ache swelled in his chest. Would it be better to grieve for her loss than to wake each day suspended in a never-ending nightmare that his absence would bring? She could learn to live with her grief. It would be a new way of living. She could move on with her life. Retrieve a sense of living. To hold on to a slender glimmer of hope that he may still return to her would feel like a cruel sentence, eating at her day by day. It would surely feel like drowning in a sea of despair.

There was always the slimmest prospect that she knew of his fate, knowing the soldiers took him to the Old Fortress, where he did not die, instead, like hundreds of others was transported to the mainland to serve a timeless sentence behind the barbwire of Haidari.

He wondered if she dreamt of him, like he dreamt of her. Did she know, if the entire length of Greece was covered in shards of glass, he would walk it in bare feet if it took him back to her? He told her every night he would return, and though, in this place, life was a fragile thing where self-preservation was sucked from every cell, it could not diminish his love for her.

Chapter 46

The weeks without him turned into insufferable months.

Alexia began to think that he could be dead, but then she thought she would know if this was so. She would feel something, but what could be worse than what she was already going through?

She went through periods of calm and busied herself with day-to-day activities. Mina visited from Lakones and told her the investigation into Theodora's death had been closed without a suspect being arrested. This news should have brought an immense relief. Instead, she continued to feel lonely and isolated. Mina pleaded with her to return home, but she refused. It would have felt like abandoning Frank.

Every day, she awoke into an everlasting limbo of not knowing, an endless nightmare. Was he warm or cold at night? Did he have enough to eat or was he losing weight? Was he ill? The thought plagued her mind that they would have tortured him and beaten him, and she wondered if it was possible for her heart to hurt anymore.

Night-time brought terrors, and instinctively, she reached over to find an empty space where she expected him to be.

She could no longer touch him with her hands, or see him with her eyes, but in her heart, she never stopped feeling him. She ached for him.

Alexia walked the lanes and narrow streets like a ghost, her mind numbed to the world around her. Nothing mattered anymore. All she desired with her whole being was for Frank to return to her, and if he was broken, she had all the time in the world to heal him.

Feelings of guilt surged and raged which Melina often bore the brunt of... 'How could this have happened?' 'Why didn't I do more to stop them from taking him away?' 'We should have stayed in Lakones,' 'We should have been more careful,' 'Why didn't they take me instead?'

Alexia's breath stuttered, and Melina would engulf her in her arms, smothering Alexia's sobs.

Her guilt was unbearable. The pain always came suddenly. From her core, it radiated outwards, from the agony of missing him. His absence was absolute. There was no refuge from its grip.

She no longer lived in the apartment. Melina thought it best and safer that Alexia moved in with her. Melina lived in a two bedded apartment opposite the shop. It had large windows and high ceilings, rugs on the floor and furnished in bold mahogany. In the main living area, a large gold-framed mirror hung on one wall, giving the illusion that the interior of the room was deeper and more spacious.

One morning, when Melina had gone to open the shop, Alexia received an unexpected visitor.

'Who is it?' she called nervously.

'It's me, Isaac.'

Every fibre in her body relaxed as the soft voice floated towards her from behind the door.

Alexia turned the key in the lock and opened the door.

'Isaac, what a pleasant surprise. Come in.'

Isaac removed his hat and kissed Alexia on both cheeks.

'Would you like a coffee? I've just made some.'

'That would be nice, thank you.'

Alexia brought the coffee and placed the cups on a low table. She sat on a couch opposite Isaac. 'Please Isaac, sit. Would you like something to eat?'

'No. I'm fine, but thank you all the same.'

'How did you know where to find me? Alexia asked curiously.

'I went to the shop. The woman behind the counter was very suspicious of me when I asked about you, but when I told her who I was, she smiled then. She said you had told her you had visited me and that I was an old family friend. She told me you were here.'

Alexia smiled. 'It's really nice to see you again. I'm glad you've come.'

'I've just returned from registering my name, like I do every morning, and I thought I will come and visit Alexia.'

She smiled. 'I'm glad you did, but it saddens me to see what's happening.'

'It's not just in Corfu. The Nazis are persecuting Greek Jews all over the country in Athens, in the north, the Dodecanese and on Crete. There're rumours that we'll be deported to camps. Some of my neighbours are talking about leaving Corfu and going to Evia and then Turkey.'

'You should go too.' Alexia urged him.

Isaac sagged visibly in the chair. 'I don't know what to do. If I were on my own, the choice would be an easy one, but taking a child on a journey into the unknown... I don't know. At the moment, it's all rumours, which one do I believe. I have a young child in my care. She is my responsibility now. Until I know for definite, I won't leave my home.' Isaac rubbed his hands on his thighs. 'Actually, I've come to visit you for a reason.'

'Oh. And what would that be?'

'It's troubled me every day. I have done a terrible thing. I can only hope God forgives me... and that one day, you will find it in your heart to forgive me too.'

'What are you talking about, Isaac? You're beginning to worry me.'

Isaac stooped his head to his knees and wrapped his hands around his head. When he finally looked at her, his eyes welled with tears.

'Isaac! What is it?'

'Two plain clothed Germans visited me; they weren't in uniform; they were dressed in suits. They were SS officers. Because I was a teacher and taught at the school, they wanted me to give them information on all the Jewish families in Corfu Town, names, address-es, their occupations. I refused, of course. I told them I could never do such a thing. They just laughed at me. They said they had ways and means of extracting the information they wanted from me. Then Amalia came into the room. She was hungry and looking for some-thing to eat. I knew immediately then I had no choice. One of the officers patted her on the head and said, I either comply with their requests, or I would never see Amalia again. It was simple, Amalia's life for information. What was I to do?

'It's so shameful. I've betrayed you, Alexia. I panicked. I didn't know what to do. Before I knew it, the words were coming out of my mouth. I told them if they promised to leave Melina alone, I would tell them the name and whereabouts of a British man who is working with the resistance. I told them about Frank.'

Her hands shook. Alexia looked at him, her shock as clear as the nose on her face. She remembered when she and Frank visited Isaac. Frank had told him everything.

Isaac's eyes tightened. 'I know I've done a terrible thing.'

The cup in her hand fell to the floor and shattered in fragments. She tried to breathe, but the air seemed to constrict her lungs. A pain of betrayal unfolded from her abdomen to her throat. Isaac stood and took a step forward, his hands outstretched, pleading forgive-ness. She, too, stood and pushed him in the chest. Isaac stumbled backwards. Alexia pressed her hand to her mouth. It felt as if Isaac had just plunged a knife into her heart. She swayed her head from side to side; her legs weak from under her. And then it came, an animalistic scream that struck Isaac harder than any physical blow could ever have done. The sound of it impregnated the air, soaking the walls, the floor, and ceiling.

He stumbled backwards, and like a thousand sharp knives, it sheared him to the core.

Isaac pleaded. 'Please, Alexia. I'm... I'm so sorry. They would have taken my little Amalia. She is just an innocent child.'

Alexia screamed hysterically. 'Get out! Get out! I never want to see you again and if I do, I promise you, I will kill you. You are already dead to me.'

Isaac winced. He looked away, his shame collapsing his face. In resignation, he turned from Alexia and left her with the air of a man walking to the gallows.

She had not the strength nor the will to spill her rage. Instead, she crumbled to the floor and heard Melina's alarmed voice swirling in her head. 'Alexia, what has happened? What has that man done? Are you alright?

Chapter 47

In August 1944, the Russian Red Army invaded Romania and continued to sweep through Bulgaria and Yugoslavia. Fearing being completely isolated, the German withdrawal from Greece was imminent. Lines of trucks, artillery, motorcycles, and soldiers moved northwards. On the 12th October, the sun rose over Athens and shone on hundreds of blue and white flags draped over balconies. The swastika was removed from the Acropolis. Church bells rang out and jubilant crowds carrying flags and placards congregated in Syntagma Square. The streets of Athens swelled with joy and celebrations, like a flowing river of humanity.

That morning in Haidari, there was no roll call. Like the rest of the prisoners who spilled out of their detention blocks, Frank stood in the warm sunshine, not quite believing what was unfolding before him.

There had been rumours for weeks that the Germans were leaving, but no one allowed themselves to believe it. The guard towers were deserted. The gates were open. It was true. There was a surge of movement, a clammer towards them. The blare of human voices, laughing, crying, an uproar of feverish joy filled the vast space around him that only yesterday, held an association with snarling dogs and sadistic guards, the crack of gunshots, the stench of fear, the endless beatings on blood-stained ground and the horror of the killings.

A fellow prisoner came alongside Frank. 'Isn't it unbelievable? We are free to go.'

'Go where?' Disorientation clouded his mind.

'Home. We can go home to our families. You have someone who is waiting for you?'

'I do.'

'Then you are free to go to them. The Germans have gone. The Russians and British are closing in. We are liberated. Can you believe it's over? I never thought I'd see this day.'

Liberated, the word sounded foreign on the man's tongue. It was a word that could send men mad with torment. It was an ideal that stretched so far from Frank. It was not of his world; it was unattainable and if he was to survive; he closed his mind to it. It was enough just to see another sunset and pray to see it rise again. In the camp, he kept it from his mind. It represented another time, another life, another Frank.

He watched the stream of people flow towards the gate.

'Liberated,' he said out loud.

Frank sank to his knees, tears staining his cheeks. He rubbed his eyes, but they were immediately filled with tears again.

It was finally over. He had survived.

Chapter 48

The day was hot, the sun already intense, warming his back in the narrow and airless street.

He stood mesmerised and watched her for a long time. He breathed in deeply, calming an ache, a driving desire to run to her. He had thought this day would never come, and he promised himself he would cherish every second and absorb every detail to its fullness.

She was wearing a blue sleeveless dress; one Frank had never seen before. He knew there would be many things that would now be new to him. Her hair was longer, tied back from her face, stretching down her back and shining in the sunlight. She had lost weight; he saw it in her face.

She was outside the shop, loading the crates with vibrant coloured vegetables, and like everything she did, she was absorbed in her task.

He thought about the last time he saw her that morning in the apartment above the shop. It felt an eternity had passed. How long had it been? Four? Five months? So much had changed. It scared him. It would be wishful thinking to imagine it had not changed her in some way.

He watched as she straightened herself and rubbed her hands along the base of her back. His eyes slid along her fingers, pressing and massaging an ache. They ran along the smooth skin of her arms, the curve of her breasts, the crease of the fabric, and he saw then the round swell of her stomach.

She heard her name being spoken. A whisper, almost. She turned and stared at a dishevelled man standing facing her. Although his clothes were unkempt, misfitting, and torn, there was something about the way he held himself that was familiar to her. Beyond the unshorn beard, his pale and dirt grained skin, the matted and straggling hair, his eyes drew her towards him. Alexia gasped. She had seen a ghost.

She moved close to him and gently placed her palm on his chest.

Frank drew back slightly. 'Don't come close to me. I smell awful, my breath stinks and my hair feels like it has things living in it.'

'I don't care. You have come back to me.' Her hand moved to his face and stroked the skin below his eyes. 'It has felt like a lifetime, but it is...' Her words caught in her throat as her voice broke. 'It is you.' She leaned heavily into his chest, and he encircled her with his arms, muffling her sobs, the love in his eyes sparkling with tears.

He inhaled deeply the familiar scent of her hair. 'There is more of you to hold now.'

Alexia lifted her head and gazed at him, at the dark shadows under his eyes. 'It has been a blessing throughout all this time.'

In Melina's apartment, Alexia filled the bathtub with boiling water, and from the surface, a warm haze rose around them.

Her fingertips gently released each button of his shirt, entrancing him with her touch and blocking the tortured hum in his head. He felt himself slipping into a dreamlike state, dissolving the internal flood of darkness.

She slipped the shirt from his shoulders and slide it over his back, letting it fall around their feet. He braced himself and flinched, knowing what her eyes would fall upon: breastbone, rib, vertebrae, and clavicle protruding taut against wafer-thin skin, pale-yellow bruising, and white scars.

She shored her resolve and unbuckled his belt, and his trousers slid freely down his legs. With no underwear, he was naked before her, and with a guiding hand, she led him to the tub.

Even as the physical remnants of his captivity assaulted her eyes, she could not even contemplate what he had endured.

Tentatively and with a deep sigh, he lowered himself into the water; he had forgotten how captivating it could be.

'How does that feel? Alexia asked, as she dipped a sponge into the bath water and lathered it in soap.

'It feels wonderful. It's weird how we take the simple things for granted. It wasn't until washing became a luxury that I longed to soak in a deep bath.'

Alexia wiped the sponge over the nape of his neck and glided it over his shoulders. Frank sighed and closed his eyes, luxuriating in the sensation as rivulets of water dripped and trickled down his back. Alexia washed him all over, with soft tender motions wiping the dirt and stains from his skin. She was erasing the months of torment and suffering from his body. Each stroke of the sponge purified him and released him from the evidence of his captivity. But what worried her most was how to heal his mind. If it could be achieved by love alone, she could cure him in an instant. What really mattered was that he was with her now and, although broken into pieces, she would invest every second of every day in putting him back together again. She loved the man taken from her, and she continued to love the man that had returned.

With scissors, she clipped at his beard, and when short enough, she shaved the short bristles clean from his face with a razor blade. When she had finished, she sat back, and satisfied with her work, she smiled, 'It really is you under all that hair.'

They ate a meal which Frank devoured, and afterwards, Alexia caught him staring at the swell of her stomach. 'You can touch it, you know. It won't break.'

He dipped his head and placed his hand against the fabric of her dress, pressing ever so slightly. 'I can't believe a life is forming and growing inside you.'

'It is. I can feel it move sometimes. At first, it felt like strange little flutters, but now, I can definitely feel it. Sometimes, it kicks so much, I am sure it's desperate to get out.'

Frank broke into a wide smile and laughed, and he couldn't remember the last time he had done so. 'Do you think it's a boy or a girl?'

'I cannot tell.'

'I've heard that some people can tell.'

'Does it matter?'

'I hope it's a girl.'

'Why?'

'Because she will look like her mother, and obviously, she will be beautiful.'

'I think you might be needing glasses. As long as our baby is healthy, that's all that matters.'

'How long has it been?' Frank said, gazing at her stomach.

'Five months now. I would have been pregnant on the day they took you, although I didn't know it at the time.'

Frank took a deep breath. 'Even though I was not here, in a way, I was.'

'You were every single day.' Alexia tucked her arm around Frank's arm. 'The sky fell on me that day and every day after that. My life no longer mattered. Without you, how could I be the woman I was? I did not know where you were. After a time, I knew you were no longer on Corfu and that they would have taken you to a prison or a camp. It was the not knowing that was insufferable. Were you alive? Were you dead? And if you were alive, what had they done to you? And as the weeks passed and turned into months, I convinced myself I had to try to live a life as best I could, whatever that may be, or whatever that looked like. Because, if I didn't, and I continued to live in my own purgatory, then they had won. I was not going to let that happen. I would be unbreakable. It would be my victory, not theirs, and if it was mine, it would be yours too and the child's growing inside me. I never stopped hoping that each day would be the day you would return. I was prepared to wait a lifetime. I knew that if you could come home, nothing would stop you, and that was the oxygen I breathed with every breath I took. We have closed a door on that time without each other, and now that you are back, and we two have become three,' Alexia cradled her stomach protectively. 'We will open a new door.'

It scared him to know, the Frank Alexia knew was not the same man who had returned to her. In the hell that was Haidari, part of that man had slipped away, and Frank hated himself for it. Alexia was the shining core of his life and he prayed there was enough of his old self left to continue to make her happy.

Chapter 49

The next day, Alexia and Melina embraced in tears of sadness and of joy.

'You will have to come and visit us.' An ache swelled in Alexia's throat.

'I will.'

'Promise me,' Alexia insisted.

'I promise.' Melina placed her palm against Alexia's stomach. 'Just try to stop me.'

She turned to Frank, and she touched his arm. 'I need to make sure this one starts to put on some weight, so I'll be bringing a big helping of my special chocolate baklava.'

'I'm indebted to you. You're a very special woman, Melina. You sacrificed everything for us.'

Fresh tears rose to Melina's eyes. 'I did what many others have done. I'm not special. And look how it has turned out. You are together again and that's all that matters.'

The sun was high in the cloudless sky. Frank could not veer his eyes from the sight of the sea, sapphire blue and speckled turquoise that kissed emerald curved bays and white sandy beaches.

The pounding of his pulse was like footsteps as Alexia opened the door to the house. Finally, to be back again, there were times he thought he would never see this day. Immediately, a gust of memories flowed through him, the same ones that filled his heart day and night during his confinement. He looked around. Nothing had changed. A pause in time. To be here, in this house, was everything to him.

He thought of what had happened and what was still to come. A life of promise and possibility unfolded before him. His chest glowed warmly.

The aromatic aroma of cooked lamb, aubergine, garlic, cumin, coriander, and cinnamon infused the kitchen. Mina had prepared a meal for them. The table was set; the pot sizzled on the stove. She did not want to intrude, but her presence would still be felt. It was her way, her welcoming home present.

He touched the sheet with his fingers; he hadn't felt anything so soft for as long as he could remember; it was a luxury that soothed the brittle edges of his mind. He sat on the bed and sank into the mattress and caught the clean washed smell that rose to meet him. It tantalised his senses, and when he felt his body relax, it felt strange not to be constantly tensed, alert to every noise, no matter how faint.

It still didn't feel real. Frank was terrified he would wake, and it had all been just a dream, but it was real. He had felt Alexia's touch; he had heard her voice, and she had washed the coating of filth and grime from his body. He pressed his hand to his face; the skin was now smooth, where she had trimmed and shaved the months of growth from his face. His first meal tasted like manna from heaven. He had drunk fresh water that was clear and not murky, and tea coloured, with dead flies floating on its surface. He had been hungry, frightened, and thirsty. He knew of no other way to be. All that would change now.

His fingers interlocked as they lay in his lap and there were tears in his eyes. Alexia came into the room, and he stretched his arms out in front of him. She crossed the floor, and he encircled her waist with his arms and gently pressed his head to her stomach. He felt her breath across the crown of his head, and the intimacy of being so close to Alexia, to his unborn child, was wondrous. Alexia ran her fingers gently through his hair and said, 'There are three of us now. We are a family, and you are home.'

The guard dragged the man from the line-up, kicking and punching him, even when the terrified man was cowering on the ground. He spat insults at him in German and, returning to the line-up, he pulled out a boy of fourteen years of age. They gave the boy a shovel and ordered him to place it at the man's throat.

'Put it on his fucking throat and stamp on it,' the guard yelled at the boy.

The man's eyes were bulging in dread, but there was also a glint of kindness, a flicker of sympathy for the boy.

'I can't. I can't,' the boy's voice cracked. 'He is my father.'

'Do it!' the guard screamed, his spital spraying the boy's face.

A dark patch spread down the boy's torn trousers and the dirt at his feet darkened in a pool of urine.

The boy stared blankly at the dark patch in the dirt. 'I can't.' His hands trembled, and the shovel toppled from his grasp.

The guard struck him hard in the face and the boy fell to the ground.

The guard kicked the man. 'You. Get up.'

The man stroked his son's face as tenderly as he could and whispered words of comfort as he wiped away the boy's tears. He turned in chilled hatred and peered at the guard.

The guard swung his leg and kicked the man again. As he dragged himself to his feet, the man grimaced in pain. The guard threw the shovel at him.

'It's your turn, Jew. Stamp on the boy's throat with the blade of the shovel.'

A creeping terror rose from the man's voice. 'You will have to kill me first.'

The guard stepped close to the man and cocked his head. 'I didn't catch that. What did you say?'

'You will have to kill me first. He is my son. How can I do such a thing to my boy?'

The guard shrugged. 'Very well.' He pressed the barrel of his rifle to the man's head and squeezed the trigger. Blood, brain, and bone shattered in all directions, spattering over the boy's face as his father's lifeless body crumpled to the ground. The guard trained his rifle on the boy and shot him twice in the chest, extinguishing the boy's high pitched hysterical screams.

The silence bored into Frank like a drill, and everything stopped for a moment. A revulsion soaked him, seething beneath his skin and with every heartbeat the man he had been, was seeping from him like liquid.

He tried to run, to escape the terror, but the more he tried, his legs grew sluggish and heavy...

He cried out and Alexia woke with a start. Droplets of sweat freckled Frank's face, and his skin soaked the crumpled sheets wrapped around his legs. She could feel his heart race, and she feared it would burst inside his chest.

Alexia comforted him with her words. 'It is alright darling. It was just another dream. You are here with me, in our bed and in our house. You are safe.'

He mumbled incoherently as she stroked his face, and soon, his breathing slowed and his muscles loosened, and before long, he sank deeper into a better place.

As the weeks passed, gradually with care and patience, Alexia was able to draw the curtain from Frank's world. A part of him wanted to stay in bed all day and block out the world around him. But when she walked into the room, it felt like she had brought a vast blue sky with her. A light emerged, and the darkness faded from his eyes.

He began to tell her about the past that dragged him in one direction and the present that lured him in another.

'I couldn't allow myself to have feelings. I put everything into little boxes and bottled it all up. I wore a mask all the time, but sometimes it slipped. I've seen unimaginable things, Alexia. The depravity of the suffering one human can inflict upon another eats at the mind. Every day, I relive what I've seen, but I try not to be overcome by it. We had to rise above it. We were better than them. We could create good from the evil that infested us, and we needed to incapacitate it, but it was bigger than us. But now the world has changed, and I need to catch up with it.

'This has always been my place, my home, my belonging. I just didn't know it until it was taken from me.'

Hope leapt in Alexia's heart and her eyes gleamed in determination. 'Whatever happens, I will be here for you. I need you and this little one will need its daddy.' She took his hand and placed it flat against her stomach. 'With all the strength in my body, I will make sure we get through this.'

Frank took her face into his hands and stared into her eyes and saw in its entirety the centre of his world glow before him. It was all he needed to see.

Chapter 50
Corfu
2010

It is evening when Damaris' last words fade from their ears, replaced by the soft pulse of the cicadas. Around them, the light is fading, thickening steadily into darkness.

'You see, it was believed Frank died when the ship he was on was torpedoed and sank. The family would have been told by letter that Frank was not amongst the survivors. For many families, there was never any closure. Without their loved one's body, there could not be a funeral.'

Rob looks at Damaris. 'And Frank would have known this.'

Damaris nods. 'Both of his parents had died before the war. He had an uncle who lived in Manchester who he never really knew. It would have been this uncle who would have received the letter presuming Frank was lost at sea.'

'So, he didn't have a reason to go back to Edinburgh.'

'He was with the woman he loved. They were about to have a baby together, and he needed time to recover from the horrors of the prison camp. He had been given a new life.'

Rob looks at the photograph of Frank and Alexia. 'You can see they are in love.'

'Yes, they were.'

He is bewildered. 'What has this to do with mum?'

'After the war, it did not sit easily with him that those who he had been close to thought that he had died. It troubled him for a long time. Finally, after seeking Alexia's approval, because he would not have done it otherwise, he phoned his friend Archie, hoping he still had the same telephone number.'

'Archie? He was the guy that was with Frank in the pub the night before he left.'

'Yes. Frank and Archie had been close friends. It was a relief to Frank when Archie answered his call.'

'That must have been some conversation.'

'In more ways than one.'

'What do you mean?'

'Once Archie got over the shock that Frank was alive and had been living in Greece, he had his own revelation.

'Back in those days, after the war, it was not like it is now. If a woman became pregnant out of marriage, and to make things worse, the father was not around, she would have been sent away and once the baby was once born it would be adopted. That was the predicament Maggie found herself in.'

Zoe looks at Damaris. 'This was Frank's girlfriend.' Her eyes widened. 'It was Frank's baby.'

Damaris hesitates and nods slightly. 'Frank never knew Maggie was pregnant. When Frank left, Archie and Maggie began to see each other, as friends at first, but as time passed, they developed feelings for each other, strong feelings. Maggie was beginning to show signs of her pregnancy, so she was forced to tell Archie. He loved her by now and he knew that Maggie would lose her baby, so he asked her to marry him.'

There is an awkward silence as this sink in, and then the enormity of it strikes Rob. 'Oh my God! Maggie and Archie, you're talking about my grandparents. Wait, what does this mean?' He presses his fingers to his forehead, trying to make sense of it. 'The baby... the baby that Maggie had is my mum.' Rob stares at the photograph. His mind races as the sudden certainty overcomes him. 'Archie isn't mum's dad, it's Frank. Then, Archie wasn't my grandad, it was Frank.'

'I know how close you were to Archie... your grandad.' Jeanie said, after you lost your dad, he was like a father to you. None of this changes that. He was still your grandad. Love is thicker than blood. Your mum always knew. Both Maggie and Archie decided they didn't want her to find out when she was older. She didn't know who her biological father was. It was brave of them.'

'Another secret.' Rob states bluntly.

Zoe leans forward in her chair and smiles at Damaris. 'And you are the baby in the photograph. You are Rob's mum's sister.'

Damaris smiles. 'Yes, Jeanie is my sister and Frank is my father, my pateras.'

Rob clutches the photograph tightly. 'Then we're related too.'

'And that is why I understand how much you are hurting. 'You see, Frank never kept his life in Edinburgh a secret from me. As I grew up, he told me stories of his life in Edinburgh, and ultimately, when I was old enough to understand, he told me the truth. I had a sister. After he died, Alexia, my mama, gave me the telephone number Frank used to contact Archie all those years ago. She didn't know if it was still his current number. I felt there was something missing in my life, but it still took me many years to phone that number. Thank God, when I did, Archie answered.' Damaris reaches for her glass. 'There's someone I'd like you to meet.'

The narrow and steep road winds, turning and twisting like a coiled snake through the densely wooded hillside. Damaris expertly and effortlessly manoeuvres the car safely around each hairpin bend bordered by ancient olive groves and crumbling stone walls. The car continues its climb above turquoise bays and emerald headlands that lounge in the aquamarine sea like giant turtles. Sometimes, as each blind bend is left behind them, Lakones is tantalisingly unveiled, enfolded within the hug of the hillside.

The hairs on the back of Rob's neck stand up. 'The views are magnificent. I never thought it would be like this. It takes your breath away.'

They reach the top of a rise, and for the first time, the road is flat. Damaris turns to Rob. 'This is Lakones. What do you think?'

Rob gasps. 'It just gets better.'

'We're at an altitude of 182 metres and some of these stone houses were built in the eighteenth-and nineteenth centuries. This is the real authentic Corfu.'

The main road crossing through Lakones is narrow and only allows for a one-way system where traffic lights sit at each end of the village. The stone houses are a diverse hue of warm mustard, salmon pink and whitewashed walls, blue and green shutters, atop with terracotta tiles.

Damaris pulls up, and the car comes to a stop. 'We'll have to walk from here, it's not far.'

Rob nods, and he and Zoe follow Damaris' lead. A breeze dislodges golden leaves that flutter like butterflies, making a sound that is of its own. The air around them is tinged in scents that drift from the foliage below. Rob can hardly believe he is here.

Finally, Damaris turns into a narrow lane, until as far as they can go, it opens into a square which Rob immediately recognises from Damaris' account from the night before. His eyes travel along the huddle of houses and fix upon one.

'We are here.' Damaris announces, and they follow as she enters the house without knocking.

Rob looks around the house that opens into an extension, almost doubling the size of the living area on the ground floor. The cast-iron stove is long gone, replaced by a modern and slimline kitchen, expertly designed with appliances and glossed wall tiles. As they move through the house, several paintings hang on the walls, all depicting a similar style. Frank must have continued to paint. The house has a pleasing flow to it, and it is bright with light from the two glass doors that open and lead into a garden.

He still has a sense of what the house must have looked like, but now, must recalibrate the image he has held in his mind.

The garden is shaded with mature trees and bathed in a warm soft light. They tread on stone paving bordered by terracotta pots emblazed in potent colour: scarlet, purple, orange and white petals leading to a patio area with a large, brimmed umbrella and Rattan chairs. Rob feels his anticipation begin to unfurl as he can see someone sitting in the shade. A hand slides into his and Zoe smiles, reading his eyes as if they were her own.

'Mama, they are here,' Damaris announces.

Her hair is still long, but now white, and pulled back from her face by a yellow band accentuating the fine bone structure under the wrinkles of her skin. She pulls herself from the chair and leans on her walking stick. There is a slight curve to her back, and a slackness to the skin under her veined and thin arms, but her dress hangs on her like it would a mannequin.

Alexia considers the new arrivals with a fixed look and an outstretched hand. Rob takes her arthritic hand in his. 'You didn't have to get up on my account,' he tells her, momentarily discomforted.

'I didn't. My back is as stiff as a board. Age doesn't come on its own. Rob isn't it? Jeanie's son.'

For a moment, he is speechless. It is her eyes that he discerns above everything else. They are the same eyes as her gaze in the photograph, strong and composed.

'It pleases me greatly that we have finally met.' Her voice is bottomless and calm, reassuring to the ear.

It occurs to him that his mum and Alexia would have met.

'Jeanie was a lovely woman. It came as a shock to learn of her illness. I'm so sorry for your loss.'

'Thank you.'

'I hope you understand your mother's hesitation. She thought she was protecting you. The last thing she wanted was to cause you pain.'

'I know that now.'

'And this must be Zoe.'

'Hello Alexia.'

'Please let's sit.' She waves her hand over four glasses and a jug. 'I hope you like orange. I picked the oranges myself.'

At the bottom of the garden, Rob notices a cluster of orange trees ladened heavily with fruit. 'You replaced your orange tree, the one the German soldier trampled, with an orange grove.'

Alexia smiles. 'When the war ended, I planted seeds and from those seeds, the trees have given me fruit every year. Whenever I'm in the garden, the orange trees remind me that from pain and suffering, good things can still happen. Hope can rise again.

'After the war, Frank taught art in Corfu Town, and he continued to paint and sell his work. Frank died from a heart attack; he was only fifty. I did not think I could live in the house after that, but the orange trees give me solace and Frank gave me the most wonderful memories. It is in this house I feel closest to him.

'Frank never met your mother, but in a way, he already knew her, for nothing could have pleased him more knowing she was brought up in a loving family, and by Archie, because Frank knew what kind of man Archie was, and he was blessed to have him as a friend and privileged to have him as the custodian of his daughter. When he died, Frank had no regrets. Age teaches us to see things for what they are.'

Rob clears his throat. 'I can see that now.' He pauses. 'I need to give you this. It was my mums.'

Rob holds out his hand, and something drops into Alexia's palm. It is a small locket attached to a chain.

With her noduled and bent fingers, Alexia carefully prises open the locket, and she takes a deep and audible breath, her face brightens and glows as she traces her fingertip over the tiny image, and then turning slightly, she wipes a single tear from her eye.

***

They are standing on Damaris' porch, looking out over a heart-shaped bay. The sun has risen over a rolling hill and already the light is blisteringly bright, tethered to the sky, that Zoe is forced to shade her eyes with sunglasses.

Zoe runs her finger along his back. Their hesitation to acknowledge their undeniable attraction now melted in their displays of affection towards one another.

Rob moves his eyes from the sea. 'An old photograph discovered by accident literally fell into my life with its mystery and secrets.'

'You'll need time to adjust and make sense of this.'

'Damaris said, she always felt something was missing. I think I've always felt the same. When Frank died, Damaris did something about it. She found my mum; she found her sister. She found the last piece of her jigsaw.'

Her response is unexpected. 'Some never look in the right place.'

He turns to face Zoe, his breath catching. 'I'm going to buy mum's house.'

'Are you sure?'

'I've never been surer.'

'And your jigsaw would be complete.'

A hopeful look spreads over Rob's face. 'There would still be a piece missing, but I've found her, and I would need her with me, and I hope she feels the same.'

Zoe takes a deep breath. 'For evermore.'

The End

Get your FREE novella, Heartland by Dougie McHale.
Click on the link: Heartland[1]

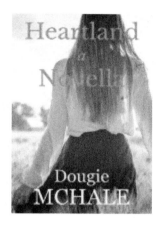

Books by Dougie McHale
Amazon.co.uk: Dougie McHale: Books, Biography, Blogs, Audio-books, Kindle[2]
Amazon.com: Dougie McHale: books, biography, latest update[3]
Connect with me at my website[4], on Facebook[5] and Instagram[6]. I'd love to hear from you.

1.   https://www.subscribepage.com/heartland

2. https://www.amazon.co.uk/Dougie-McHale/e/B013B5ZN-

   PC?ref=sr_ntt_srch_lnk_1&qid=1678315767&sr=1-1

3. https://www.amazon.com/stores/Dougie-McHale/author/B013B5ZN-

   PC?ref=ap_rdr&store_ref=ap_rdr&isDramIntegrated=true&shoppingPortalEnabled=true

4. https://dougiemchale.com/

5. https://www.facebook.com/www.dougiemchale

A note from the author

Thank you for reading my book. Reviews are really important to me, and it would mean a lot if you could leave a short review.

As an author, I love getting feedback from readers. Thank you for your kind consideration.

If you'd like to be first to know about any of my books, please visit me on my website and sign up for occasional updates about new releases and book promotions. I'd love to hear from you:

Acknowledgements

Heartfelt thanks to Sheona, my wife, for her continued support and constant encouragement. Thanks to Tracy Watson, Maggie Crawshaw, Anne Clague, Lisa Richards and Dilys Killick. As my advanced readers they have given me invaluable feedback on all of my novels. A very special thanks to Maria A. Karamitsos for her editorial skills, advice and time. She has made me a better writer and I will be for ever grateful.

Printed in Great Britain
by Amazon

25204624R00165